Defending
A Lady

☆ ──────────────────────────── ☆

Chase had just set another pack down beside the mule when he heard the crude imitation of a jackass's "Whee Haw," and a roar of laughter behind them. He wheeled around to see five cowboys watching them load the mules. One of the cowboys was a big man with a mean face and shoulders of a bull. Chase turned to see where the man was looking. Seth and Kally were bent over a pack and he was showing her how to rope it. In her tight new blue jeans, Kally presented a pretty nice view, but no gentleman would have responded the way the big cowboy had.

Chase reached the cowboy in two long strides. His feet were set solidly when he stopped, and he swung a doubled-up, hard fist into the cowboy's face. The cowboy's lips spurted blood and he went down hard, but wasn't out. As the cowboy gained his knees, Chase brought an uppercut from the ground that caught the cowboy on the end of his chin. The blow was so hard it brought the man up on his tiptoes before he fell headlong into the street, raising a cloud of dust. He lay still, but Chase wasn't through with him yet. . . .

· ☆

SPIRIT'S GOLD

STUART DILLON

Harper Paperbacks

Harper & Row, Publishers, New York
Grand Rapids, Philadelphia, St. Louis, San Francisco
London, Singapore, Sydney, Tokyo, Toronto

This is a work of fiction. The characters, incidents, and dialogues are products of the author's imagination and are not to be construed as real. Any resemblance to actual events or persons, living or dead, is entirely coincidental.

Harper Paperbacks a division of Harper & Row, Publishers, Inc.
10 East 53rd Street, New York, N.Y. 10022

Cover art by Darrell Sweet

First printing: July, 1990

Printed in the United States of America

HARPER PAPERBACKS and colophon are trademarks of Harper & Row, Publishers, Inc.

10 9 8 7 6 5 4 3 2 1

*To my wife Lee, for being
a patient computer widow.*

*C*hase Wade glanced at his cards, folded them, and threw them into the discards. Leaving his coat on the back of the chair, he stood and rolled up the sleeves of his white shirt as he walked toward the open door of the hotel bar. The desert country was warmer than usual for this early in the spring.

Chase leaned against the door frame, enjoying the breeze blowing in off the desert. It was warm, but cooler than the sultry, still air of the saloon. He lifted his wide-brimmed, flat-crowned hat and ran a hand through his thick, neatly trimmed black hair.

Across the street, the afternoon train had just pulled in. Chase carefully studied each man as he stepped off; he was always on the lookout for another gunman—especially one he might know. He didn't see any. A couple of the men were drummers, carrying their oversize sample cases. The rest were just ordinary men, happy to have come to the end of a long, tiring train ride. From their dress, Chase suspected they had come to join the track-laying crews,

1

pushing hard to lay the rails on to El Paso. Some might be miners on their way to Silver City.

If they were going on from here, it would have to be by stage or horseback. The rails had been laid past Albuquerque, but this was the end of the line for now.

Chase took a last look down the dusty street, past the train station, in hopes that his friend Seth might be riding in. He didn't see him. As he started to turn back into the bar, a striking, dark-haired woman in eastern dress appeared in the doorway of the train. Without waiting for help from the conductor, she swung gracefully off the train step onto the platform. The conductor set her two large bags off for her.

Chase watched a moment, wondering what would bring a woman like her to Albuquerque. She obviously wasn't a dance-hall girl or entertainer. There was something very different about the way she carried herself. He could see she was no ordinary western woman.

She looked around the platform, then moved resolutely toward a man standing near the station door who had been observing the new arrivals more closely than Chase. As the man turned to speak to her, the sun reflected off the badge on his vest. Chase couldn't see the sheriff's face, but he was always glad when it was someone else's job to watch for trouble coming into town. He hoped he wouldn't have to wait long for Seth. If he did, some young gunman might recognize him and he would have to use his gun again.

Turning and walking back to the game, Chase called to the bartender to bring him a drink. "Deal me in," he said to the men at the table as he took his seat with his back to the wall.

Chase had ridden in the evening before and gotten a shave and haircut before checking into this big, new hotel. It hadn't been here the last time he was in Albuquerque—five, maybe six years before. The town had grown.

Chase paid the bartender for the drink when he brought it, and then looked at his cards. Dressed as he was in a black suit with expensive boots and black hat, Chase might have been taken for a gambler. But any man familiar with men of the West, like those in the game, would know better. Although Chase was in his early thirties, his face reflected the hard living he had packed into those years. He had the slim waist and broad shoulders of a man who had spent much of his life in a saddle. He wore his six-gun low on his leg, resting in a tied-down, fast-draw, *pistolero*'s holster. Time and much use had polished its dark grips to a high luster.

Chase tossed in another hand. These low-stake games bored him. He was used to gambling with miners who would risk all the dust they had found in several months' digging on one turn of the cards. Or with cowboys who would risk all their pay from a trail drive on one hand. This game was just something to do while he waited for Seth.

He picked up his new hand and studied it. It wasn't even worth drawing to. He tossed it into the discards, and looked up to see a man he recognized coming through the door from the hotel lobby. It was the sheriff he had seen across the street a few minutes earlier. He hadn't realized then that it was Ben Taylor.

Chase rose and stepped forward to meet him. "I didn't know you were the sheriff of Albuquerque, Ben. Thought you were still taming boom towns like me."

"'Lo, Chase," Ben returned coolly, ignoring his outstretched hand. Ben wore his six-gun tied low, like Chase's. The hair protruding beneath his hat was streaked with gray, but his handlebar mustache was totally white. He was a good twenty years older than Chase, but the way he moved said he could back up the badge he wore.

"I've been here a couple years now, since the railroad hit town. With the cattle goin' out of here, they need a sheriff to handle the trail crews when they get liquored up. I keep the peace here. That's why I came lookin' fer you, Chase."

"Don't reckon I was hard to find. I just rode in last night from up north. I'm staying here at the hotel."

"You must have showed up after I'd already gone out to my ranch. This mornin' my deputy told me a new gun was in town, so I came to see who it was. Don't help a whole lot, seein' it's you, and as sheriff, I've got to ask you how long you figure on bein' here?"

Chase was having trouble understanding Ben's hostility. They had known each other for years. He tried to keep a friendly tone in his voice as he answered. "You don't think I'd cause any trouble do you, Ben? You know me better than that."

"Yeah, I know you. I know what you can do with your gun or your hands if you get riled. That's why I'm askin'. I don't want no fast guns like you in my town." There it was again, the voice of the sheriff, not a friend. Ben wasn't as tall as Chase's six feet, nor was he as muscular, but Chase knew him well enough to know he meant business.

The crisp edge in Chase's voice revealed his agitation as he tried to explain. "I didn't come to Albuquerque to cause trouble...."

"I know you don't start trouble," Ben shot back, "but we both know where there's a fast gun as well known as you, trouble's bound to come lookin' fer you. Payday fer the cowboys is only 'bout a week away—first of the month—so I'd jest as soon you wasn't around when the ruckus starts. I'll have my hands full as it is," Ben finished, looking Chase straight in the eye.

"Damned if it don't sound like you're running me out of town, Sheriff Taylor." Chase's voice lowered and his eyes changed from their usual blue to a cool gray as he returned Ben's steady gaze. "Nobody's ever run me out of any town. I don't want any trouble with you, Ben, but I'm not about to let you run me out of town either. Is this how you treat all your old friends?"

"If that's what it takes to keep the peace here. I'm keepin' my hand clear of my gun, and I expect you to do the same, but I don't want to go up against you if some trigger-happy cowboy comes gunnin' fer you."

"I haven't seen anyone I recognized since I got into town, except you and Larkin over at the livery. I was hoping no one would recognize me. I won't be here long."

Sheriff Taylor looked skeptical. "You've only been here a few hours, and if that woman from the train knew you was here, it ain't gonna take long fer others to find out."

Chase looked surprised. "What woman?"

"I met the train this afternoon, like I always do, and this high-falutin, eastern-dressed woman got off and asked fer you. She knew your name. I didn't know then you was in town, so I jest walked her to the hotel."

"Did she say what she wanted? Not some woman I made a widow of, I hope." Chase had had too many run-ins with the vengeful friends and relatives of men he had killed in his years as a gunfighter to not be concerned about strangers on his trail.

"No, she didn't," Ben snapped, obviously not interested in answering questions. "To be honest I couldn't figure what a lady like her wanted with the likes a you. Didn't look like your kind of woman. She's an oriental half-caste. Got slanty eyes like a Chinee, and pretty snobbish iffen you ask me."

"Beats me," said Chase, pushing back his hat and resting his hands on his hips, careful to keep them clear of his gun. "I saw her getting off the train, but even from a distance I'm sure I'd have recognized her if I'd ever run into her."

"I don't know nothin' 'bout her business, and I don't care to, but I carried her bags upstairs to Room 9."

"Guess I'll have to go find out later," said Chase, shaking his head.

"I didn't come to talk about the woman. I still need to know what you're doin' in town and how long you plan on stayin'?"

"It's personal business. Couple years ago, in a

poker game, I won a ranch up in the high country of Colorado. The way it sits now, it's not worth the money I chucked in the pot, but with help I can make it into a real ranch. I've had a bellyful of gunfighting."

"Where'd you get that fool idea? You know well as me, young guns eager to make a name fer themselves ain't likely to leave a gun like you alone."

"I'm going to find a way to make it work. This ranch is a long way from nowhere. It'll take a few years to fix it up and raise enough cattle for a drive. I'm hoping when I disappear my name will fade into the past like some of the others who quit."

"I ain't sayin' you can't do it, but you'll have to stay clear of towns for a good long while."

"That won't be hard. I'm sick of all of them. The last town I wore a badge in, I had to gun down some drunk miners; men who probably never had a six-gun in their hands before. A crooked claim-jumper and his bunch put them up to it. I took out him and his boys, but not soon enough. He'd already poured enough liquor into the miners to convince them I was working with the bunch that was jumping their claims. They pulled on me. It was either take them out or let them cut me down. After it was over I threw my badge in the street and rode. I'm sick of killing for a living. I've been doing it too long. I'm hanging up my gun for good."

"Don't 'pear to me as if you've hung it up," Ben said dryly.

"I haven't yet," Chase admitted, "but I'm going to—I can promise you that. I wired Larkin earlier, since he was the only one I could remember from here, and asked him to send word down to Mexico for my old trail pard, Seth Wakefield, to meet me here. You remember Seth. We scouted for the army together when they were rounding up the Apaches. Anyway, Larkin got word back from him that he'd likely be here today. Soon as he comes we'll be heading for my ranch. When we get it rebuilt, I'm hoping we won't have much use for guns."

"Sounds like you're gettin' smart. Not much room fer men like us no more. That's why I got married, bought a little ranch, and settled here."

"Guess you saw it before I did. Anyway, Seth'll come running when he hears he's got a place to put down roots. He's older than you, but neither of us has ever had a place to call home."

"Sounds like you'll likely be out of town before the first then. I'd feel a whole lot better if you was." Ben wasn't backing down.

"Chances are we will, but if Seth doesn't show by then I'm going to wait for him. I'll stay out of the poker games when the cowboys hit town if it'll make you feel better. But you're not going to run me out of town, Ben." Chase wasn't a man to back down either.

"I won't—less you do somethin' that makes it my business as sheriff. If that happens, I'll do my job."

"Fair enough," Chase replied. "I hope there's no trouble either, but you know if someone brings it to me I'll finish it. If Seth shows today, it won't take long to make our plans. We'll load a packhorse and be out of here tomorrow before noon."

Ben's eyes narrowed. "Before the first, Chase." Then he turned on his heel and walked out of the bar without another word.

Chase went back to the table and picked up his money. He rolled down his sleeves and slipped into his coat as he walked toward the bar and ordered another drink. He sipped it slowly as he thought about the conversation he had just had with Ben. He had always liked the man and they had never had a run-in before now. They had even worked together a couple of times, cleaning up some pretty rough towns. It wasn't like Ben to come after him the way he did. Something was going on that Chase didn't understand. He would keep his eyes open, and his back to the wall, until he had a chance to talk it over with Seth.

As he finished his drink, he remembered the woman upstairs. He turned and walked toward the hotel lobby. Chase didn't have any idea what this woman might want, but he had never been one to ignore or hide from possible trouble. Besides, his curiosity was getting the better of him. He couldn't help but wonder how she knew him, and more than that, how she knew he would be in Albuquerque. There was only one way to find out.

*C*hase stopped at the front desk to speak with the clerk on his way upstairs. "I'm expecting a friend today—name of Seth Wakefield. You can't miss him. He's tall and skinny—like an old scarecrow. If he comes in, give him Room 4 across the hall from me," Chase said, handing the clerk some money. "Tell him I'm in Room 5. If he doesn't find me there, I'll meet him in the bar later." The clerk mumbled the room numbers, nodded, and made a note in his ledger.

Chase mounted the steps two at a time and strode down the hall to Room 9. Always the wary gunfighter, he hesitated and checked his six-gun before knocking. This woman could be more than she seemed. She could still be someone with an old score to settle. She wouldn't be the first woman to carry a derringer and know how to use it. He wasn't partial to snobbish eastern women, but for the moment he didn't have anything better to do. He would find out what her business was, and get it settled before Seth arrived.

Chase straightened his coat and rubbed the dust from the toes of his boots on the back of his pants legs before knocking. His knock was answered immediately by a low, clear voice from inside the room. He opened the door and stepped inside, removing his hat.

Standing by the window was the most beautiful young woman he had ever seen. She was small; barely five feet tall. Her dress was expensively tailored and very fashionable. She was a mature woman despite her size. The well-rounded bodice of her dress and upper body tapered to a tiny waist. The skirt hugged her hips for a few inches below her waist and then fell in small pleats almost to the floor. Chase had never seen so much woman in such a small package.

"I take it you are Chase Wade," she said, walking toward him. Her long black hair fell in natural waves below her shoulders, framing her delicate, lightly tanned face. She had high, narrow cheekbones with a perfect nose and mouth. Her eyes were almond-shaped, giving her an exotic, almost mysterious look.

"I am, but I don't know who you are, ma'am."

"I am Miss VanDerVeer, and if you are through looking me over, I need to talk with you." It was obvious from the cold, crisp edge in her voice that she wasn't flattered by his visual appraisal. "I have been looking for you in small towns all over the West for nearly a year now. Most of them were not the kind of places I care to be." She motioned for him to take a chair by the door as she sat on the edge of the bed.

She continued, "I am sure you were not expecting me, but now that I see you, I will have to admit you are not exactly what I expected either."

Chase sat down. "You're right. I don't know what

you want, or how you found me, and I sure I don't understand why I would be a surprise to you. If you've been looking for me, I'd guess the people you've talked to told you plenty about me. Otherwise you wouldn't be here." Chase relaxed a little; she didn't sound like she was looking for trouble.

She nodded. "I have heard a lot about you and nearly every other gunfighter in this part of the country. I talked to a great many lawmen and army officers, and you were recommended above all the others. They said you were quick to use your gun, but you had never run afoul of the law. They also said you were honest, and if you gave your word, you would keep it. Sheriff Beal in Santa Fe told me you were coming here."

"That explains it," Chase mumbled to himself. Tom Beal was an old friend he'd stopped by to see on his way down. He was glad to have an answer to at least one of his questions. "I reckon you heard the truth, ma'am, but that still doesn't explain why I'm a surprise to you."

"Well, you are not at all what I expected. I had several other men pointed out to me; gunmen like you who might be able to help me. None of them looked anything like you. They all looked—I cannot explain—somehow hard and ruthless. Even the ones who were well dressed and carried guns with fancy grips."

"I know the kind of men you mean, but I'm not one of them. I only wear a suit when I'm in town. On the trail I wear range clothes, same as a cowboy. Never was one for fancy guns either. To me a gun's just a tool. Plain works as well as fancy. I like a shave every morning and a bath when there's enough water, but other than that I guess I'm pretty much like the other men you saw."

"That is where you are wrong, Mr. Wade." She had been watching him closely as he spoke. "From where I am sitting I do see a difference. If I had run into you on the street I would never have picked you for the man I was looking for. Granted, you do not look like a rancher or a businessman. There is something in your eyes..." She looked at him appraisingly. "Not hate or meanness like I saw in so many others. But that is not important now. If you can live up to your reputation—and I heard it from so many men I have no reason to believe otherwise—I would like to hire you to take me into the desert. I need to travel near a place called Pike City. I also want you to buy me a rifle and instruct me in its use."

Chase interrupted before she could go on. "Whoa, just a minute, little lady," he said as he got to his feet. "If I was still hiring out my gun, which I'm not, I'd have to know a lot more about why you want to go into that country. That's a long, hard trip even for an experienced desert man, much less a fancy eastern woman like you."

Chase could tell by the determined look on her face that he was not getting through to her. He went on to paint the hardships of desert travel.

"It's hotter than Hell out there, and some places there's hardly enough water to survive. What there is is sometimes so bad-tasting you only drink it to keep from dying. Pike City's been a ghost town for years. It's right at the start of the canyon country. Some of those canyons are so hot you'd swear your skin was frying, and they run on for miles. Some clear up into Utah. I've known men to go in and never come out."

She didn't flinch. "I know of the hardships. That is why I want to hire you to take me in—into one canyon in particular. You will know how to find the water and get me to my destination and back. I do not know a great deal about this country. But before I started looking for you I lived for two years in Kansas, learning what I could about the West. I can ride a horse and I am a lot stronger than I appear."

Chase was still shaking his head. "If you'd found me a couple months ago we might have talked about it. It's not that I'd mind spending a few months in the desert with a beautiful woman, but my gun isn't for hire anymore. I'm waiting for an old friend to get to town so we can go to my new ranch. We're settling down; hanging up our guns. And even if we weren't, I wouldn't want the responsibility of taking a woman like you into the desert." Chase backed toward the door.

Miss VanDerVeer jumped to her feet. "Just what do you mean—a woman like me? I thought a gunman would do anything for money. I have the money. It never occurred to me that you would refuse the job."

Chase walked back toward her. "I'm sorry, ma'am. Like I said, if you'd have come around sooner we might have talked about it. I don't know what else to tell you."

"First, I need to know what you meant by 'a woman like me'!" She was now standing very erect, her shoulders thrown back.

Chase smiled. "You should be able to look at

yourself and answer that question. You're dressed like you just stepped off a train from Philadelphia. You seem to hold yourself above the kind of people you've run into out here. Sheriff Taylor said it a little less politely, but maybe it fits. He said you were one of those snobbish eastern women. Are you?"

The young woman now held Chase in the piercing gaze of her snapping ebony eyes. "The sheriff saw me just as I wanted him to. The way I expect most people to see me. It has not been easy traveling around as I do. First I am a woman alone, and second I am of mixed heritage. As I am sure you know, there are those who would take advantage of me for either reason. I find it best to keep my distance."

"Where did you come from?" Chase realized this woman was still raising more questions than she was answering.

"I was raised in Boston by a wealthy aunt and uncle before I went to Kansas. My father was a Dutch ship captain and my mother was from China, but I do not see that this has any bearing on my request that you take me to Pike City. I still need your help."

Chase shook his head. "What you've told me—that you were raised comfortably in Boston—only confirms what I did think. That you aren't prepared physically to make such a trip. Besides, you've done a lot of talking and I still know only where you want to go—not why."

"All in good time, Mr. Wade. Before I tell you any more, I need to know how you view me—aside from your appraisal that I am too soft for desert travel." She sat back down on the edge of the bed waiting for his answer.

Chase moved back to the chair and sat studying her face for a moment before speaking. He wasn't sure how honest he could be with a woman like this. "If I'm not out of line, I'd like to say that when I first walked into this room, I thought you were the most beautiful woman I'd ever seen. After talking with you, I can see you are a woman with a strong purpose—even if I haven't gotten out of you what it is. I suppose if you weren't such a high-class lady I'd ask you to join me for supper."

"I was not looking for your compliments, Mr. Wade," she snapped back. "I am offering you a business proposition—nothing more. You will do well to remember that. For now, I must decide if you are a man I can trust—a man I can tell more of my story to."

"I don't see that it's a question of whether *I* can be trusted," Chase shot back. "You've already checked me out. You're the one avoiding the questions. My father taught me how to treat a lady before I lost him when I was twelve. If I didn't still remember those lessons I'd have walked out on you by now." His patience was wearing thin.

She looked at him in silence for a moment before she spoke. "Alright. First, my full name is Kally VanDerVeer. You may call me Kally if you wish. I am not as much of a snob as the sheriff thought. And to show you I am not really as I appear, I will agree to dine with you, Mr. Wade—to discuss my business proposition."

"Whoa! My name's Chase. If I'm going to call you Kally, you'll have to call me Chase."

"I'm sorry. When you're raised in Boston, it's

hard to break the habit of not using first names with people you're not well acquainted with. That's one of the reasons I went to Kansas—to get some of the 'Boston' out of me—but mostly I wanted to get away from my aunt and uncle, and prepare for this trip."

Chase sat back in his chair and listened as Kally continued. "I taught school in Kansas and saved all the money I could. Most of my clothes I brought from Boston, and the rest I made myself. I visited a lot with the families of my students. Most of them were farmers, but they had a saddle horse or two and they taught me to ride. I rode every chance I got."

"Excuse me for interrupting, Kally, but knowing how to ride a horse is only the beginning of what you'll need to know to make a trip like this. I'm afraid you're just not..."

"Please hear me out, Mr. Wade. It doesn't matter that I'm an eastern woman who only knows how to ride a horse. I'll go to Pike City, with or without your help."

Chase smiled again. He was beginning to admire this young woman's spunk and determination. "Alright, I'll listen, but you haven't said anything yet that convinces me either of us should make this trip."

"When I was able to ride a horse well enough, I quit my job and started looking for a man to take me. It didn't take long to realize some of the men I found could have been more of a danger to me than anything I might run into on the trail. That's one reason I want to learn to use a rifle. Any reason beyond that is none of your concern."

Chase nodded. "I can understand why you'd worry, but if you hired someone like me to take you,

you wouldn't need a gun yourself. It would be his job to protect you."

"I would expect him to protect me from others, but who will protect me from him? I'm not so naive that I would not understand how a man might feel after being on the trail with a woman for several months. I want to make it clear from the beginning: my only interest in you, as a man, is that you can take me where I want to go. That's all. When I learn to use a rifle, I'll sleep with it." From the tone of her voice, Chase had no doubt that she would.

"You speak real plain when you need to, Kally. I like that. I understand your reasons for wanting to learn to use a rifle. I suspect there may be more to it, but for now I'll accept what you've said. Besides, there are plenty of reasons for knowing how to use a gun in the desert.

"But you're talking like you still expect me to take you. I've told you my gun's not for hire. It'll take all summer for Seth and me to fix up the ranch for the winter."

"But couldn't you put that off for a while if something more important came up, something that might make it worth your while?"

"I reckon we could. This gal named Kally is convincing me a lot more quickly than that snobbish Miss VanDerVeer could have. You just might be woman enough to survive such a trip. Knowing how to ride helps, but Kansas really isn't the West anymore. The desert can be hell, even for a man who's used to it. You've never experienced the kind of heat I'm talking about; you would have to toughen up in a hurry. You'd have to leave all those fancy clothes behind and wear men's riding gear. There's not much privacy for a woman. Baths will be few and far between. Most of the time you'll be more worried about finding enough water to drink."

"I don't care what you say, I'm not changing my mind." Kally stood her ground.

Chase tried another tactic. "Besides the hardships, we haven't even talked about the dangers. Did you know the Indians are back in the desert?"

Kally's expression didn't change. "No, I didn't know about the Indians, but that doesn't alter the situation. I'll still get to Pike City, somehow!"

Chase admired her, but he was still concerned for her safety. "My friend Seth and I helped the army dig the Apaches out of the desert and canyons a few years back, but they didn't stay on the reservations long. The army is out in full strength trying to bring them back. But even with the army on their tail they don't hesitate to lift a scalp if they get the chance. The two of us out there alone would be a prime target, but then if I was going, it wouldn't be just the two of us. Seth would go. Of course we'd need a couple of Mexican or Indian wranglers to handle the pack mules. It will take a lot of supplies for a trip like you're talking about."

"In that case the Indians wouldn't be much of a threat, would they?" Kally said, as if winning a point for her side.

"No," Chase admitted. He could see he wasn't going to scare her off. "But you still haven't told me why you want to make this trip."

"I haven't told you because you haven't said you'd take the job. My reasons will have to be kept secret from everyone but those who accompany me. The fewer people who know, the better. Like I said earlier, I assumed the kind of man who would take the job would only be interested in the money. My reasons wouldn't be important."

"With some men you'd be right, but when I sell my services I earn my pay. I can't seem to get across to you the dangers involved in such a trip. My job wouldn't be just to guide you, I'd become responsible for your safety, even your life. I'd have to know a whole lot more about where you were going and why, then weigh the dangers for all of us. Telling me it's a big secret doesn't tempt me at all."

"Mr. Wade, you are one of the most infuriating men I have ever met, but I still believe you are the man to take me on this trip. What is it going to take for me to convince you?"

Chase had never met a woman like this one. If she had spent a year in this country, traveling between towns on trains and dusty stagecoaches trying to find him, it was obvious there was little he could say to change her mind. Besides, if he didn't take her she would find someone else to, likely someone less capable of doing the job right.

The ranch had sat idle for several years already, so another year wouldn't make much difference. Chase knew the trip to and from Pike City alone would take two months or more, and he had no idea how long Kally's business would take beyond that. He had to figure at least most of the summer. He and Seth wouldn't mind wintering in Albuquerque and heading for the ranch next spring. Chase made a quick decision, as he usually did.

"If you can convince me there's an important reason to make this trip—reason enough to warrant taking all the risks and facing all the hardships—I'll take you, but I won't charge you a penny. I have to keep my word, even to myself, and when I said I wouldn't hire out my gun again I meant it. If you've got a good reason for this trip, I know Seth will be ready to go along. He's an old warrior from way back. I've never known him to pass up a chance for a little adventure, especially when there's a pretty gal involved. I have enough money put aside to start the ranch when we get back, so I wouldn't have to charge you if you bought all the supplies."

"Of course. I'll pay for everything."

"You've said you believed I was a man of my word. Now you'll have to put that to the test. I can't make a decision about taking you on this trip until I know everything. Whatever it is will be your secret. If, after you tell me, I decide not to make the trip, no one else will ever know of our talk. Everything you say will stay right in this room. If you can't take that chance, then I'll still enjoy your company at supper tonight, but I won't take you."

"That sounds pretty final, but at least you've given me some hope. I've never been close to a man since my father left. I don't like men much, but I know I can't make this trip alone. I'm really not comfortable even talking about making this trip with you, but the fact that your friend Seth and the wranglers will be along will help some. I don't like having a strange man in my room. If this didn't have to remain a secret, I would have met you in the dining room."

Chase's patience was wearing thin. "I can understand that, but are you going to tell me or not?"

"Alright, Chase Wade. I've got to believe you'll keep your word about not telling if you decide not to go with me. I know I could never stand up to you with a gun and I sure couldn't whip you in a fight, but you'd better believe that if you turn down my offer and then let any of this out, I'll spread the word Chase Wade doesn't keep his word, especially to a lady."

"You'll never have to spread that word."

Kally got up and paced the floor in silence as she tried to put her thoughts in some kind of order. After a moment or two she began her story in a low voice.

"It's not a long story, but it's all true. My father is, or was, in the canyon where I want you to take me. He may be dead, but I can't rest until I know for sure. I haven't seen him since I was about nine. He left me with my aunt and uncle while he came out West to find gold so he could buy a home and raise me." Kally stopped for a moment and looked intently at Chase before going on.

"I didn't hear from my father for six years. Then one day a box arrived from him. Inside were three gold bars. A year later another box came with three more bars, along with a letter and a map. He had discovered gold, lots of it. The first box came from Utah, the second from Nevada. The letter said he was being followed, so I might not hear from him again. I never did. That was why he sent the map. If I didn't hear from him, I was to follow the map to the gold, and take in only twenty mules to carry it out. He said even though they couldn't carry out half the gold that was there, I would be rich. I would never have to worry about money again."

Chase had difficulty not interrupting her at this point. He had heard many stories like this before, but he let her continue. The look in her eyes told him it was this story that drove her.

"I've tried to accept that my father is dead. I haven't heard from him in so long. But something inside won't allow me to let go of him. I have to know, to see some remains, something that will tell me he's really gone. Besides, if he gave his life to find the gold for me, it would all have been in vain unless I go in there and bring some of it out. I know that's what he wanted." Kally was fighting back the tears, but wouldn't give in to them.

"I've thought a lot about that gold. It can change many things for me, but even if we don't find it, I have to make this trip. If you and your friend Seth are willing to help me, I'll make you full partners. We can all come out rich and you and Seth wouldn't be risking your lives just to help me."

Chase stood. "You can stop there, Kally. I've heard enough. You won't have to worry about my telling your story. I've probably heard at least a thousand other stories about lost gold mines, most with maps to go along with them. Those dumb enough to believe the stories have paid a lot of money for a map some swindler had drawn up in his room only hours before. All the lost gold mines I ever heard of stayed lost."

"I assure you," Kally insisted, "this is not like those stories."

"As far as I'm concerned, it is. I'm certainly not

prepared to risk all our necks to go chasing into the worst country in the West after a fairy tale. I'll see you at seven. I'll buy you the best supper in town, and in the morning I'll put you on a train back to Kansas. Use the money you've saved to open a dress shop, or something. Burn that map and accept the fact your father is dead. You'd have heard from him by now if he wasn't. Go back, find a good man, and start building yourself a new life."

Kally said nothing but started digging in one of her bags as Chase walked toward the door. As he reached for the knob, her voice stopped him.

"You've listened this long. Just take a minute more to look at this. What I told you was no fairy tale. My father's word was as good as yours. He never lied. I have a very detailed map only my father could have drawn. And it's not a gold mine. It has to be a cave or a hole of some kind, with tons of these in it."

Chase turned and walked over to the bed. On it, lay four gold ingots. Beside them lay a map burned into what looked like the back cut from a buckskin shirt. The map clearly showed Pike City and a canyon to the north of it Chase had never been in. He remembered it as a box canyon, but the map showed it twisting and turning for miles.

She was right, this wasn't a hastily drawn map. It was very detailed, with numbers, landmarks, bells, and mules burned in very carefully with a nail or pointed instrument of some kind. The drawings were not crude. Even the ears of the mules were long, to distinguish them from horses. Chase had no idea what some of the symbols meant, but if Kally's father had drawn the map for her, he obviously believed she would be able to follow it. Chase was sure they could figure it all out when they got to Pike City.

Kally picked up one of the ingots and handed it to Chase. The date stamped on top was 1538. He couldn't read the writing. The sides and bottom of the ingot showed the tiny pits of a sandy clay mold. A little of the clay still clung to the bar. Chase rubbed off some and looked at it closely. He had seen that color clay in the canyon country.

Kally looked intently into Chase's face as he studied the gold. "The words are Latin. I read Latin, but they aren't words I recognize, probably names of men or a place. I've read all I could find about Coronado and the Jesuit priests who were in this country over three hundred years ago. From what I've found out, I'd say this was gold taken from the Indians, then melted down for transport to Mexico, and later Spain."

Kally had Chase's attention now. He continued to study the gold and the map as she went on.

"I don't know what happened, but the gold never left that canyon. Somehow my father found it, and I believe it's still there. I had the clay assayed, but all they could tell me was that it came from the Grand Canyon country. Each ingot weighs exactly one troy pound. I cashed in two of them so I could finish my schooling and make the move to Kansas. I wasn't able to save much from my teacher's wages, but with what I have and what the rest of the ingots will bring, I can easily finance the trip. You must take me. If my father is still alive, or if there is anything of his left, I've got to find it. I can't let his death be for nothing."

"I'll see you at seven," said Chase as he headed for the door.

"Wait!" Kally called after him. "You can't just leave me standing here. I've got to have an answer. Where are you going?"

"To see if Seth's rode in yet. If not, to find you a good horse and round up twenty mules. Hide those ingots and map. Lock this door and don't open it for anyone but me."

*C*hase reached the lobby just as Seth came through the front doors of the hotel. It was easy to see that he had been on the trail a long while. His clothes were dusty and well worn. Chase hurried to meet him, holding out his hand.

"It's about time you showed up, you old bag of bones." Chase was clearly happy to see his old friend again. "Larkin said you got my message, but I sort of thought you might get here ahead of me. Must have had too many señoritas to take care of first." Chase laughed.

Seth took his hat off and hit it against his leg, sending up a cloud of dust. His hair was long and heavily streaked with gray. "I'd have been here sooner, but I did have some unfinished business with a certain little señorita," he admitted in his deep bass voice, giving Chase a wink. He hadn't shaved in a while, and the stubble on his face was pure white. He was a good four inches taller than Chase, but stood in a natural slump, giving him the appearance of being older and less agile than he really was. Even Chase had never been anxious to get into a fight with him, with fists or guns.

"Y'all serious about this ranch thing?" Seth asked with a twinkle in his light gray eyes. "Truth is, this señorita says she's in love with me an' I reckon I love her. Anyhow, I'd like to bring her up here later if this ranch deal's on the level."

Chase was a little surprised at his old friend. In all the years he had known Seth, he had never heard him talk about settling down with a woman. Although Seth was old enough to be his father, he was one of those ageless men whose love for adventure rivaled that of any man years younger. When things got too slow for him he headed down to Mexico, found some little revolution, and got a job teaching rebel peasants how to fight. Besides, he had always been able to find a warm bed with some pretty Mexican señorita.

"You bet it's on the level."

"Come on an' tell me about it over a drink." Seth motioned toward the bar. "I've got a heap of trail dust to wash down. We can talk there as well as standin' here holdin' hands."

They walked into the bar and ordered whiskey. When the bartender brought the bottle and glasses they carried them to a table in the corner. Chase waited until Seth had downed the first drink and had poured a second before he spoke.

"I don't reckon I pulled you out of some important war, did I?"

"War—hell!" Seth exclaimed. "This was the worst yet. I had a little band of peasants who didn't like what the government was doin' with taxes an' the like, but they sure didn't wanna fight. We had one run-in with the Mexican regulars an' got whupped pretty bad. The message y'all sent me was bein' carried by a Mexican with a wagon-load of rifles for us. He'd have made it, but the regulars hit him a day out of where we was holed up in the hills. He jumped off the wagon an' ran like hell. He got your message into camp, but the regulars got the guns. We didn't have a chance without 'em, so I sent the men home. They're probably back diggin' in their gardens an' talkin' about what great soldiers they are," Seth finished with a laugh.

"Same old Seth."

"Of course I didn't get half the pay they promised me, so I'm broke as usual. You're gonna have to pay for these drinks, Chase. Any chance you could loan a friend enough to get a bath, haircut an' shave, an' maybe some new duds before we head out?"

"You've got it." Chase nodded. "You should have known I wouldn't expect anything different."

"Now tell me about this ranch. Where does she set? I reckon settlin' down on a ranch sounds pretty good to me about now. Besides, don't know nobody I'd rather throw in with than you, Chase. We always did make a mighty good team."

"You know that's mutual, Seth. I wouldn't have sent for you otherwise." Chase slapped him on the shoulder. "The ranch is in the high country of Colorado. Right at the end of the good grazing land. Sets right on the first jump of the Rockies. Can hardly call it a ranch though. Not even a corral or lean-to barn on it. Cabin will need some fixing, but it sits up high among the tall pines. The main range is a wide, long valley with a river running right through the middle.

Guess it's about the prettiest country I've seen in a long time."

"Sounds good to me."

"Cabin will likely get snow in the winter, but I don't expect much in the valley. I rode out to look it over before riding on down here. I'm going to hang up my gun when I get there, and put up a permanent peg for my hat. There'll be a couple of pegs for you, too, Seth, for as long as you want them."

"You're paintin' a mighty pretty picture." Seth downed his second drink. "Not 'cause I'm gettin' old, mind you, but there's not much room for men like us no more. First the beaver went, then the buffalo. We run out of Injuns to chase. The little Mexican revolutions are playin' out an' the boom towns are dryin' up. Just let me get cleaned up an' into some new clothes, while you get the supplies an' load 'em on my packhorse. Then I'll be rarin' to go."

"Here's the money you'll need." Chase handed him several bills. "I'm as anxious to go as you are, pardner, but pour yourself another drink. Something's come up we need to take care of. I promised a young gal we'd help her first. It may take us a few months, but the ranch'll be waiting when we get back."

"Y'all ain't changed a bit, Chase."

"You don't have to come along, but the truth is I'm going to need your help. She wants us to take her over into the canyon country, near Pike City, and help her bring out twenty mule loads of gold."

"Aw, Chase, I thought I taught you better'n that. This gal wouldn't happen to be a real looker, would she?"

"Probably the most beautiful woman I've ever

met. She's half oriental, and about as much woman as I'd ever want to handle. But that doesn't have anything to do with it. Her father told her about the gold, and then disappeared."

"That explains it. I never saw a pretty woman you didn't wanna help. I don't reckon the location of the mine is a mystery an' she just happens to have a map that'll lead us right to it?"

"That about covers it," Chase admitted.

"Come on. Don't tell me some pretty little filly can make you believe a story like that? We've both been on enough wild goose chases to last us a lifetime. I can understand you wantin' to be with this almond-eyed, little beauty, but you'd be a heap more comfortable at the hotel here in town. If you need a last fling before we hit the ranch, we can ride over an' get into a couple good fistfights with them wild Texas cowboys."

"I know what you're thinking, but this is different."

"Sounds like the same old story to me. Besides, as hot as it is already this spring, the canyon country'll be unbearable by summer. Y'all go ahead an' enjoy this gal for a couple days while I rest up, have a few more drinks, an' play a little poker with your money. Then we'll go on up to the ranch an' sweat for somethin' that'll pay off someday."

"I knew you were going to feel this way, so why don't you get some of that trail dust soaked off. You're in Room 4 upstairs. Stop at the desk and tell them to send you up some hot water. We're meeting Miss Kally VanDerVeer for supper. You'll have time enough to make up your mind about her. After that I'll have a couple of things to show you."

"Y'all know me. Never pass up a chance to have supper with a beautiful woman, but I'm not likely to change my mind about nothin'."

"Okay, if you still don't want to go along, after you meet Kally and see what she's got, I'll give you a map and enough money and supplies to get started at the ranch. I've already given her my word I'd take her. I'll join you as soon as we get back."

"Y'all know me better'n that, Chase Wade," Seth answered with the same old twinkle in his eye. "Pretty woman or not, I know you wouldn't be goin' on this wild goose chase unless she'd done a heap of convincin'. I can think of a lot cooler places I'd like to spend the summer, but if you happen to find somethin' to load on them mules for the trip home, you just might be needin' my gun. Y'all know I'll be right beside you as long as you need me."

"Thanks, pardner. I knew I could count on you. Now why don't you take the rest of that bottle with you. You can get your insides good and cleaned out while you're scrubbing the outside.

"I'm going to find Kally a good desert horse and see what I can find in the way of mules. I'm in Room 5 and Kally's in Room 9, but she won't let anyone in but me. We'll meet you in the dining room at seven."

"This is all gettin' mighty interestin', boy. I'm gettin' right anxious to meet this mystery woman." Seth picked up the bottle and headed for the stairs.

"One other thing." Chase stopped him. "Ben Taylor's sheriff here. He's actually gotten married and settled down on his own place. But he's a might more nervous than the old days. Practically tried to run me out of town."

"Sure don't sound like the Ben Taylor I recollect."

"Seems things get pretty heated up around here after the cowboys get paid on the first. He's afraid we'll get mixed up in some fighting and doesn't want to get caught in the middle of it."

"Ben knows we don't go lookin' for a fight. In the old days he'd have backed either of us if we was in the right."

"That's what I thought, but I told him we'd be out of here by the first as long as you got here by then. Maybe best if we just stay clear of him while we're in town."

✳

Chase walked to the livery. He stopped by the loafing lot to check on his horse. Ranger was a big chestnut he had owned for almost ten years. He was the best horse Chase had ever had. He could work cattle and make the long rides across the desert with little water. He was surefooted, and could handle narrow mountain trails with ease. Chase would not have traded him for the ten best mustangs in the country.

Chase gave Ranger a couple of more loving pats and then went to find Larkin, the man who owned the livery. He was standing in the big doorway out front.

"That's one fine horse you've got there, Chase. Don't suppose you'd care to sell him or maybe do some tradin'?"

"Not on your life," Chase returned. "But I am in

the market for another good horse and some mules with packsaddles. Can you help me?"

"Jest might," Larkin said as he threw away the stick he had been whittling and slipped the knife into his pocket. "I sort of fell into the horse an' mule tradin' business by accident. Someone was always comin' in here wantin' to sell onè, or buy one, like you. Got way too many mules right now. Not many prospectors needin' 'em anymore, an' the railroad's about put the packers out of business. I bought a few here an' there, but can't seem to get rid of 'em. How many was you thinkin' about?"

"Twenty?"

"That would about clean me out, but I wouldn't be sorry to get rid of 'em. Reckon I've got that many packsaddles around somewhere too. I'll throw 'em in with the mules. Ain't got but three or four here. No room for 'em. They're out to my place, but I can have 'em here in the mornin' if you want."

"I haven't heard the price yet."

"We won't have a problem with the price. Jest make me a fair offer, an' they're yours. I've plenty of horses too. What'd you have in mind?"

"It's for a woman. She's small, so I thought I might find a smaller horse she wouldn't have much trouble mounting. It's got to be desert bred, and not a mustang. They don't have enough bottom for the long hauls."

"I've got a nice little paint, jest right for a woman. Let's go look."

They climbed the pole fence of the side lot. It was clear Larkin did more buying than selling. Chase spotted the paint, but after watching him for a moment realized he was young and probably just rough broke. Kally could mount him easily, but he was too green for this kind of trip. Besides, Apaches were partial to paints and Chase didn't want to have to worry about having their scalps lifted over a horse. He wasn't too worried about Apaches, but some of them were still out there with the road agents and rustlers he hadn't told Kally about. Not that it would change her mind.

Chase watched the other horses for a few minutes. As they moved around, he suddenly saw the horse for Kally. He was as big as Ranger and almost the same color. Chase climbed down and worked his way to the horse's side.

"His name's Pacer," Larkin called from the fence. "I sort of figured if you knew horses, you'd spot him. He's one of mine. Desert bred, but mostly Morgan. Think he's got some Walker in him too, because of his gait. He's well broke an' cattle wise, sound as a dollar. But he won't be cheap."

Chase gave Pacer a once over. His hooves and teeth were good, and he had been shod recently. He was gentle and responded readily to Chase's pats. Chase was sure Kally would need a leg up, but with her light weight, this horse would probably outdistance Ranger in an all-out run. Chase gave Pacer one last pat, walked back, and climbed over the fence.

"Looks like you just sold a horse and twenty mules with packsaddles, if we can get together on the price."

By the time they had reached the front of the livery again, they had made a deal. Larkin promised to have the mules and packsaddles at the livery early the next morning. He didn't have a used saddle small enough for Kally, but sent Chase to see Señor Perez. Larkin said he made nice Spanish style saddles in all sizes.

Larkin had been right. It took Chase only a few minutes to pick out a smaller woman's saddle with matching saddlebags. He had planned to get a used one, to save Kally a little money, but he knew a comfortable saddle was more important. After he had moved the saddle and other gear to the livery, he stopped by the big supply store for the blankets and tarp for her bedroll, and a canvas sack for her personal items.

Checking his pocket watch, he picked up his stride. He barely had enough time to get a bath before supper. He knew it would be his last hot one for a long time.

After cleaning up, he picked up the things he had gotten for Kally and knocked on Seth's door. He was not surprised when there was no answer. Knowing Seth, he would already be downstairs in a poker game or at the bar.

Chase walked down the hall and knocked on Kally's door, identifying himself. He heard the lock turn, then the door swung open. Kally had changed dresses and had stacked her long hair on top of her head, where it was held in place with an ornate Spanish comb. He was speechless as he looked at her.

Chase knew this woman was different from any he had ever met. She was not only the most beautiful he had ever seen, she was the most fascinating.

She had changed to higher heeled shoes, and the elegant dress she wore was made from a shiny white fabric that contrasted with her raven hair and naturally red lips. She was like a picture out of a mail-order catalog, in one of those dresses western women only dreamed about.

"Are you going to stand there all day, or would you like to come in?" Kally asked, breaking his trance.

"You look lovely tonight, Miss Kally," Chase responded in his most gallant voice.

"Thank you, Mr. Wade." Kally was visibly uncomfortable with his compliments, and avoided his eyes.

"Seth got here, and he's waiting for us downstairs, but we need to take care of a little business before we go. Here are some things you'll need for the trip," he said, dropping them near the door. "I'll show you what to do with them later. Do you have a pen and paper? We need to make a list of the rest of the things you're going to need."

Kally rummaged through her bag, glad for a change of subject.

"I found you a horse this afternoon, as well as twenty mules with packsaddles. We'll pick those up in the morning. Shouldn't be too hard to find a couple of wranglers to take care of them on the trail. I also got you a saddle and saddlebags."

"Sounds like you've had a busy afternoon. I've waited so long for all this, I can't believe things are happening so quickly." Kally pulled paper, pen, and ink from her bag as she spoke.

Chase went on. "We hope to be ready to leave right after dinner tomorrow, so we don't have time to waste. I'll have to bring Seth back here after supper to see the map and gold. It won't take long to find you a rifle in the morning. Now if you're ready to write, I'll start the list."

They were fifteen minutes late getting to the dining room by the time Chase had explained everything and Kally had written it all down. Seth was waiting at the bar and watched them come in. Chase felt proud as he escorted Kally into the room, and all eyes turned in their direction.

Seth met them at the table, looking like a new man after a bath, haircut, and shave, and decked out in his new trail clothes. Chase introduced him to Kally.

By the time they had gotten through the introductions and were on a first-name basis, Chase could see Seth was as taken with Kally as he had been. She was obviously uncomfortable being with two admiring men, but by the time they had ordered supper and had had a couple of cups of coffee, she seemed to relax some and was at least enjoying Seth's company. She was little more than polite to Chase, and when he spontaneously reached out and touched her arm while they were talking, she pulled back unexpectedly, startling him. She had obviously not spent much time in the company of men.

Over supper, Chase and Seth discussed the plans for the morning in a low voice so they wouldn't be overheard. When they had finished eating and drinking a final cup of coffee, Chase suggested they go back to Kally's room.

Chase nodded to her as they closed and locked the door behind them. She went directly to her bag and laid out the gold and map on the bed. Seth picked up one of the ingots, turning it over and over in his hand, quietly studying every inch of it. He wet his finger and wiped it along the ingot, then touched his finger to his tongue. He was silent as Chase and Kally both watched him intently. Then he said only two words.

"Spirit's gold."

"What do you mean—'spirit's gold'? They're the gold bars Kally's father sent her." Chase was surprised at his old friend's strange reaction.

"Go ahead, Kally, tell him what you told me."

As she finished retelling her story, Chase cut in, "I don't know much about this kind of thing, but I remember hearing of priests coming into a lot of this country. I've heard of Spanish helmets and breastplates being found as far north as Kansas and Colorado. Those bells on the map could be Spanish mission bells. It all makes a lot of sense to me."

"I can't argue with what you're sayin', either of you. Now I see why you decided to make this trip. I've strained enough seep water through my teeth out in them canyons to know the taste of the clay. It's the same clay the molds for these were made from."

Chase nodded and went on, "You know how that country is always changing. The earthquakes, with rocks falling all over the place, have completely changed the landscape. It's possible one of those earthquakes shook the mission down and covered it with rock, along with the gold. That could be what Kally's father found."

"I'm not superstitious about this sort of thing, but the Injuns are. They seem to know somethin' about the cave dwellers who lived in them canyons a long time ago. They wasn't the kind of Injuns we know today, but no one seems to know much about 'em. They lived an' then just seemed to disappear off the face of the earth. Spooky iffen you ask me," Seth added.

Kally shuddered, but didn't speak.

"I've been up into some of them cave dwellin's an' there's not a bone or sign of any of 'em dyin' there. Just bits of pottery an' such. Not many clues to what happened to 'em. The Injuns are scared to death of them canyons. Say they're full of spirits of the old ones. We'd better look for Mexican wranglers, Chase, we won't get Injuns to go no farther than Pike City."

"Okay," Chase agreed, "but now what do you think about making this trip into the desert?"

"I think like you. I've been lookin' at this map. The man what made it knew where the gold was alright. It wasn't made in no hurry."

"I've seen a lot of phony maps, but I think this one's the real thing," Chase agreed.

Seth was bent over the map now as he spoke. "I can't make out all these symbols. These wavy lines must mean there's a stream here somewhere.

"Me an' Chase know the way to Pike City, Kally," Seth said as he straightened up and handed her the map. "I think once we're there we can follow the map one step at a time an' find that gold. The Injuns may call this spirit's gold, but from now on we'd better call it Kally's gold." Seth laughed.

"No, Seth, I forgot to tell you. Kally's a generous woman. She's offered to cut you and me in for equal shares of whatever we find. I guess if we find it we'll just call it our gold."

"That's mighty generous of you, Kally," Seth said

with a smile. "I never dreamed I might settle down with a little gold in my pocket. I've been broke all my life. Y'all just might change all that. But for now, Chase, if Kally'll trust you, you'd better take the map an' keep it safe. We've got a couple other problems to worry about."

"Not you too," Kally said. "Chase has already pointed out every problem imaginable, trying to convince me not to make this trip. Now what?"

"I take it you need the money from them ingots to pay for this trip?"

"That's right, I do."

"The only place to exchange that much gold is the bank. The minute we change it the word'll start spreadin'. In less than an hour the whole town'll know about it. In a few days everybody in Santa Fe will know too. By the time we load all our supplies an' pull out of here with twenty mules, we'll have a heap of gold-hungry men on our back trail. Ben may keep the known gunhands out of town, but I've already seen some men I recognize who wouldn't think twice about shootin' us in the back if they thought we was on the trail to some gold."

"You're right, Seth. I don't know why I didn't think of that sooner," Chase agreed.

"What can we do?" asked Kally. "Go to another town to cash in the gold and somewhere else for supplies?"

"That wouldn't do anything but waste time," Chase said. "People would catch on real fast. What are you thinking, Seth?"

"It's gonna cost Kally plenty to outfit us for this trip, but for a couple of no-goods it'll only take a few days' rations. If they picked us off in our sleep they could take over our mules, supplies, an' the map an' be on their way. First thing we'll have to do is split the night an' stand guard, startin' the first night out."

"I can already see that," Chase agreed. "What else?"

"If Kally's daddy was followed, goin' in an' out of that canyon at least twice we know about, it's hard to know how many men caught on to the fact the gold was there. No guessin' how many of 'em might still be wanderin' around that canyon tryin' to find it. Don't know how many guns might be waitin' for us when we get to Pike City. Them are my questions, but I don't have answers to even a one of 'em. Guess we'll just have to take 'em as they come."

"You know as well as I do, Seth, we'll have to take out anyone who comes after us. We can't take the chance of them coming back with more men to pick up our trail. I think we should ride straight across country instead of following the main trail. We'll have to do some zigzagging, and it'll take us longer, but we can't take a chance on having anyone still following us by the time we reach Pike City."

"I understand exactly what you're saying," Kally said, the strength of her determination filling her voice again. "I know you're right, and although I hope nothing like that ever has to happen, I want you to know I'll stand up to it. I didn't just get one right man to take me in, I've found two. I am thankful to both of you. But...." Kally hesitated a long time.

"But what?" Chase encouraged. "Is there something you haven't told us?"

Kally stood erect again. "No, of course not. I've

told you everything you need to know."

"Y'all just might make a real western gal after all, Kally," Seth said with a chuckle. "Me an' Chase'll do our best to get you in an' out with the gold. We're not anxious to share it with nobody else along the way. Now I'm goin' to bed. You two stay up an' talk if you like, but we've got a big day tomorrow. I'll see you at breakfast. We should be to the store by the time it opens. It'll take a spell to load the mules. An' we're sure to have a heap of rubberneckers around to watch."

"We'll be down bright and early," Chase said as Seth started for the door.

"Oh, Chase, before I forget." Seth stopped and turned back toward them. "I talked with Ben this afternoon. Ben's a proud man an' still fast with a gun, but he told me somethin' he couldn't tell you. His eyesight's goin'. He plans to back up his job or die tryin', but inside he's afraid. In a shootout with a cowboy he manages to get in close enough to see, but a real gunman's likely to make it a long shot. He just can't see good enough to hit his target at any distance. That's why he's tryin' to keep all gunmen out of town. He asked me to apologize to you for the way he acted."

"I'm sorry to hear that, but it explains a lot of things. I'll try to talk with him before we leave; let him know there's no hard feelings."

"Thought you might. Good night, you two."

Chase folded the map and slipped it into his shirt. Kally put the gold back into her bag. Then Chase spent the next few minutes showing her how to roll her blankets into a bedroll in the tarp he had gotten her.

The canvas bag would be for the personal items she would need on the trip. He encouraged her to think of any things she might need and get them in the morning. The only trading post where they could stop later probably wouldn't have what she could get here.

She would need to leave room in her saddlebags for ammunition and jerky and anything else she might want to get to easily without unrolling her bedroll. Kally was all business and took in all the information he had to give. She was a quick learner. Chase knew he wouldn't have to repeat any of his instructions.

"That's enough for tonight, Kally." Chase could tell she was tired from all the excitement of the day. So was he. "I'll come by for you on the way to break-fast, early."

"Good night, Mr. Wade. Thanks again for all you've done for me today. I know you and Seth will get me to my father's gold, no matter who..." Kally stopped suddenly. "No matter what happens." She closed the door quickly before Chase had a chance to respond.

Chase turned toward his own room. This was a strange woman. Sometimes he felt like he already knew a lot about her; at other times he wasn't sure he knew anything. The only thing he was sure of was that he wanted to know more about this mysterious woman who pulled back so quickly from his touch. He felt sure there was more to Kally VanDerVeer's story than what she had told them.

4

*C*hase was up early and shaved by lamplight. He dressed in his trail clothes, rolled the rest of his gear in his bedroll, and picked up his saddlebags.

The door to Seth's room stood open. He had already cleared out and would be waiting for them in the dining room. When Kally opened her door, she was ready to go. She wore a plain cotton dress with low-heeled shoes, and her hair was down around her shoulders again. Kally had already laid the gold ingots out on the bed. After Chase slipped them into his saddlebags, she handed him a roll of bills, which he tucked into his pocket.

"I hope with the ingots that will be enough. I saved out some to buy myself trail clothes, but that's all I have," Kally said as she locked the door behind them.

"I'm sure it will be," Chase assured her. "You might even have some left."

Seth was already seated at a table drinking coffee. When they joined him and had each poured them-

45

selves a cup, they found the pot was almost empty. He had been up awhile.

"You two are gonna have to start gettin' up earlier," Seth said with a grin. "It may be hard on you for a while, Kally, but we'll have to be up an' eatin' by first light when we get on the trail. I'm sure you'll do fine. It's Chase I'm worried about. He's been playin' cards all night an' sleepin' half the day for so long he's probably gotten soft." Seth winked at Kally.

"You don't worry none about me being soft, you old hoot owl. Kally and I'll both do just fine. It's not our fault you don't sleep much."

"It's a durn good way to stay alive," Seth answered with a chuckle. "But I was just funnin'. You're not late. Truth is I didn't sleep much last night—too much to think about. I hope you both like ham an' eggs. I ordered for all of us before you got here."

"Suits me," Kally said.

"You'd better eat hearty, Kally, before you have to start eating Seth's cooking," Chase warned.

"Y'all know what you can do iffen you don't like my cookin'."

"Yeah, but the only thing I hate worse than your cooking is my own," Chase answered.

"Do you two always get up on the wrong side of the bed, like this?" Kally asked as the girl brought their orders. "I intend to do my share on this trip. And I *can* cook."

"A Boston schoolmarm cookin' over a campfire?" Seth questioned with a mischievous grin.

"Wal, I reckon I kin cook plumb good. No harder to burn grub on a fire than on the stove, an' it'll be a heap better'n either of y'all kin do," Kally shot back.

"Well, I'll be. Did you hear that, Chase? Spunky little cuss, ain't she? We just might make a western gal out of her yet. She's even startin' to talk like regular folks," Seth added, slapping himself on the leg.

"Don't appear she'll be a tenderfoot for long," Chase agreed. "I, for one, will look forward to her cooking."

"I'm not making any promises, so you better eat your ham and eggs," Kally came back as she dug into her breakfast.

Over breakfast, Chase and Seth decided Seth should take the gold to the bank as soon as it opened. Since he had just ridden in the day before, he could concoct some story about finding it in Mexico and outfitting to go back for more. While he waited for the bank to open, he would stop by the store, put in their order, and get someone to start stacking the supplies out on the boardwalk so they would be ready to load onto the mules.

Kally had trail clothes to buy and packing to finish, and Chase was to take care of things at the livery.

Seth took Chase's saddlebags so they wouldn't have to expose the gold in public. They left the hotel and Chase hurried to the livery where he found the mules already hitched in a string with packsaddles on them. Larkin wasn't around, so he went to the loafing lot and found Ranger, Pacer, and Seth's old mare, Maude. He led them into the livery and saddled them up. He then went back for Seth's packhorse and was throwing a packsaddle on him when Larkin appeared with the bills of sale in his hand. Chase paid him and put all the papers in his back pocket, except for the one for Pacer, which he slipped into his shirt pocket.

"Thanks, Larkin," Chase said. "By the way, you wouldn't know of a couple Mexicans who are good with stock that might be looking for work, would you?"

"Don't know if they'll go, but the two boys what brought in the mules this mornin' are right good hands. They're brothers, about twenty or so. I use them when I've got work for 'em. Oldest of about ten younguns, so I know the family could use the money. They're in the side lot. I'll get 'em for you."

Larkin returned with two ragged Mexican boys trailing along behind him. He introduced them as Carlos and Roberto.

Chase looked them over carefully before making his offer. "You boys be interested in hiring on as wranglers for me? I'm heading for Mexico—probably won't be back for a few months."

"*Sí,* Señor Wade," Carlos answered. "We would like the job, but we have no horses, and we'd need new clothes and boots for such a long trip."

"I'll pay you twenty-five dollars a month and grub, furnish you with horses and used saddles, and advance enough for clothes and boots. Can either of you use a rifle?"

"*Sí,* señor. We are pretty good shots, but have only one old rifle between us."

"Larkin will have good horses and saddles for you, but you'll have to help stand night watch to pay for them. I'll buy you rifles, but they'll come out of your pay too. Here's two months pay for each of you. Buy clothes and bedrolls, and say good-bye to your family. Get back here pronto and bring the mules to the supply store. We're riding right after dinner."

"*Sí,* señor. We'll be at the store, ready to go, in an hour. *Gracias,* Señor Wade."

The boys turned and headed for the horse lot as Chase and Larkin negotiated a price for their horses and saddles. Chase paid him, mounted Ranger, and led the other horses to the supply store. He tied them at the rail. The boardwalk was already piled high, but Seth wasn't back yet. As he turned toward the bank, Seth came walking toward him.

Several people had followed him out of the bank and stood on the boardwalk watching him. A buzz of excitement was already growing in the street. Chase saw a couple of gamblers he recognized, and one he was sure he knew, but couldn't place. The people were starting to drift up from across the street, in hopes their curiosity would appear less noticeable. Seth was right. They could expect an audience until they got out of town—and beyond.

Seth handed Chase his saddlebags. "Y'all pay for the supplies. With what little we're gonna have to buy on the trail, Kally should have quite a bit left, whether we find the gold or not. That fool banker was a durn sight louder in our negotiations than he needed to be. Everybody in the bank knew what was goin' on. No way we'll get out of here without company today."

"I'm afraid you're right." Chase slipped the bills of sale out of his back pocket and into the saddlebags. "I got us a couple Mexican wranglers, named Carlos and Roberto. They'll be here in less than an hour with the mules. I'm going to take Kally's horse to her and help with her bags. Then we'll go to the gun shop after her rifle. Put the boys to work loading the supplies when they get here. Kally and I'll get back to help as soon as we can."

Chase reached the front of the hotel as Kally came out the door, dragging her suitcases, saddlebags, and bedroll behind her.

Chase dismounted and rushed toward her, reaching for her bags. "Give me those. I thought you hired us to help. You don't have to do everything yourself, you know."

Kally stood looking at him belligerently, then reluctantly let go of the bags, and they dropped in a heap on the boardwalk.

"Come on, I want you to meet your new horse. His name's Pacer. Here's the bill of sale; it's made out in your name. Whatever comes of this trip, at least you'll have your own horse. I think the two of you'll get along real good. He's a beauty.

"But first, let me look at you." Chase stopped Kally. "You sure don't look like a Boston school-teacher in those western duds." Chase had hoped she would look more like a young boy, but in her close-fitting pants and western shirt, there was no doubting she was all woman. She had found a hat almost identical to the ones Chase and Seth wore, and her boots were plain, but expensive. Her hair was tied back loosely with a ribbon below her shoulders. It would protect her neck from the hot sun.

She had dressed as closely as she could to the way the men were dressed, right down to the big, red neckerchief around her neck. Chase liked her even better in her western gear than he had in her fancy dresses.

"You look real good, Kally. But how do those

boots feel? You're going to be stuck with them after we ride out of here today, so you'd better be sure they're comfortable."

Kally nodded as she tucked the bill of sale into her shirt pocket and walked up to Pacer, calling him by name and petting him. It was obvious they would be good friends. Pacer pushed his nose into Kally's hand, begging for more attention, while Chase tied on her bedroll and saddlebags.

"He's a grand horse, Chase. I couldn't have picked a finer one myself. I love him already."

"I'm glad you like him. I wanted to get a smaller one so you could mount by yourself, but size and endurance are more important for this kind of trip. Seth or I can give you a leg up, or you can find a rock to stand on."

"Pacer is just fine. I told you I'd pull my own weight on this trip, so don't worry about my getting on him. I know there are a lot of things I can't do yet, but mounting Pacer is not one of them." With that, Kally grabbed the saddle horn and vaulted into the saddle. It was obviously not the first time.

"If you'll adjust my stirrups for me and hand me one of those bags, I think it's time we got them checked in and found me a rifle. Seth will be waiting for our help."

Chase did as he was told, then grabbed the remaining bag and swung into his saddle. Kally reined Pacer around and led the way to the Wells Fargo office. Riding behind her, Chase could see she sat the saddle well. A few days on the trail would tell, but he was already having a hard time thinking of her as a tenderfoot. She was full of surprises, but Chase wanted to know more. He now felt responsible for her; responsible in a way he had never felt about a woman before.

When they reached the office, Kally lifted one leg over the saddle horn and slipped to the ground with the suitcase before Chase could step down from Ranger. She checked the bags until their return.

When they came out, she had vaulted back into the saddle and was heading up the street by the time Chase was back on Ranger. They stopped at the gun shop and bought three new Winchesters. He laid two aside for the wranglers. Then he showed Kally how to hold the third one and had the gunsmith mark where to cut the stock so it would fit her. Chase paid him a couple of dollars extra to get the stock shortened by noon.

By the time they got back to the supply store, the mule train was waiting, along with a number of onlookers. Chase handed the Mexicans their new rifles and a couple of boxes of ammunition for their saddlebags. Kally got four boxes so she would have extra for practicing.

"I'll show you how to load your rifle first chance we get." Chase wasn't smiling now as he spoke to Kally. "I want you to carry it loaded, with extra cartridges in your pocket and two full boxes in your saddlebags. An unloaded gun won't do any of us any good."

Chase and Kally started helping get the supplies into packs. Chase and the Mexicans carried them to the mules and Seth tied them on. Chase sent Kally to help Seth so she would learn how to tie a diamond hitch, the standard knot used on all packs. Until she learned to tie and untie it, she wouldn't be able to get things out of the packs she might need on the trail.

Chase had just set another pack down beside a mule when he heard the crude imitation of a jackass's "Whee Haw," and a roar of laughter behind them. He wheeled around to see five cowboys watching them load the mules. One of the cowboys was a big, tall man with a shock of red hair sticking out from under his hat. He had the mean face, short neck, and broad shoulders of a bull. He stood a head taller than Chase and outweighed him by fifty or sixty pounds.

Chase turned to see where they were looking. Seth and Kally were bent over a pack and he was showing her how to rope it. In her tight new pants, Kally presented a pretty nice view, but no gentleman would have responded the way the redheaded cowboy had.

Chase was an experienced gunfighter who had learned to control his temper long ago, but he couldn't control it now. He reached the cowboy in two long strides. His feet were set solidly when he stopped, and he swung a doubled-up, hard, glove-covered fist into the cowboy's face. It exploded right where Chase had aimed it. The redhead's lips spurted blood and those nearby could hear the cartilage break in his nose.

He went down hard, but wasn't out. The cowboy shook his head and started to get up. Chase shifted his feet and waited. As the redhead gained his knees, Chase brought a right uppercut from the ground and caught the cowboy on the end of his chin. The blow was so hard it brought the man up on his tiptoes before he fell headlong into the street again, raising a cloud of dust. He lay still, but Chase wasn't through with him yet. He waited.

"My goodness!" Kally exclaimed to Seth. "What in the world brought that on? That cowboy is almost twice Chase's size, someone could get killed!"

"Chase might just kill him at that." Seth chuckled.

"But what for? What did he do to Chase?"

"Well, honey," Seth drawled. "Busy as we was here, teachin' you to tie packs, guess we didn't realize what a pretty picture you were, all bent over in your new britches. Didn't you hear that jackass bray?"

"I did, but what has that got to do with it?"

"It was meant for you," Seth explained. "If he'd whistled at you, it wouldn't have been too gentlemanly, but wouldn't mean much more'n he thought you was a pretty gal. The jackass bray meant more'n that. The cowboy thought you was pretty alright, but he was sayin' he wanted to do more'n just look. That's why Chase got so mad. I've seen him in a lot of fights, with fists and guns, but I've never seen him lose control like this. He's usually as cool as a chunk of ice."

"I saw a couple fights in Kansas, but nothing as brutal as this. As soon as one man went down, it was all over."

"Kansas is pretty tame, now that the trail drives are over, but this country is still wild. It takes hard men like Chase to tame it. Y'all won't find many harder than him, no matter how big they are. He learned his fightin' from some of the roughest, toughest boys in the West—the wild Texas cowboys who pushed herds up the big trail. He learned good, an' fast. He got whupped some at first, but not bad. His face don't look like that cowboy's is goin' to when Chase gets through with him. I've always been glad Chase an' I were friends. I'd never want to go up against him when he was riled.

"When y'all hired Chase to take you on this trip, you bought more'n a gun. Givin' that cowboy the worst whuppin' of his life is just a sample of what he's prepared to do for you on the trail."

Kally hadn't taken her eyes off the man lying at Chase's feet. "But why don't they quit? Chase has already beaten him badly."

"When y'all fight a man as big as that one, you don't quit 'til you've took all the fight out of him. Besides, Chase seems to have more'n a passin' interest in fightin' for your honor. I've never seen him go into a fight so mad. He's always been one to stand up for the women, but I ain't seen him take such a personal interest before. You'd better watch yourself, little lady. I'd say Chase Wade's interest in you *was* personal."

Kally bristled. "His interest may be personal, but I already told him mine wasn't."

"Have it your way, Kally, but don't say I didn't warn you."

By this time the big cowboy was starting to move and trying to raise himself up.

Chase spoke again. "Don't bother getting up, Red. Just crawl over to the lady, kiss her boot, and see if you can think of any nice words to say."

The cowboy didn't move.

"Start crawling!" Chase commanded. "And say those words good and loud. Let's see some of the lung power you used on that jackass bray."

The cowboy ignored Chase and started to push himself up again. Chase took a step forward and planted his boot on the cowboy's neck. He stomped his face down hard into the two or three inches of dust on the street and held him there until he quit struggling.

One of Red's friends called from behind Chase. "That's enough, mister. You're gonna kill George. Let 'em up before y'all drown 'em in that dust."

"Now there's an idea," Chase responded in a cool voice. "You can be sure I will if he don't start crawling, but you keep your nose out of this until I'm done with him. Then I'll give you any satisfaction you think you've got coming. Fists or guns, makes no difference to me. Any yellow skunk that'd ride with the likes of him is lower than a snake's belly anyhow. In case you have any ideas about hurrying this along, you better look over where my pard's standing. He doesn't wear that iron for decoration." Seth loosened his gun in its holster, just to make sure the cowboys understood.

Chase pulled his boot off George's neck. George slowly lifted his head, coughing and wheezing. He shook his head a couple of times and then started up again. This time Chase made a double-handed fist and brought it down with all his might on the back of George's neck. George flopped back into the street, raising another cloud of dust. Chase tipped George's head to the side with the toe of his boot, so he could breathe, and waited again. This big cowboy was young and strong, but he had met his match in Chase's fury.

When George moved again, it was on his hands and knees toward Kally. Chase followed slowly, watching his every move. When George reached

Kally, he touched his lips to the toe of her boot. His lips were so split and mangled he had trouble with the words, but he made a real polite speech. Kally tried to mumble an acceptance of his apology, but had to turn away at the sight of his horribly smashed face. Chase pulled George to his feet and sent him in the direction of his friends with a boot to the seat of his pants.

As his friends caught his crumpling body, Chase moved out into the street and faced them. "I don't have time for any more games." Chase's voice was still tinged with ice. "Now that I'm facing you, my partner's out of this. It's just the five of you and me. If any of you feel lucky—reach."

Chase stood relaxed with his hand well above his gun butt. He waited one minute. Two. Then five.

"Well, in that case, I suggest you five gutless coyotes run for your horses—not walk—I said run, and hightail it out of town before I decide to do the sheriff a favor and clean the riffraff off his streets. Now get!"

Chase turned to the crowd that had gathered. "The rest of you people get on your way too. The show's over and we've got work to do. Go on home or about your business and let us do our work in peace. All of you—get!"

Several of the onlookers fell down trying to get out of the way. The cowboys were already running down the street toward their horses, nearly dragging George. By the time they had gotten George on his horse and galloped out of town, most of the townspeople were out of sight or well on their way.

Chase had the street to himself, except for Seth,

Kally, and the two wranglers. Even the store clerks were staying inside out of sight.

Chase walked over to Kally. "I'm sorry you had to see that side of Chase Wade so soon. I'd hoped that could have waited until we ran into some real trouble on the trail, but no man insults a lady friend of mine that way. I may only be your hired gun, but I feel responsible for your honor as well as your life. I hope you can accept my apology, Kally."

Kally's face still reflected the horror of what she had just witnessed. "I accept your apology, Mr. Wade," she said in a controlled voice. "There's no reason to apologize. I admit it was all pretty shocking, but I'm beginning to understand more about the West and why I need someone like you at my side on this trip. Seth explained to me what happened, so perhaps I should thank you for what you did. I'm just thankful it's over without anyone getting killed. Now, let's get the rest of this stuff loaded and get out of town." As Kally turned away from Chase, she had trouble believing the two men who made up Chase Wade. A few moments ago, his face had been so hard and tight it looked as if it had been chiseled out of granite. Even from where she had been standing, she could see that his eyes had lost all color and had filled with hate and anger. Now, his eyes had turned back to their brilliant blue and his face was again relaxed and handsome.

Chase wasn't sure how Kally was feeling about him and what had just happened. He had hoped she would never have to see that side of him.

Kally, Seth, and the wranglers had already gone back to work. As Chase started to join them, Ben

Taylor stepped out of the barbershop and walked toward him.

"I saw it all from inside," Ben said as he reached Chase. "If I had any sense I'd have stopped you; I've seen you in action before. But George has beaten up several other cowboys the last couple weeks an' he only got what he deserved. I should thank you for gettin' him out of my town, but it's just like I said it would be. You did everythin' you could to make it a shootout. Did Seth talk to you?"

"I'm sorry it happened, Ben, but I wasn't looking for trouble. I understand what you're doing and I hope you can make it work. We're almost loaded. We'll just have our dinner, pick up a gun from the gunsmith, and be out of town in an hour or so. I've always liked you, Ben, and I wish you luck." Chase extended his hand and Ben took it this time.

"I always liked you too, Chase. I'm sorry if I pushed you too hard yesterday. A man don't have to be no mind reader to figure out what you'n Seth are fixin' to do. Word of the gold is all over town. I've been watchin' people real close an' I've seen a couple of hard lookers who might have a mind to follow you. To show you there's no hard feelin's on my part, leave town up there by the livery. 'Bout half a mile out, there's a couple big trees with some shade. Reckon I'll just get my horse an' follow your trail out to the trees. After you go on, I might set there a spell in the shade an' rest. If any varmints was to come along an' disturb my peace, I might just have to toss 'em in jail for a day or two. Good luck, Chase."

Chase stood a minute and watched Ben walk away. He could understand the older man's terror in his secret, but Ben did a good job of hiding it. Chase could only hope he had put enough money aside to retire to that little ranch of his before a fast gun ended his career and made his señorita a widow.

They finished the loading and Chase went inside and paid their bill. They had dinner at a little Mexican restaurant near the supply store, where they could keep an eye on the horses and mules.

Chase quietly filled Seth in on Ben's plan. Seth and the wranglers headed for the trail by the livery, and would stop to fill all their canteens, while Chase and Kally rode to the gun shop to pick up her rifle. Chase loaded it for her and shoved it in her scabbard. They mounted up and quickly caught up with Seth and the mule train.

*S*eth led them west for an hour after passing Ben's shade trees, then turned straight south. Chase and Kally rode at his side while the wranglers followed with the pack animals. As they rode, Seth explained his plans for the route they would follow.

"We'll ride south until about noon tomorrow when we get to a long, rocky ravine. You should remember it from our scoutin' days, Chase." Seth looked over at his partner.

Chase nodded. "From there we can turn west and leave a crooked trail for anyone following."

Seth went on explaining to Kally. "If we're gonna throw off any followers, it's gonna mean more dry camps and rougher ridin', and takin' more time than we would if we followed the Old Santa Fe Trail to where we can head north to Pike City. The question is not *will* we have followers; the question is simply how many."

Chase and Seth both knew even a crooked trail wouldn't throw off anyone who could read sign, at least not until they reached a place called Death Canyon.

Seth, Chase, and a whole troop of cavalry had driven a large band of Apaches into that canyon when they were scouting for the army. They had spent a month in the narrow, high-walled canyon trying to flush the Indians out. It wasn't until they sent for reinforcements that they finally got the last ten Apaches to surrender. The cost of getting those ten Indians to the San Carlos Reservation had been too great.

It would take them at least a week to ride through the canyon, and there were only two water holes. Actually they were reservoirs or cisterns, *tanques* the Spanish called them, hidden high above the trail. Few white men knew where they were. Seth and Chase wouldn't have known either if they hadn't caught the Indians using them. If they could stop anyone following them before they reached the canyon, the canyon would stop any who came later. It would be too hot and dry to ride the canyon without knowing where the water was, and it wasn't possible to carry enough water to make it to the other end.

Kally shuddered at the thought of what might happen if someone was following them. This trip wasn't like she had thought it would be when she made her plans. Exchanging the other gold bars in Boston had caused only a little to-do, but then she had not left town with mules and a load of supplies afterward either. After the attention they got in Albuquerque, she knew the men had good reason to expect they would be followed. She had already seen the other side of Chase Wade with his fists. She had no reason to doubt he would be even more deadly with his gun.

Even though she had cut Seth and Chase in for full shares of the gold, they both still acted like they worked for her. She liked Seth, he was honest and straightforward with her, and he had the same twinkle in his eye she remembered her father having. She had mixed feelings about Chase. It wasn't that she didn't trust him. She had from the beginning. But his interest in her protection was too personal. It made her uncomfortable. Seth's words of warning during the fight hadn't helped either. She only hoped he would keep his distance.

During all her years of planning, and the months of looking for someone like Chase, she had thought of the man who would take her as just a hired gun. He would be a gentleman, keep his distance, and simply guide her to the gold and help her get it out. It was never to have been personal. There simply was no way she could let a man get close to her; there never would be. She shuddered again, but this time it was not in fear of what lay ahead.

Kally tried to get her mind off what had happened in Albuquerque and concentrate on what they might run into on the trail. Before they reached Pike City she would have to tell Seth and Chase what might be waiting for them there. She hadn't told them in town because she hadn't wanted to say anything that might make them change their minds about taking her. It would be a while before they got to Pike City. She would wait until they were too far along to turn back. Besides, she wasn't sure she could tell them about

Pieter's plans without telling the rest—and she had never told that to anyone.

As they rode along in silence now, Kally tried to sort out all the feelings she had been avoiding. Chase was an unusual man. So much different from what she had thought a gunfighter would be. She had always found a way to avoid men in the past, but she and Chase would be together for many weeks on the trail. This time she couldn't run and hide.

"Kally—Kally?"

She was suddenly aware that Chase was calling her name. "I'm sorry. I guess I was daydreaming. This all does seem pretty much like a dream to me about now."

"I thought we'd ride back a ways and give you a chance to try out your rifle. You need to get used to it. We can shoot today, and a couple times tomorrow. After that, we won't be doing any shooting unless we have to. A gunshot can be heard for a long way in this country. We don't want to give anyone following us that kind of clue to where we are."

The two of them turned their horses and rode along their back trail for a couple miles. When they reached a small knoll, Chase pulled up and dismounted. He watched as Kally slid from her saddle. It was obvious that if she had ridden every chance she got, she must have had plenty of chances. Kally didn't say anything, but rubbed the seat of her new blue denims with both hands.

Chase took two empty cans he had picked up in town from his saddlebags, while Kally pulled her rifle from its scabbard. He stepped off one hundred paces, set up one of the cans, and came back to where she stood. Chase spent the next few minutes showing her how the lever-action worked. He made Kally pump out the cartridges and reload the rifle until she could do it quickly. He showed her how to hold the rifle, line up the sights, and slowly squeeze the trigger. Chase stepped back and let her shoot at the can. Her first shots were a little wild, but before long she started nicking the can and then hitting it center. When her shots became more consistent, Chase took the second can out farther while Kally reloaded again. He suggested she hold the rifle a little higher. Soon she was hitting the can with every shot. Chase let her reload one more time and shoot at both cans. When she finished, they were only mangled pieces of tin. Then he showed her how to clean the rifle.

"You surprised me again, little lady," Chase said with a smile. "I can see you've done a lot more riding than you let on. You said you'd never shot a rifle, but you'd have a hard time making anyone believe it. You're a lot better shot already than I thought you'd ever be. But you're doing better all around than I expected. We'll shoot a couple times tomorrow so you can get more comfortable handling the rifle, but you already shoot as well as some men."

"Thank you, sir. I'd say coming from Chase Wade, that's quite a compliment. I have every intention of being the best I can at riding and shooting. I know I have a lot to learn, but you'll find I'm a good student. I won't need a nursemaid. From the sound of things you and Seth will have your hands full. I don't intend to slow you down or get in your way."

"It doesn't appear to me you'll do either, Kally."

"One more thing, Mr. Wade. I've been thinking

about what happened in town this morning. I'll have to admit I was more than a little surprised at the other side of Chase Wade, but I've already learned enough about life in this country to understand what you did and why. I'm still sure I found the right man to take me to the gold. I also thought about what might have happened if I'd hired a man like that cowboy for the job. I don't think I have to explain what that thought did to me."

"No, guess that's pretty plain."

"All I'm trying to say, Chase, is that I hired you to do a job and I'm not going to stand in the way of your doing that job the best way you know how. We're partners now, and I'm going to trust your judgment—yours and Seth's—to do what's best for all of us."

"Thank you, Kally. It helps to know how you feel. The going might get a little rough before we're done with this trip, so I'm glad you're beginning to understand a little more about how life really is in the West. I don't know why, but what you think of me does make a difference. A lot of people look at me simply as the lesser of two evils. They hire me because I'm a killer, pin a badge on me to make it legal, and pay me to rid their towns of all the other killers. Once the dirty work is done, and the town tamed, they fire me. I guess it makes them feel less guilty, having me do their dirty work for them. It costs them plenty for what they think will be a clear conscience."

"I assure you I would never feel that way about you. Besides, we're partners. I'm not paying you for anything. Whatever you get I'm sure you'll earn. But now I'm beginning to understand why your gun isn't for hire anymore. You don't seem to be the kind of man who would enjoy doing that for a living." Kally had been watching Chase as he explained a part of his life he obviously wasn't proud of. Here was a man with a deep sense of loneliness and separation from his world that she longed to know more about, in spite of herself.

Chase had been keeping an eye on their back trail ever since they had stopped. "There's no one behind us yet. Really don't expect anyone for three or four more days. Come on, we'll let our horses stretch their legs on the way back. Turn Pacer loose and let's see what he's got. I suspect he's real fast, but we'd better find out before we have to put him to the test."

"Good. I've been hoping for a chance to let him run."

"We need to get back and take over the mules so Carlos and Roberto can try out their rifles too. By the time they get back, it'll be almost time to make camp."

Kally vaulted into the saddle and urged Pacer into a run. Chase didn't catch her until they reached the mule train. That answered two questions: Pacer was very fast, and Kally sat the saddle like she was glued to it. She had what it took to be a western woman all right. She wasn't going to be near the trouble Chase had thought at first.

Chase let Kally lead the string of mules and he brought up the rear until the boys returned, obviously having enjoyed their rifle practice.

They made a dry camp that night, as they would the next two. Kally was learning much about the desert and the trail. Although she had ridden a lot, she had never spent such seemingly endless hours in the saddle, and walked around more than a little gingerly when she got off Pacer that evening. The smaller saddle helped, but she couldn't remember another time when every single part of her body hurt the way it did now. She had worn her hat so low to keep the sun off her face that sometimes she could scarcely see where she was going, but the skin on her face was already feeling the results of the sun and dry wind.

As they set up camp, Chase showed Kally how they would have to water the stock when they were in a dry camp with no river or stream nearby. He showed her how to pour a measure of water out of their canteens into a bucket for each of the mules.

Chase and Seth wanted to keep an eye on the boys for a couple days before letting them stand guard, so they flipped a coin for first watch. Chase won and Seth headed for his blankets. Chase told them good night, and started up to the top of a knoll where he would have a better view of their camp and back trail.

"Let me go with you." Kally ran to catch up. "It's too early for me to go to sleep. Besides, I need to learn how to do this too. I'll be taking my turn as soon as I catch on to what I'm supposed to do."

By now, Chase had learned it was futile to try to argue with her. She had a mind of her own, and it was obvious she planned to learn how to do everything they did, and as soon as possible.

"Alright, come on." Chase waited for her to catch up. "The first thing you have to do is learn to be invisible." He taught her to walk softly and lose herself in the shadow of a big rock. He instructed her in a low voice. "Memorize every rock or clump of mesquite in sight. If any of them should suddenly grow a new lump—shoot it. Watch large areas at a time and keep your eyes moving. They'll play tricks on you if you stare at any one spot too long.

"Stick close to that rock. When the moon's out there's enough light for any rifleman to pick you off if you step out of those shadows," Chase warned her, and she knew he meant business.

The hours of watch passed slowly, but they exchanged few words except for Chase's instructions and a few questions from Kally. Chase had never spent time with a woman like this on the trail and he was unsure how he felt about it or about her. She was very different from other women he had known. Not simply because of her background; something mysterious—almost ominous—surrounded her.

Kally was unaware of Chase's thoughts, but was curious, herself, to know more about the man she had caught a glimpse of at target practice. For tonight they each settled for their own thoughts and a few polite words swallowed up by the still darkness.

As the moon cleared the eastern horizon, a coyote standing on a lonesome ridge miles away let out a howl that rang across the silent desert. Kally stepped closer to Chase, but stood her ground without a word. Seth soon came to relieve them, slipping so silently from the shadows he gave Kally a start.

She and Chase walked back to camp, and Kally watched him roll out his blankets next to his saddle and prop his rifle against the saddle horn. He unbuckled his gun belt and slipped his boots off, putting both within easy reach. Kally imitated everything he did and was soon in her own bedroll, not far from his. A moment later she reached out and pulled her rifle in next to her.

During the next couple of days, Kally practiced her shooting and proved she was every bit as good as Chase had thought. On the fourth evening, Seth led them up out of the long ravine they had been following, and about two miles later dismounted at the edge of a steep-sided arroyo. They hadn't been on any trail and there was no trail into the arroyo. It had very steep, rocky sides. Seth carefully led his mare over the side and slowly picked his way down at an angle, in an attempt to give Maude surer footing.

"Where in the world is Seth going?" Kally asked, eyeing the hot, rocky expanse that lay ahead. "It's getting late. Shouldn't we be looking for a place to camp? We're out of water."

"He doesn't have to look; he's headed for camp now."

"You're not serious? That place is steeper and rockier than the ravine we've been traveling."

"The Indians and a few desert men are the only ones who know about this place. There's a nice cool spring at the bottom, and green grass for the stock. You can even take a bath tonight if you like."

"I'm beginning to think you've been out in the sun too long, but I'll accept your word for it for now," Kally said, looking at Chase in disbelief.

"You'll see. Now go on and follow Seth. Just watch your footing and take it slow."

Chase turned and told the wranglers to hold the pack train until he and Seth could get back to help with the animals. He led Ranger over the side and followed Kally down. It was slow and tedious going. Chase, watching Kally, couldn't help but admire the way she had taken to the trail and followed their instructions. She was doing fine.

As they got close to the bottom, Kally pulled back sharply on Pacer's bridle and slapped him on the neck. "What's the matter with you, Pacer? I didn't tell you to get in a hurry."

Chase laughed. "There's nothing wrong with Pacer. He just has a better nose than you. He's thirsty, and can smell water down there."

When they reached the bottom, Chase and Kally had to walk quickly to keep up with their mounts. The horses led them to a large spring surrounded by green grass. The little overflow that ran from the spring and disappeared into the rock bank at its lower end was surrounded by willows. The horses drank from the rivulet, while they got a drink from the main spring. Seth had already slipped Maude's saddle and set it to one side of the blackened area where fires had burned in the past. Chase started to loosen the cinch on Ranger.

"Go on with Seth." Kally stopped him. "I'll take care of the horses."

Chase looked at her a moment. "On one condition. You'll stop being so bullheaded about doing your share. Let me saddle Pacer in the mornings. It makes me tired watching you having to jump to get a saddle on his back. You're going to end up spraining your back—or worse—and holding us up a day or two while you recover. You don't have to prove anything to us; you're doing your share and more."

She stood looking at him with that stubborn, independent expression he was coming to know well, then slowly broke into a smile. "Alright, you've got a deal. Pacer *is* a little tall for me, but I wanted you both to know I could take care of myself. Now get going."

It didn't take the four men long to bring the mules down. They let the mules drink long, then pulled their packs and turned them loose on the green grass. Kally had already gathered some wood and started a fire. In a few minutes they were all having a cup of hot coffee.

Chase set down his empty cup, picked up a bucket and towel, and walked up the stream a short way from the others. He tossed his hat and kerchief on the ground. Slipping out of his shirt, he began washing up.

"My goodness!" Kally exclaimed to Seth. "What are all those small, round scars on Chase's back?" She had been lying on the cool grass watching him, suddenly aware that it was the first time she had ever watched a man take off his shirt.

"Lessons," Seth replied.

"Lessons? I don't understand."

"Well, little gal, them's bullet scars. Y'all don't get to be the gunman Chase is without bein' awfully lucky, good, or a fast learner. I reckon he's all three. No one wears a badge in some of them rip-roarin' boom towns, full of drunks lookin' for a fight, without gettin' a nick or two. It's taken more'n luck to bring Chase as far as he's come with that gun. He's gone up against the best of 'em, but he's the one what's still around to tell about it. If y'all look close, you'll see none of them scars is in a place what matters much."

Kally watched in silence as Chase finished washing up and came back to the fire. She would wait until after supper for her bath.

"Guess we'd better hurry if we're gonna get supper before dark," Seth said, watching the quickly setting sun. Kally helped him get the meal together, and they ate as Seth and Chase discussed the watch.

"I don't see any reason to climb back up that steep bank to stand watch," Chase said as darkness began to fill the arroyo.

"Nope," Seth agreed. "Anybody tryin' to come down would roll rock an' we'd be ready for 'em by the time they got here."

Chase sent Roberto up the arroyo, away from the stock, to stand watch where he could hear anyone coming down. Carlos was to relieve him, and Kally insisted on taking the next watch. Since the men felt sure they would hear anyone coming in as soon as she did, they agreed. Chase would relieve her.

Kally wanted a bath before going to bed, so Chase carried a couple of buckets of water to a secluded place in the willows for her. She thanked him and waited until she could hear the two men talking around the fire before she undressed and took her bath. As she started to wash her neck, she let out a muffled cry of pain. Unprotected spots on the sides of her neck were sore and sunburned. She was thankful for the dim lighting; she knew she didn't want to see what the hot sun and hours in a saddle were doing to her skin. In a little while, she joined the men by the fire, and they all turned in.

Later, Kally stood her watch without incident. Chase came out an hour early to relieve her, but she stayed with him, hoping it would give them a chance to talk a little. She found the watches to be long and lonely.

"Are you worried, Chase? I mean about someone following us down here. It seems so remote to me."

"Not really. Not many people know about this place, so most will likely ride right on by." Chase was quiet for a moment and listened for any sound in the night. "Does it scare you to stand watch by yourself now?"

"No, I'm fine," Kally assured him.

"Guess that doesn't surprise me. Nothing much surprises me about you anymore. You're quite a woman, Kally VanDerVeer."

Kally felt uncomfortable again and changed the subject. "You haven't told me much about yourself, Chase. I would really like to know more."

"Not much to tell."

"Where are you from? What about your family? You said your father died when you were young. What happened to him?"

"He was shot when I was twelve."

"Was he a gunman too?"

"No, a homesteader. All we had was a little sod house on the Kansas prairie, east of Abilene. But the railroad was coming into Abilene and there was a man who tried to buy up all the little homesteads the railroad would need for the right of way. My pa didn't want to sell, but that didn't matter to the man. It was easy for him to push Pa into a fight and kill him. Pa wasn't the only one." Chase's voice was flat and emotionless.

"That's terrible! Couldn't the sheriff do anything about him?"

"I always thought the sheriff was in on it, but I never could prove anything."

"What happened to you and your mother then?"

"My mother was already gone. Guess she wasn't cut out for that kind of life. They said she ran off with a drummer. I don't even remember her. My father raised me. Taught me what he knew and made sure I stayed in school."

"Then you were all alone—after he was killed? What did you do?"

"The woman who ran the boardinghouse took me in and kept me in school for a couple more years. I did odd jobs for her to earn my keep and ran lots of errands for the local businessmen to earn money on the side. I needed to buy a gun."

"But you were still a child," Kally protested.

"The crooked real-estate man was still in town. He got rich off the railroad deal and owned the biggest saloon in Abilene."

"You were going to kill him?" Kally's eyes were wide in disbelief.

"You're damn right I was. I saved every cent I got so I could buy a six-gun, but the gunsmith wouldn't sell me one—said I was too young. Then one night I found a drunk cowboy passed out in an alley." Chase stopped and looked at Kally; he really didn't want to finish this story. What he was about to tell her was an act he had regretted all his life.

"What happened?" Kally wasn't about to let him stop now.

"I took his gun and gun belt. I slipped out of town and practiced with it every chance I got, until I was good enough."

"You went after the real-estate man?"

"One day I walked down the street and called him out of the saloon. He thought I was too young, and just laughed at me. A crew of Texas cowboys was in the saloon and they pushed him into it. I outdrew him."

"You killed him?"

"For my pa."

Kally stood silent for a long time. Chase couldn't believe he had told her that story. He had never told anyone else, except Seth. He wasn't sure why he had. This woman was making him do and feel things he had never felt before. She stirred things in him no other woman had ever touched. He wasn't sure if he wanted to take her in his arms or get as far away from her as he could. It was a moot point. A strange wall stood between them; a wall Chase didn't understand and didn't know how to fight.

Kally started toward camp. "I'd better get to bed. My watch is over."

Chase was watching her go in silence when suddenly she stopped and slipped back into the shadows near him. "Thank you, Chase, for telling me what you did tonight. It helps me to understand a lot of things. I . . ." Kally's voice trailed off.

"Kally." Chase started to reach out for her, but she turned abruptly and disappeared into the darkness.

She lay on her bedroll for a long time thinking about all Chase had said, and all the feelings of compassion she had for a young boy she felt she understood and knew so well. Those feelings brought her a step closer to the Chase Wade who had given away a part of himself tonight. A gift she was afraid to accept.

Kally had come on this trip so sure of where she was going and what she was after. She hadn't bargained on Chase Wade. Now, the only thing she did know was that she had to tell him what might lay ahead in Pike City. She drifted in and out of sleep the rest of the night.

They were up early and climbing the steep bank shortly after first light the next morning. Seth reached the top first and dismounted with two burlap bags they had brought along to carry the gold. Chase led the way back to where they had come up out of the ravine the day before. After circling in their own tracks, they made a new set of tracks that led away from the arroyo and around its upper side.

Kally looked back as Seth started sprinkling the sand he had put into the burlap bags. "What's he doing?"

"An old tracker's trick. He'll salt the first twenty or thirty feet of the trail where we went over the bank into the arroyo, covering the scars left by the horses' and mules' shoes on the rocks. He'll drag the sacks over our tracks back to where we circled, sprinkling sand over that too."

"I see. Then anyone following us will think we went right on past the arroyo." Kally pointed back at their new tracks.

"It will only slow down a seasoned tracker a little, but most men won't realize we ever went down there. They'll ride right by that spring, but, believe me, they're going to need some water. Since we won't come to more water for two days, that may turn back some of our unwanted company.

"Come on. Seth will catch up with us in an hour or so. Let's make some time."

*C*hase and Kally led the way down the trail, with the wranglers and mules falling in behind. They would cover as much ground as possible. Seth would catch up as soon as he could. Chase knew Seth could handle himself if he ran into trouble, and Chase could take care of Kally and the rest, but he would feel better when they were all back together again.

Chase was beginning to enjoy the time alone with Kally, but now he was no longer sure what he should or even dared to say, and was even more afraid of what she might ask.

Kally spoke first. "Do you think Seth's trick will work back at the arroyo?"

"I hope it'll stop some of them anyway. The problem is some could know about the spring there too."

"Some of them? How many do you think there might be?"

"Hard to say. But with as much interest as we stirred up in Albuquerque, there could be two or three bunches, maybe more."

"Does that worry you?"

"Yeah—I'd be loco if I said it didn't. But don't worry your pretty head. Seth and I can take care of them, and you." Chase didn't want to worry her, but he knew they could be jumped at any time.

They rode another few minutes in silence before Kally spoke again. "You didn't tell me what happened to you—where did you go?"

"Go?"

"After you killed the real-estate man? I've been wondering what happened to you after that." Kally looked over at Chase.

"Reckon I panicked some. The same sheriff I thought was in on the deal was still in town, and I wasn't sure what he'd do to me. I just wanted to get away from there. One of the cowboys loaned me a mustang and gave me the name of the rancher he worked for in Texas. It meant riding across the Indian nations and into Texas alone, but I got away from the sheriff and eventually found the ranch. The old man gave me a job and by the time he was ready to send out another drive, I went up the trail as a drover."

"It sounds like a hard life for a fourteen-year-old boy."

"By that time I was fifteen and wasn't much of a boy anymore. Those drovers were a rough bunch. I learned a lot, and in a hurry. I practiced with the six-gun every chance I got, and had lots of practice with my fists. If I hadn't gotten real good with both, I'd never have reached sixteen."

"Obviously you did," Kally said with a grin.

"After five years at that, I heard the army was looking for scouts—that's where I met Seth. We rode together for the next five years. Seth taught me everything he knew about scouting and tracking. We were friends right from the start. I suppose in some ways he was like the father I'd lost too soon."

"It sounds like that was a good time for you—the time you spent with Seth."

"I reckon it was, while it lasted. After we got the Indians rounded up and onto the reservations, our job was pretty much done. My reputation as a fast gun was spreading by that time. I was offered a job as sheriff in a boom town, and we split up. After that it was just cleaning up one wild town after another. Got so I hated it." Chase was staring off into the distance. Suddenly his attention came back to Kally, and he looked over at her.

"That's enough about me. Now it's your turn."

"My turn?"

"Well, all I know about you is the story of your father and the gold. There's got to be more."

Kally hadn't expected his attention to turn in her direction so quickly. "Not a lot," she said, not knowing how much she wanted to tell him.

"That's not fair, Kally VanDerVeer. I told you more than I've ever told any woman in my life. Now it's your turn to even the score." Chase was smiling, but the look on his face told her he wanted an answer.

"Actually I don't know a lot about my parents, but I'll tell you what I do. According to my aunt, my father and his brother inherited a whaling fleet from their father, and were both ship captains at an early age. They didn't get along too well, and my father never liked whaling, so he eventually took a job with another company. As captain of a cargo ship, he sailed the South Seas and to China, bringing cargo back to California."

"Is that how he met your mother? In China?"

"I have no idea how he got her away from her father who, I understand, was a powerful warlord. But she left with my father and later I was born on his ship. My mother and I lived with my father on the ship, but she never set foot in China again. We were very happy in those days. I think my parents were very much in love; even as a small child I remember the warmth and kindness between them."

Chase interrupted her. "I've been wondering how you ever got a name like Kally. It doesn't sound Dutch *or* Chinese to me."

"You're right, it's really not either. My mother actually named me Ki Li, but the old doctor on the ship wrote it down as Kally and it stuck."

"What happened to your mother?"

"She got very sick and died on the ship when I was about seven."

"Is that why you and your father left the ship?"

"After her death there was a deep sadness in my father I never saw leave him as long as we were together. I think he would have stayed at sea, but about that time my mother's father found out where we were and demanded her return. He was very powerful and was able to have all the ships owned by my father's employer banned from China until she was returned, but since that was impossible, the ship owners simply dismissed my father. Of course, he wouldn't have let her go anyway, so even if she had been alive, I suppose we would still have had to leave the ship."

"Where did you go?" Chase asked as he looked back over his shoulder hoping to catch sight of Seth.

"Father's first mate, a Spanish man, went with us to Sacramento. They left me with the old woman we rented a room from, while they went prospecting for gold. Since the first mate was Spanish, I've always wondered if he was the one who told my father about where the gold was in the canyon. As a child I remember the man being quite a storyteller on the ship; always telling stories of great adventures and lots of treasure."

"Did they ever find gold in Sacramento?"

"Not much. They obviously didn't do too well at prospecting. When they gave up on it, my father had only enough gold to buy us two train tickets to Boston. He left the mate behind, but they may have had plans to meet later, I never knew for sure.

"I know now how hard it must have been for him, but he asked his brother to look after me until he found gold or a job so he could come back for me. I think my uncle was happy to take me in, but I always felt his wife thought I was some kind of heathen oriental. They had lots of money. Uncle had built their father's whaling fleet into a big company by then. I had a private room, went to the best schools, and was well taken care of, but I missed my father so much and always felt painfully alone." Kally spoke as if to herself. She seemed almost oblivious to Chase's presence until he interrupted her thoughts.

"I think I understand how you felt, Kally. I have spent so much of my life alone." Chase's sense of loneliness mirrored Kally's and he quietly shared her moment of pain before speaking again. "Didn't your aunt and uncle have any children of their own?"

Chase looked over at Kally as he spoke and could see the expression on her face change. Her eyes narrowed and she chewed nervously at her lower lip. "Children?" she asked blankly.

"Your aunt and uncle? Did they have other children?" Chase was watching Kally, curiously.

"Children—yes—yes, they had a son. He was about four years older than me. His name was Pieter." An edge of hatred filled her voice as she spoke his name.

"I don't reckon a boy that much older would have been much company for you as a child." Chase had the feeling he was talking to himself. Kally was staring ahead, ignoring his comment.

Chase turned his head quickly and his hand automatically went to his gun butt as he heard hoofbeats approaching. He relaxed as he saw Seth riding up alongside the pack mules.

"Well, I reckon that'll keep 'em off our trail for a spell," Seth said as he joined them. "I covered our tracks for a mile or two. Did I miss anythin'?"

"Kally and I've been talking...." Before Chase could finish his sentence, Kally broke away and rode on ahead without saying a word to either of them.

"Looks like you upset her a might. What was you talkin' about?"

"I'm not sure what I did. She was telling me about her childhood when all of a sudden she got real jittery. I don't know what, but I suspect there's something she's not telling us."

"Now's no time for games. Iffen she's got some-thin' to say, she best get it out."

"Did you see or hear anything back there?" Chase asked as he swung around in his saddle to scan the horizon on their back trail.

"Didn't need to hear nothin'. Learned a long time ago you got to be most careful when it's quiet—an' it's so durn quiet out there you could hear a bug crawlin'."

He was right. If Chase hadn't been listening so closely to Kally he would have noticed it himself. It was as if a strong wind had suddenly stopped blowing.

They rode the rest of the day with fewer than a dozen words passing between them. They called Kally back to keep a closer eye on her, and Chase and Seth took turns riding to the rear of the mule train to check their back trail. Kally was quiet and withdrawn, but did her share of watching too.

They made a dry camp that night, and then one the next night in a deep, rocky gulch. Kally said little, and avoided Chase's questioning looks, but fixed them supper. They were sitting around the fire drinking a last cup of coffee when Kally suddenly jumped to her feet. Her sudden movement startled the men who thought she had seen or heard something, and they were on their feet in one quick motion.

"What is it, Kally?" Chase whispered as his eyes encircled the darkness around them.

"I didn't hear anything," she assured them, re-alizing they had misunderstood her quick movement. "Sit down. I have something I must tell you." The tone of her voice gave them little choice but to obey. The battle that had raged within her all day was finished and her course of action was clear, at least to her.

"I know you're concerned about who might be following us, and I don't want to add to that concern, but there's something I should have told you before we left Albuquerque. Back then I didn't realize the danger I was putting us in. The last few days have taught me a lot about the seriousness of this trip."

Chase interrupted, "What are you talking about, Kally?"

"Pieter." She let the word lie there.

"Who in tarnation is Pieter?" Seth asked impatiently.

"Isn't that the cousin you told me about earlier?" Chase was watching Kally with a bewildered expression. "What has he got to do with this?"

"The map. He stole it from me once when I was still at my uncle's house. I told on him and they made him return it, but later, after..." Her voice trailed off for a moment. "Later he bragged that he'd made a copy of it. I doubt he had time to make a very detailed copy, but he could have gotten enough down to get him as far as Pike City, or somewhere between here and there." In the firelight, the expression in Kally's eyes was a combination of fear, regret, and utter confusion. It was the fear that she felt the deepest.

Chase and Seth realized a reprimand would be wasted on someone who had already punished herself more than they would ever feel was necessary.

Chase spoke first. "What kind of man is this Pieter?"

The fear in Kally's eyes ignited into rage. "He's a bad man—mean, selfish, arrogant—capable of anything. I know he wouldn't stop at murder. We never got along, even as children, and he hates me. He'd like nothing better than to beat me to the gold and take everything my father meant for me." Kally was on her feet and her whole body pulsed with the anger expressed in the fevered pitch of her voice.

"It's alright, Kally." Chase moved to her side. "We'll take care of him if we run into him. One more skunk won't make that much difference now. Chances are he'll be stymied in Pike City, waiting for you to come along with the real map. As long as we know about him, we can be watching for him."

Kally pulled abruptly away from Chase as he reached out to comfort her. Her eyes were ablaze with fear and anger. "Don't worry. I'll kill him. I've waited so long. . . ." Kally turned and was swallowed up by the darkness as she went to her bedroll and sobbed quietly into the night.

Chase started after her, but Seth stopped him. "Leave her be, Chase, a woman's got a right to lay claim to things she figures belong to her alone."

None of them got much sleep that night. Everyone was extra cautious on guard, and Chase, having the last watch, walked up the steep bank of the gulch and back a half mile or more, sniffing the air and looking for a glimmer of fire. He didn't see, hear, or smell anything. He rolled everyone out at the earliest hint of dawn, and they were on their way at first light.

Seth was jumpy. As they reached the top of the steep gulch bank, they stopped to let the horses and mules rest from the difficult climb. As they waited, Seth gave voice to his apprehensions.

"My neck's itchy as hell this mornin'. If anyone was comin' they should have been here by now."

Chase nodded.

Seth went on. "We should be to that box canyon by tonight. There's a good spring and lots of green grass. It'll be the last decent graze for the stock 'til we break out of Death Canyon on the floor of the desert, well above Fort Apache. After that we've got a week of hard travel to the Salt River."

Chase led Ranger over to a big rock, bigger than a log cabin, sitting on the edge of a high bank, as he spoke. "I'm not about to argue with that itchy neck of yours, Seth. Think I'll just sit here in the shade a spell. You'll have good trail to the box canyon. I'll wait here until I have just enough time to catch up with you before dark. Unless you see me before that, don't go into the canyon to camp. Just water the stock and fill the canteens."

Seth nodded in agreement and started to lead the others away. Kally turned and rode over to where Chase was already sitting in the shade. "I'd like to stay with you."

She spoke quietly, but there was a forcefulness in her request that defied argument. He nodded, knowing a day in the shade and out of the saddle would be good for her. She slipped from her horse and led him to where Chase had left Ranger behind the big rock. She pulled her rifle and sat down next to Chase in the shade.

"Does Seth's itchy neck mean we're going to have trouble?" she asked softly.

"It's been right more times than not, but I don't feel anything yet. Checked things out good early this morning and I found nothing, but that doesn't mean somebody couldn't be close. Might have camped in the ravine and let their fire go out. We'll just set here and watch. Fine if we don't see anything, but Seth'll feel better knowing somebody's watching his tail."

"I'll have to admit that I'm tired. I could use a day out of the saddle, and the sun." Kally seemed to be over her soreness from riding, and Chase could see her face was much more tanned than when they had started. The sore, sunburned areas on her neck were beginning to heal and were peeling.

"I'm afraid you'll be a lot more tired by the time we get you to Pike City. We're just over two weeks from the Salt River and another four weeks or more from Pike City."

"Will it be hard traveling the rest of the way?"

"It'll ease up when we get to the Salt. We'll have a week of all the water you want and plenty of graze for the stock. But after that it's three weeks across nothing but open desert. The water will be bad and it will really start getting hot. Don't know what to expect after Pike City. Just heat, lots of it."

Kally was listening, but said nothing in response to Chase's dismal description of what lay ahead. She was bone tired, and if it hadn't been for the strength of her determination, she might have given in to it. The day before had been one of the most difficult and exhausting in her life. She was surprised Seth and Chase hadn't been angrier at her for withholding the information about Pieter, but she wasn't sure how they really felt about that or about her. She hoped the fact that Chase allowed her to stay with him now proved he wasn't really angry.

Kally was surprised at how comfortable she was beginning to feel with Chase. She wasn't sure that there was anything more she was ready to say to him today, but she felt a warmth when she was with him that she'd never felt with anyone before. It dispelled some of the loneliness that had become so much a part of who and what she was.

She looked over at him for the first time in several minutes. They had a good view of the trail and he was searching every inch of the horizon for any movement. Suddenly he realized she was looking at him and turned toward her. Their eyes met and held for a long moment. A moment after Kally looked away, Chase reached out and grabbed her arm.

She jerked her head back in his direction. He was holding a finger to his lips.

Kally sat motionless and scarcely breathed as she listened.

Chase didn't say a word, but pulled her down with him and pointed toward the edge of the bank.

They snaked up to the edge and lay perfectly still. In a moment, Kally heard it too. It was the crack of horses' hooves on rock. Soon four men rode into sight on the opposite side of the gulch. One man was leading a packhorse. Chase recognized the man in front as one of the gamblers he had seen in Albuquerque. It was clear the riders were stopping where they had seen fresh tracks from the horses and mules breaking over the edge of the bank. The four men pulled up their horses and looked across the gulch to where Chase and Kally lay motionless just out of sight.

"*L*ooks like Seth's itchy neck was right again," Kally whispered softly, with her mouth near Chase's ear. "Can we pick them off from here?"

"No! It's too long a shot. We couldn't be sure of taking them all from this far away." Chase really thought Seth's hunch had been wrong this time. He should have known better. He didn't want Kally in the middle of this, and he certainly didn't want her killing anyone unless she had to.

"I can help," Kally said resolutely.

"You're pretty good with that gun, but I don't think you're ready to kill a man." Chase was watching the four men as they began to make their way down the far side of the gulch.

"I have as much—maybe more—reason to keep them from getting to my father's gold. Tell me what to do."

"You can back me up, but this has to be done my way—close and sure. If I don't stop them all, shoot anyone trying to get away before you help me. Do you understand? Your life, and everyone else's, may depend on it."

Kally nodded.

"Now stay out of sight." Chase was over the bank and gone before she could say anything else.

Kally moved into a better position for shooting and watched. She knew she couldn't do anything to help Chase, but her heart was now pounding so wildly in her throat that she could hardly breathe. He was wrong about her not being ready to kill a man, but it had never occurred to her that she would ever have to kill anyone but Pieter. She had planned that day for so long. But now she knew she had to be prepared to do whatever Chase needed from her.

Chase had worked his way almost halfway down the bank by now. He slipped between the rocks and stopped behind a large boulder beside the trail where the men would be coming up. It fully concealed his body. The four men would be in single file and broadside to Chase as they circled his hiding place. Kally could see Chase checking his gun, his whole body alive and alert, and his normally handsome face was hardening to granite.

The gambler and his friends had reached the bottom of the gulch and were starting up the bank toward Chase. He could hear them talking, but couldn't make out their words yet. As the clacking and clicking of the horses' hooves on rock came closer, Chase again checked the looseness of his gun in its holster. He had to do this right and quickly. Now the voices came clearly.

"I just don't figure how they carried so much water," one of the men was saying.

"Beats me," another said. "If their canteens are as empty as ours are when we jump them, we'll be in a heap of trouble. I figured on them taking care of that for us. These horses can't go much longer without water."

"That's as far as you go, boys," Chase said in a hard voice as he stepped out from behind the rock. His feet were planted squarely in the pathway and he was ready to respond at the slightest movement from any of them.

"We'll go where we want," the gambler shot back. "Take him, Frank!"

Frank, obviously the only gunman in the bunch, was on the horse behind the gambler. He tried. So did the other three. Chase's gun was only a blur from where Kally lay gripping her rifle so tightly her knuckles had turned white. His gun bucked and spat smoke and flame. The four men were flung from their saddles like rag dolls by the heavy slugs from Chase's gun. The horses shied and backed down the trail a short way. Chase quickly reloaded his gun before walking to each man and rolling him over with the toe of his boot. He slipped his gun into his holster. They were all dead. He spoke softly to the horses as he gathered up their reins and led them slowly up the bank to where Kally was getting to her feet. She was trembling and all the color had drained from her face.

Chase didn't seem to notice. There was work to be done.

"Get Pacer. You go on ahead and tell Seth his hunch was right. Tell him I think it might be safe to camp in the box canyon tonight." Chase was barking orders like an army sergeant.

Kally nodded.

"I have some things to take care of here. If there's anyone else out there, that gunfire ought to bring them running. I'll wait around awhile and see. I only wish we could be sure this was the last of them."

Kally was on Pacer by now, and Chase handed her the reins of the extra horses. "Tell Seth not to expect me until dark."

Kally moved down the trail without a word, then turned in her saddle and called back to him, "Be careful, Chase."

Chase turned and walked back down to where the bodies were strewn on the trail. He moved in close to a big boulder and watched the far side of the gulch for almost an hour. When no one else showed up, he began to search the bodies. Any papers he found he put in a pile and burned. He found two gold watches and almost a thousand dollars in cash between them. He put it with what was left of Kally's money. Even after they bought more supplies in River Bend, there would be quite a bit left. If there was no gold, at least Kally would have enough to make a new start.

Chase rode into the box canyon to join the others just at dusk. Seth had not set up camp yet; he was waiting to see what Chase had to say. The mules and packhorses still had their packs on and were grazing on the lush green grass around the big spring.

"How's that itch feel now, Seth?" Chase asked as he swung down out of the saddle and walked toward Seth and Kally.

"Seein's how you're back in one piece, boy, I'd say pretty good. Who were they?"

"One of those gamblers and his friends from Albuquerque. Don't know why I didn't smell them coming. Guess my nose isn't as good as your itchy neck, pardner."

"Y'all didn't see nobody else back there?"

Kally was taking in every word, but didn't speak.

"Nope. I waited as long as I could and still have time to get here before dark. Unless you're working up another case of itchy neck, I think we'll probably be alright here for one night. You'd think if anyone was very close behind that bunch, they'd have come to see what the shooting was about."

"Reckon I don't have the itch no more, an' I'm inclined to agree with you, but if we're wrong, we'll be trapped like fish in a barrel."

Chase stood silently a moment as he surveyed the canyon in what little daylight was left. It was as he had remembered. "Doesn't look to me like anyone could get in here. There's only room for one horse at a time to get through that entrance and there aren't even any good places on the rim where they could shoot down on us. Guess I'm willing to chance it for tonight."

"If we can get out of here by first light in the mornin', we could be campin' at the head of Death Canyon by tomorrow night. I'd lay odds that once we're in that canyon our worries about pole cats in the wood pile will be over. Besides, this is a right nice campin' place; the last until we reach the Salt. What do you think, Kally?" Seth looked at Kally for the first time since Chase's return.

"It looks real nice here," Kally said softly. "You know I trust your judgment as far as how safe it might be." Her voice was strained and she seemed distant as she spoke.

"That settles it then," Seth said as he turned to leave. "I'll tell the boys to unsaddle the stock an' have one of 'em get over by the entrance an' keep an eye open."

Chase nodded to Seth as he left, but he was watching Kally, trying to decide what he might say to her. Kally was slipping the saddle from Pacer as he spoke.

"Are you alright, Kally?"

She turned back in his direction, but didn't make eye contact.

Chase went on. "I'm sorry you had to see Chase Wade in action again today. That's the man I had hoped to leave behind, but doesn't look like that might happen, at least until this trip is over. I hope you can understand that, Kally."

Kally was searching Chase's face now, and then looked directly into his eyes—as if looking for something. Chase felt immobilized by the strength and intensity of her gaze. He waited for her to speak.

"You're a gunman, Chase. That's why I hired you. I understand it's what you do for a living, but I have also come to realize that it's not what you are—inside. Already you have shown me pieces of yet another Chase Wade. The real one. You did what you had to do today. It's not something I will soon forget, but I know it had to be done."

Chase wasn't sure how to respond to this lady who seemed to know him better already than he had ever allowed anyone to know him. At times like these when he would have expected her to be frightened and upset, she was more calm and collected than he could ever have imagined a woman would be. He remembered back to the afternoon when he had stood outside her door and wondered if she would be a threat to him. Now he was beginning to wonder if she wouldn't have been less of a threat if she had been holding a derringer on him when he opened that door.

Before he could say anything more, Kally turned back to Pacer as she spoke, "You must be starved, let's get some supper. I want to take advantage of all this water to take a bath and wash my hair tonight."

Chase knew their conversation was over for now.

It didn't take them long to get camp set up and supper on. When they had finished and Kally was cleaning up the dishes, Chase took a plate of food and cup of coffee to Roberto who was standing watch at the entrance and then walked outside for a look around. He stood silently for several minutes, but neither saw nor heard anything in the still darkness. He had expected anyone following to have caught up with them long before now. This first bunch hadn't found the water and chances were any others following would have had the same problem. If Ben was lucky, back in Albuquerque, he just might have discouraged any others who had similar ideas. As Chase walked back into the canyon, he was feeling better about the chances of anyone being able to track them this far. By tomorrow evening their worries about anyone being behind them would be over. Then they would only have to worry about what was up ahead.

By the time Chase returned to the fire, Seth was cleaning his rifle and Kally was ready for her bath.

She gathered up a change of clothing, soap and towel, and followed Chase, who was carrying two buckets of water for her. They found a place where four large rocks provided the privacy of a small room. Kally stepped inside and thanked Chase as he set the buckets down nearby. He returned to the fire and filled Seth in on what had happened earlier with the men he had killed, and they made plans for the next day's journey.

Kally came back and sat on a rock near the fire, brushing her hair dry. She volunteered to relieve Roberto on watch. Chase and Seth would take the next two. Things were quiet all night.

Carlos stood guard at the entrance the next morning as the others prepared for an early start. Kally carried a plate of breakfast out to him. As she reached the entrance she found Carlos had dozed off and one of the mules had wandered outside the entrance. She kicked the bottom of Carlos's boot and shoved the plate into his hands.

"Eat this. It's almost time to pull out. One of the mules wandered off. I'll go get him while you eat, then I can take your plate back and pack up."

Kally made chirruping sounds at the mule as she dashed out the entrance in hopes of catching him before he got too far. Chase looked up from saddling Ranger just in time to see her slip out of sight. Independent cuss, Chase thought to himself as he decided it would be futile to try to stop her now. He turned back to his work.

Suddenly his attention was yanked back to the entrance as a piercing scream echoed into the small canyon from outside. It was Kally's voice and the screams came over and over again. Seth caught up with Chase as he ran toward the sound. Carlos had dropped his plate and was standing wide-eyed with his gun at the ready, but he had made no move to go outside. Chase and Seth charged through the entrance, only to hit the ground instantly beneath a barrage of whining bullets. They rolled clear of the entrance and found cover inside the rock wall. Bullets continued to ricochet off the rocks for several moments.

Chase and Seth were back on their feet, guns drawn. They stood listening for a moment, looking at each other.

"Do you think they've killed her?" Chase asked as a tightness formed around his mouth and eyes.

"Don't even think it, boy. They're not that dumb. Y'all can bet they're plannin' to use her to get to us an' the map."

"I hope you're right, Seth. How could we have been such damn fools? We both know better than to let our guard down—ever. If they hurt or kill Kally we'll be to blame." Chase's anger was directed at himself as much as outside the canyon.

"Pull yourself together, Chase. We've been in tight spots like this before. The most important thing now is to keep our heads an' stay in control. We can worry about who to blame later. What's our next step?" One of Seth's strengths had always been his coolness under fire. One of Chase's weaknesses was his inability to remain detached.

"I'm going out to get her, Seth. It's my fault she's out there and I'm not going to let her die for my stupidity."

"Runnin' out there into a hail of lead an' gettin' yourself killed ain't gonna help Kally. I've suspected all along there's somethin' special going on between the two of you, but that's no reason to throw out your common sense, boy. I'm bettin' we'll be hearin' somethin' from them real soon. No sense chargin' out there half-cocked until we know what they're up to."

Chase stood looking at Seth for a moment. Everything in him wanted to take action now, but he knew Seth was right.

"As soon as we find out who they are an' figure out what their game is, we can make some plans." Seth sat down with his back against the rock wall and waited.

Chase paced impatiently along the canyon wall near the entrance, but kept out of sight. As he walked past Seth he hissed, "Why don't they . . . ?" He didn't have a chance to finish.

He was interrupted by a loud, harsh voice from outside the entrance. "Alright, Wade! Y'all were a little quicker than I figured. We should have gotten you an' Seth when you run out. Don't matter much, though. We got your little slant-eyed woman. Pretty little thing. She's all tied up to a nice warm rock out here. Why not make it easy on all of us, especially on your little Chink? Jest toss them guns out an' come on out with your hands up. All we want is the map an' supplies. We'll let you take your woman, horses, an' enough water to get you back to the arroyo where the spring is."

Chase and Seth both knew he was lying. No man in his right mind would leave the two of them alive to come back and take them out. And if he knew who they were, he would have to know they would be back.

Chase's mind was racing in search of an answer, but now his voice was calm. "I'm afraid you've got me at a disadvantage, friend. You know my name, but I don't know who you are."

"I've got more'n one advantage on you, Wade. Y'all should remember me, though. You put a bullet through my shoulder up in White Plains a couple years ago. If that's slipped your mind, y'all might remember I was scout for the troop what come out to help your bunch in that Death Canyon fiasco. The name's Speed Evans."

"You're damn right I remember you," Chase shouted back. "I remember the army tried to hang you for stealing rifles and selling them to the Indians. I also remember the reason I only winged you was because you were hiding behind your men instead of standing out like a man." Chase would have liked to say more, but knew Kally's life might depend on him keeping his wits about him.

"Why, that's plumb unfriendly, Wade. After all the favors we've done fer you. We took out three parties back there on the trail. We'd have gotten that other bunch, but that nosy sheriff throwed us in the hoosegow fer a couple days. Some trumped up charge 'bout disturbin' the peace. Anyhow, there's nobody on our back trail now. It's just your party an' mine. It's lucky I know this country well as you. We stopped in the arroyo to fill our canteens. Got plenty of supplies an' enough men to send one back fer more water if we need to. We can wait as long as you."

"Wait as long as you like, Speed. I thought I'd

take a nap while you were waiting. Hope you boys'll be quiet out there so you don't disturb my sleep."

"Alright, Wade. I'm through bein' nice. I said we could wait, but I'm an impatient man an' I have no intention of waitin' long. I'm givin' you a choice. Either you an' your boys throw out your guns an' come on out here, or I'm gonna kill your little Chink gal."

"I always knew you were a fool, Evans, but I don't think you're fool enough to kill the only one who can take either of us to the gold. I've got the map alright, but it's no good without the woman. Her daddy drew it with clues only she knows, so it's worthless if you kill her."

"I reckon I can believe that, Wade. Otherwise I'm sure you wouldn't have brought her. You an' Seth could've brought out the gold lots easier without her taggin' along. That don't change things a heap, though. Even if we cain't kill her, she's still our ace in the hole."

"I'm listening," Chase yelled. "What's on your mind?"

"Me an' my men'll get you an' Seth one way or another. We've got you bottled up in there. All we have to do is bide our time. One night, we'll slip in an' kill the both of you an' take the map an' everythin' else we want."

"You're scaring me to death," Chase taunted. "You know the only way you'll ever kill either of us is to back-shoot us."

"You're right, friend. Not gonna bother us to back-shoot you. That's why I say sooner or later we're bound to get you. In the meantime, if you haven't come out by dinnertime, me an' this little Chink'll have a real party. Guess you've heard how I like my women—screamin' an' hollerin'. If you don't wanna join our little party by then, I'll let my men have a little fun with her. None of us ever had a slant-eye before. Heard they're real good at pleasin' their men. Of course, after travelin' with you, she'll want to find out what a real man is like. I'm sure you'll be able to hear how much she likes it from in there."

Chase's fingers closed tightly around the butt of his six-gun as anger welled within him. Seth put his hand over Chase's and looked him straight in the eye. Chase's hand relaxed as his mind drew together all his resources.

"You can do what you want with her as far as I'm concerned, she's just another payday to me. But if you do what you say, and kill her in the process, none of us will ever find the gold. She can't tell you anything about the map until she gets a chance to work out the clues, so she's no good to you without the map—and we've got it. She might be just as happy to cut you in to take her the rest of the way, if you're nice to her. All you've got to do is take out me and Seth, and get the map. She's got a real temper, though. I wouldn't get her mad if I was you."

Evans was silent. Chase hoped he had given him something to think about. He turned to Seth. "I think Kally will be alright for a while. At least until Evans decides what to believe. Now that we know who we're up against, you got any ideas?"

"I've been thinkin' on it, but haven't come up with no plan yet. If he believed any of what you said, Kally could be alright for as long as a couple days, but she's gonna be mighty uncomfortable if they keep her tied to a rock out in the sun all that time. She's got to be scared to death too, so we don't dare leave her out there long. There's no figurin' a man like Evans. He could change his mind any minute or do somethin' loco for no reason at all. Right now it looks like a Mexican standoff. He can't get in an' we're not about to walk out into his guns."

"I'm not waiting two days. Not even the rest of this one. I don't trust that skunk out there with Kally for a minute. We've got to figure out exactly where they are. Let's see what we can find out."

"Be careful, Chase. Y'all know I'd go down for Kally too, but I'm not the man you are with a gun. I wouldn't have a chance of gettin' 'em if they get you first. Evans would win. He'd take me out, get the map, an' have Kally too."

Chase didn't answer. He told the Mexicans to stay out of sight, but to keep their rifles ready. He and Seth went down on their bellies and snaked their way alongside the rock walls until they could see some of the rocky terrain outside. They couldn't see much. They lay silent and listened.

It was a good hour before they heard the lookout rattle rocks as he changed position. He was behind a big rock straight across from the entrance, less than a hundred yards from them. They watched closely and once in a while caught glimpses of him as he lit a cigarette or moved around.

The problem now was that they didn't know which direction the others were from the entrance. They could be on either side. Chase was impatient and couldn't make a move until he knew their position, but a desperate plan began to form in his mind.

A few minutes later Kally gave him what he needed—the last piece to complete his plan. She yelled out in fury, "I told you I don't know anything without that map. Kill me if you like, but you'll never find the gold." Her voice came from the left of the entrance and not far away. Chase knew how determined she could be. He didn't dare leave her much longer. Evans wouldn't take much of her tongue-lashing. He turned to Seth and motioned for him to go back for his rifle. Seth nodded and wiggled back through the entrance.

Chase knew his scheme was wild, but it was so wild it just might work. He could see the lookout was already bored and distracted by Kally's shouts, and he hoped Evans was counting on them to wait for dark before they tried anything. The element of surprise would be in their favor. He was banking on that—and his gun—to give them the edge they needed. It wasn't much, but it was all they had.

Seth was back with his rifle and looked questioningly at Chase. "Y'all know you're loco to even try this?" Seth whispered close to Chase's ear. It was more of a statement than a question.

Chase knew Seth was with him, no matter what he thought of the idea. He gave Seth instructions and a rundown of his plan as quickly and quietly as he could. The success of his plan called for precision on both of their parts.

They both crawled forward as far as they dared. The lookout was still distracted. Chase slowly eased to his feet. Seth had his rifle trained on the rock where the lookout was hiding. In that instant, Chase pulled his six-gun and leaped out of the entrance in a hard run to the left. He didn't try to hide the noise he made. The lookout came up fast and the crack of Seth's rifle was all the assurance Chase needed to know the man was dead.

The enemy camp was now in full sight. Kally was tied to a rock just off the trail. Evans had been hunkered down in front of her, still talking, when he heard the first shot. He snapped to his feet in a turn. The two other men close by were on their feet and grabbing leather. Chase kept running until Evans's first shot missed him and ricocheted off a rock somewhere nearby. He hit the ground rolling and his first shot found its mark. Evans was thrown back by the heavy slug. He crumpled to the ground as a hail of bullets kicked stinging bits of rock all over Chase.

Chase took a chance on catching a bullet to make sure of his aim. His six-gun belched and roared. Both of Evans's men went down. They weren't moving, but Chase caught a glimpse of movement from Evans out of the corner of his eye. As he turned back to finish the job, Evans was flung back again before Chase could squeeze off a shot. The ring of Seth's rifle came from right behind him.

Chase leaped to his feet and ran forward. A quick check found all three men dead. Evans had gone down hard. He had two slugs in his chest, one from Chase's six-gun, the other from Seth's rifle.

Chase reloaded and holstered his gun before he turned his attention to Kally for the first time since the shooting had started. She was slumped against the rock sobbing quietly. Chase cut her bonds and helped her to her feet.

"Are you alright, Kally? He didn't hurt you, did he?"

Kally looked blankly into his face, as if she didn't know who he was or where they were. Then she collapsed into his arms. The combination of fear and sitting out in the sun for so long was too much for her. He picked her up and carried her back into the canyon. He was surprised at how light she was in his arms, almost like a child. The warmth of her body next to his was something he had thought about often. Seth had gone ahead to roll out her bedroll, then went to his saddlebags for a bottle of whiskey.

Chase carefully laid her down as she began to come to. She began thrashing around and crying out. "No—no—you'll never touch me again—never. I'll kill you, Pieter. I'll kill you." Chase and Seth exchanged bewildered glances as Seth poured a sip of whiskey between her dry lips. She sat up choking as the bitter liquid started down her throat. Kally looked from one man's face to the other as she regained an awareness of what had happened.

"Chase—Seth—are you alright? When I saw you come running, I was sure you'd be killed. I never saw anyone do anything as brave as that. Did you kill them? Are they dead?" Kally's questions seemed to be coming faster than she could express them. She reached out and grabbed both of their hands. "I can't believe you're both alright."

"We're alright, but how about you? You had us worried to death," said Chase, looking at her more closely. She didn't seem to remember what she had said as she was coming to.

"They didn't hurt me, although I have no doubt

they would have if you hadn't worried them about my tie to the map. Evans was an animal." Kally shuddered. "I knew he would have done all he threatened, and more. I don't know what I would have done if he had. . . ." Kally slumped back onto her blankets as she turned her face away from the men.

8

Kally was still dizzy and somewhat dazed. She assured the men she would be alright and insisted they do what needed to be done so they could leave the canyon as soon as possible. She promised to rest, get cleaned up, and be ready to leave as soon as they were.

Seth and Chase went back to gather up the horses and packhorses left by the Evans bunch. They were accumulating more extra stock than they needed. The Mexicans took what they might need from the packs, in way of supplies, as well as the guns and cash. They packed away the extra guns and supplies. Chase put their cash with the rest of Kally's money. They hid the packs behind boulders and figured the buzzards or coyotes would soon take care of any other evidence that Evans and his gang had been there.

By the time the men had finished cleaning up, saddling their horses, and had come back to help the Mexicans load the pack mules, Kally was moving around and had freshened up in the spring. Her face was still flushed, but she looked a little better. All of them were anxious to get out of the canyon and put

110

the horrors of the morning behind them, but they took time enough to eat a little jerky and left-over biscuits before they hit the trail, heading for the mouth of Death Canyon.

The day was more than half gone by the time they were on their way, but none of them was anxious to spend another night in the box canyon. Even though Chase and Seth were quite sure there would be no more followers, neither of them was willing to take that chance again. Their last mistake had almost cost all of them their lives.

Chase watched Kally as they rode. She was sitting her saddle straight, but he could tell she was exhausted. He was thankful they would have only a couple more hours on the trail before they would have to stop for the night. Chase couldn't forget Kally's words and her obvious terror as she had regained consciousness after her rescue. Something more had happened between her and Pieter than the stealing of her father's map. Chase was sure of that now. He was determined to find out what.

Since the horses and mules were well rested from the extra time in the canyon, they were able to make good time during the rest of the afternoon. Chase let Kally ride up front with Seth, and he dropped back to bring up the rear. He would keep a close eye on their back trail until they were well inside Death Canyon.

Seth and Kally rode along in silence most of the time, except for Seth occasionally checking to see if Kally was feeling well enough to keep riding. She assured him she was fine.

"If you're alright up here alone for a couple minutes, I think I'll go back an' check on Chase," Seth said as he reined Maude around and rode back to where Chase was bringing up the rear.

"You alright, boy?" Seth asked as he turned Maude and rode up alongside Chase. "Y'all had a rough time this morning."

"I'm fine, Seth. I want to thank you for backing me. We both know I couldn't have done it without you. Kind of like the old days, wasn't it?"

"We're pardners, ain't we? I don't see as how we had a whole lot of choice. Kally's neck was on the line."

"Is she okay?" Chase asked. "I've been worried about her."

"Says she is, but she looks plumb tuckered out to me. Hasn't said much of anythin' since we left the canyon."

Chase didn't respond right away, and they rode along in silence for a few minutes. "You heard what she said when she was coming to. How do you figure it?"

Seth shook his head. "Hard to say, but I'd bet the whole pot she's got good reason to kill that no-good cousin of hers. She's got a real burr rubbin' her about somethin', iffen you ask me."

"Whatever it is, I think it's time she let us in on the whole story. I'd guess it's more than she needs to keep bottled up inside. Something's really eating at her. You think she'll tell us if we ask?"

Seth was quiet as he thought a moment. "I don't see she's got much choice. If it's got anythin' to do with what's waitin' for us in Pike City, we need to know, an' now. I better get back to her. I reckon we best get this settled tonight." Seth rode on back up to the front of the mule train.

They were all relieved when it was time to stop and camp for the night. Now that they had all had a chance to relax after the excitement of the morning, tiredness was beginning to fill every inch of their bodies. The Mexicans had been talking between themselves in Spanish all afternoon. It was obvious they weren't used to all the killing that was going on.

They made a dry camp that night, but they still had plenty of water to get them to the first *tanque* in Death Canyon. Seth sensed they could all use a little cheering up, so he fixed one of his famous desert stews for supper. It had been about the only dish of Seth's that Chase could stand. He was never sure what was in it, but had enough sense not to ask.

The men both insisted that Kally take the night off from supper chores and night watch so she could get rested up before the next day's ride. She argued at first, but they insisted that if she didn't she might get sick and hold them up where they were for a day or two. They all knew they wouldn't be safe until they got well into Death Canyon, and that was still several hours' of riding away.

After supper, Roberto took the first watch and Carlos went to check on the animals before turning in. Kally sat looking into the fire as the men casually discussed how far they were from Death Canyon, and how long it would be before they came to the first water. They purposely avoided any talk of what had happened that morning. It was done, and they were all anxious to put it behind them.

Chase couldn't get Pieter out of his mind. He

knew Seth would leave it up to him to get some answers out of Kally. Chase was reluctant to put Kally through any more that night, but knew he wouldn't sleep until he knew what she was hiding. Besides, the safety of all of them might depend on it.

At last, he looked over at Kally, who was still lost deep within her own thoughts. "Kally, I know you've had a hard day, but Seth and I have talked it over and feel like we have no choice but to ask you what Pieter has done to make you hate him so much. More than once you've talked of killing him."

Kally looked at Chase for a moment without any change of expression, as if she was not sure what he was saying to her. Slowly her whole body seemed to tense up and the old fire was back in her eyes. She looked curiously from Chase's face to Seth's as she tried to determine what she could do to avoid the question.

"Do you remember what you said when you came to this morning?" Chase asked.

Kally shook her head.

"I don't remember your exact words, but something about killing Pieter and about him not doing something ever again. It didn't make a lot of sense to us."

Suddenly her shoulders dropped and it was obvious she didn't have the energy to protect the secret she had carried as a penance for so long. Maybe it was better to get it all out in the open. Then she wouldn't have to worry about Chase getting too close. He wouldn't be interested in her any longer and they could get on with finding the gold.

Kally's voice was quivering as she began. "I didn't

tell you the whole story about Pieter. He was always a bully, as long as I can remember. He didn't get along with his father at all; he never wanted to work and was usually in some kind of trouble. He considered himself a real ladies' man, and was constantly fighting and whipping other young men over women or anything else he thought was worth a fight. He had gotten into a big fight with his father over money. My uncle wouldn't give him the money he needed to go after my father's gold." Kally hesitated.

"Did he fight with you too? You said earlier you didn't get along with him," Chase said.

"He hated me right from the first. He had been an only child and had always gotten everything he wanted. I'm sure he didn't get any less because I was there, but somehow he believed I was cheating him out of something that was rightfully his. I tried my best to avoid him, especially as I got older, but he took great joy in tormenting me whenever he could. I spent a lot of time in my room alone, just to avoid being around him. I think that made him as angry as my being there." Kally's face was taking on a contorted look of pain as she seemed to begin reliving those difficult days in her aunt and uncle's home. She took a sip of her coffee, seemingly unaware it had grown cold.

"One night, when I was about sixteen, I had gone to my room right after supper because my aunt and uncle had gone out to the theater and he was being more obnoxious than usual. I took a long hot bath and slipped into a nightgown. I was planning to read in bed until bedtime. Suddenly my door flew open and Pieter was in my room before I knew what was happening." Kally's voice was calm and steady now as she determined she would finally set her secret free.

"He grabbed me, tore my nightgown off, and threw me on the bed. I was too frightened even to cry out. He was so strong, and so much bigger than I that it mattered little I was digging my fingernails into him and fighting with all my might to get free. He said a lot of vulgar things to me, including something about making a real woman of me. He hurt me so badly I thought I was going to die before . . ." Kally's voice cracked as the tears welled up into her throat.

"It's alright, Kally." Chase tried to help ease her pain. "You don't have to finish. We know what happened."

Kally looked at him a moment, then shook her head. "He said if I told my aunt and uncle, he would tell them I invited him to my room, took off my clothes in front of him, and begged him to . . . I knew they would take his word over mine, so I said nothing. My aunt already disliked me. I don't think I could have told them what had happened anyway. I never wanted to tell anyone about that night."

Kally stared into the dying embers of the fire again, as the men wrestled with what they should say to her. Before they could say anything, her head suddenly jerked back up and she looked intently at both men. "That's why I'm going to kill him. He not only took my virginity, he took any chance I ever had of falling in love and marrying a man. He made me dirty and ugly. No man would ever want me now." She had tried to avoid Chase's eyes, but now she was drawn to them with such force she had to look directly at him. His eyes were full of such hate and anger that she got up and ran into the darkness.

"Kally," he called after her, but she didn't stop. She had been right about the hate and anger, but she hadn't given him the chance to explain that they were directed against Pieter, not against her. His only feelings toward her were of love and deep concern. He wanted nothing more than to take her in his arms and hold her close.

Chase looked at Seth. He didn't know whether he should follow her or leave her alone for now.

"Go on after her, Chase. She needs to know we don't hold none of this against her. Sounds like she's gotten mighty messed up in her thinkin'. Talk to her."

That was all the encouragement Chase needed. He got to his feet and followed her into the darkness. She was slumped down next to the dead stump of an old ocotillo sobbing softly when Chase found her.

"It's me, Kally," Chase called out as he approached, so he wouldn't frighten her. "Are you alright?"

Kally rose quickly to her feet, and looked at Chase with a combination of hurt and anger. "Don't bother yourself about me, Mr. Wade. I can take care of myself. Your job is only to get me to the gold and back, and I'd appreciate it if you'd keep your disgust to yourself and just do your job." Without another word, she marched back toward camp.

"But, Kally. Wait. You don't understand...." Chase's attempts to stop her were to no avail. She climbed into her bedroll that she had pulled to the opposite side of the fire from where Chase had laid his. Kally was so exhausted she soon fell into a deep, druggedlike sleep.

It was a long night for Chase. He was too upset to go to sleep, so he took the next watch. He had never been so confused about his feelings for a woman, or hers for him. He had known from the beginning there had been an impenetrable wall between him and Kally. Now he knew that wall was made up of her fears and confusion about what Pieter had done to her. It was a relief to finally know what it was, but now she had misunderstood his reaction to her story. He knew she was only a victim of her cousin's brutality. He could never hold that against her, and it certainly made no difference in how he felt about her. Somehow he would have to make her understand that.

Part of his problem was that he wasn't sure how he felt. He had never known a woman like her. He had met a few respectable women in his travels over the country, but most of them would not have been comfortable spending any amount of time with a gun-man. So most of his experience with women had been with the saloon girls. They were easy to love—and to leave—and they had never meant any more to him than a fulfillment of his sexual needs and a pleasant pastime. Kally was different. Although he had been attracted to her physically from the beginning be-cause of her outward beauty, he was beginning to realize he was drawn to her in a way he had never been drawn to a woman before. She had an inner beauty—an inner strength that drew him deeper and deeper into her very being. Was it love? Infatuation? Or fascination? He wasn't sure.

He wasn't sure of anything anymore, except his hatred and his anger, directed toward Pieter. Chase hoped they would find him waiting for them in Pike City. Pieter would pay, and pay dearly, for shattering this fragile China doll.

9

Kally was still sleeping soundly when the men began to stir at dawn the next morning. Since there had been no sign of trouble all night, they decided they would let her sleep a little later. They would ride into the relative safety of Death Canyon today anyway. Chase built a fire, and Seth put on some coffee.

"I reckon you wasn't able to get through to Kally last night," Seth said as he poured a cup of coffee a few minutes later. "That little gal's been carryin' a heap of horse manure around with her when it comes to that cousin of hers. Can't say I blame her for wantin' to blow his head off."

"Well, she sure answered a lot of questions last night, but now she thinks we're going to hold what he did against her. I've got to convince her somehow that she's wrong."

"Just how do you feel about her, Chase? You've always told me you could never get serious about any woman, but it appears to me there's somethin' goin' on between the two of you."

"I thought I understood women, but this one's

120

a real mystery to me, Seth. In some ways there's been some kind of a bond between us almost from the start. She's easy to talk to and I've told her things I've never told any other woman. We've become good friends, but I find myself wanting it to be more than that, lots more. I see now why she felt she had to keep me at a distance, but I'm not sure I can convince her she's wrong about how she feels. I want her, Seth. Like I've never wanted a woman before."

"I understand what you're sayin', boy. That's how I felt about my wife."

"The young Indian squaw you were married to?"

"To me, she wasn't no squaw. She was the most lovin' an' excitin' woman I ever knew. Running Deer was my wife, an' I loved her. I couldn't do enough for her. The few months we had together in that little cabin up in high lonesome were the happiest of my life. Closest to settlin' down I ever got, I reckon."

"She was killed, wasn't she?"

"I lost her to a war party from another tribe. I followed 'em for weeks, picking off one or two at a time until I got 'em all. I had my revenge, but it didn't bring her back to me. I ain't never found no other woman I felt the same about—except maybe this little Carmen I met on my last trip. That's why I never married again."

Chase felt closer to Seth than he ever had. "I never thought I'd get married, or even want to, but I reckon all the talk about starting up the ranch and hanging up our guns has gotten me to thinking more about wanting to share that with someone. But when Kally gets this gold, she can go back to Boston and have any man she wants. Why would she settle for a broken-down gunfighter with a poor excuse for a ranch somewhere in Colorado?"

"What broken-down gunfighter? You're still the best around. Besides, if we find the gold, your share will make you as rich as Kally. Y'all can go back an' build that ranch up to the best in Colorado, or go off anywhere you want to build her a big, fancy new place. Didn't it ever occur to you, boy, that you might be the man she wants?"

"That's what I'm hoping, but I'm scared, Seth. I wouldn't admit that to anyone but you. For the first time in my life I'm fighting something I can't use my gun or fists on. What if I can never get her over this fear Pieter has put in her? Right now she won't even let me touch her."

"I'm no expert on women, Chase, but I do know time an' love can heal a heap of things. You'll just have to be patient with her. But I've been watchin' you together since we had dinner with her that first night an' I'd say the two of you have the same thing Running Deer an' I had. A love like that's worth fightin' for, boy. Don't let her get away from you."

"Thanks, pardner. I'm ready to fight whatever it takes to get that little gal." Chase poured himself another cup of coffee and looked over at Kally's bedroll. She was beginning to stir.

Suddenly Kally sat up and looked around. "You should have called me when it was time to go," she said as she realized it was sunup. She scrambled to her feet and rolled up her bedroll.

"It's alright. We can spare the time, an' you needed the rest," Seth assured her.

"I'll be ready in a minute," Kally said matter-offactly as she splashed a little water on her face and brushed out her hair. "Did I miss breakfast?"

"No. Here's a cup of coffee," answered Chase, handing her a fresh cup as she walked toward them. "We waited on breakfast until you could join us. As soon as we're done we'll pull out. The boys have packed up everything but what we'll be needing for breakfast, so it won't take long."

"Y'all look a whole lot better this mornin', Kally," said Seth. "Reckon that extra sleep was just what you needed. Can't tell you how sorry we both are about yesterday. Just thankful we was able to get you out of there in one piece. An' about last night. It don't make . . ."

Kally cut Seth off before he could finish. "I'm going to saddle Pacer. Isn't it time we were getting on the trail?" Without waiting for a response, she turned and headed for the horses.

Seth and Chase looked at each other and both shrugged their shoulders. They had a cold breakfast.

By noon, they were at the entrance of Death Canyon and soon were following the trail along the floor of it. The old trail twisted and turned, and the narrow walls of the canyon reflected the sun's intense afternoon heat. The trail was so narrow in some places they had to ride single file. Kally was thankful for the excuse not to have to talk to the men. Not that she had been talking. She had decided before falling asleep the night before that they would all be better off if she kept her distance so Chase and Seth wouldn't feel like they had to be sociable. Now that they knew the kind of woman she was, their interest would only be in the gold.

The heat was almost unbearable as Kally wiped the perspiration from her forehead and back of her neck as they picked their way along the narrow trail. Chase was leading the way, and Seth was bringing up the rear. Kally sat high in the saddle, filled with determination that she would make it to the gold and bring out enough to buy her the place in society she had always dreamed of having. As she thought about the big house and beautiful clothes the gold would buy her, a deep wave of sadness and extreme loneliness swept over her and she fought to keep back the tears. She realized her old dream had lost its polish. It didn't hold the same satisfaction and fascination for her that it had for all those years of planning and dreaming.

Something had changed in her since the start of this trip. She had come to Albuquerque very much alone, but she had left there with two men who had changed her life. Seth had become like the father she missed so desperately and Chase—she couldn't find the words to express how she had come to feel about him, even to herself. He may have been the only real friend she had ever had. She had tried to convince herself all along that it was merely friendship, but she knew it was more, so much more. She felt more alive, more like a woman, when she was with him than she ever had in her life. Now she had even lost his friend-ship.

In some ways Kally was glad her secret was out. At least she could stop worrying about them finding out. But she suddenly realized that last night's confession had destroyed the only family she had ever felt a part of since her mother's death. She cried softly into her kerchief as she pretended to wipe the perspiration from her face. Her loneliness was more unbearable than the heat of Death Canyon.

Late in the afternoon, Chase raised his hand for them to stop, and swung down off Ranger. "Roberto—Carlos—bring the buckets so we can water the stock." Chase headed for the rock bank.

Kally couldn't see water anywhere. There was nothing but bare rock around them. Not even the slightest dampness. She watched Chase curiously as he began to climb the rock bank, fitting his boots into old, nearly hidden niches in the rock. Roberto handed him a bucket and soon he was handing down buckets of clear, cool water. They had come to the first of the *tanques* Chase and Seth had told her about earlier. As she splashed the cool water on her face and wet her kerchief before putting it back around her neck, she was thankful Chase and Seth had known where the water was.

It took them almost an hour to water the stock and fill their canteens before they were ready to move on. Kally was glad for an excuse to be off her horse and stretch her legs as she helped with the watering. Now, more than ever, she would do her share of the work. It would keep her mind occupied and help pass the time.

Two days before they rode out of the canyon they came to another hidden *tanque* and repeated the same watering process. Chase watched Kally carrying buckets of water too heavy for her. He knew she would never complain, and was even more sure she would not allow him to help, so he watched her from a distance. Kally hadn't spoken to him for days, except to answer his questions with an abrupt yes or no. Chase wasn't sure how much longer he could stand her silence. He knew that on the other side of the stoic look she wore like a mask was a woman consumed by guilt and loneliness. He was beginning to realize he cared much too much to let her stay in the prison she had built around herself. He would break in—somehow.

Kally fixed supper that night and then took the second watch, after Carlos. Chase lay on his bedroll thinking about what he was going to do until he heard Seth preparing to go out and relieve Kally on watch. "Let me take the next watch, Seth. I'm wide awake. Besides, maybe I can get her to talk to me."

Seth waved his hand in agreement and lay back down on his bedroll.

Chase slipped into his boots, buckled on his gun belt, and walked out to where Kally was. She was surprised when he approached her.

"I was expecting Seth," she said flatly.

"I know, Kally, I just—I mean I wanted to talk with you," Chase stammered as he tried to remember the words he had rehearsed; afraid she might leave before he could have his say. "I can't stand seeing you do this to yourself."

"I'm not doing anything to myself except what's best for all of us. This is strictly a business deal. You don't have to like me. I'm sure when it comes to the gold, it doesn't matter if I'm a proper Bostonian or no better than your whore friends." Kally bit her lip, but wouldn't allow the tears to surface.

"Stop it, Kally!" Chase shot back. "Don't ever say anything like that again. If you'd get off that stubborn high horse of yours just once, you might give a man a chance to have his say." Chase stood with his hands on his hips, blocking her path.

Kally was so surprised at his quick reaction and the tone of his voice, she was speechless for a moment, and looked at him wide-eyed. "I don't think there's anything you could say that will change what's happened," Kally said as she recovered.

"Well, ma'am, you won't find out unless you shut your pretty little mouth and let me say what I came out here to say."

Kally looked him in the eyes and realized he wasn't going to let her go until she listened, so she stepped back and stood quietly—waiting. "I'm listening," she said in a voice still tinged with belligerence.

"I'm not real good with words, Kally, but there's something been gnawing at me for a long time now. I've felt there was something special about you from the time I first saw you in Albuquerque. The more time we spent together, the stronger that feeling became. I've never met a woman like you, but I liked what I saw. I liked it a lot. It didn't take me long to realize it was more than outward beauty. There's something inside you, Kally, something deep, and warm, and beautiful."

Kally was looking at the ground now, trembling slightly as Chase spoke.

"I think I knew almost from the start we could be more than friends, but there was something—something invisible—that always stood between us. I could never even reach out and touch you. After you told us about what Pieter did to you, I knew that was a wall of fear and I was so angry..."

Kally interrupted, "Chase, you don't have to say . . ."

"Yes, I do have to say it, so be quiet and listen." Chase was not going to let her stop him now. "I was angry and disgusted, but not at you, Kally. At Pieter. All I wanted to do was kill him for what he had done to you. None of that was your fault, and it doesn't change the way I feel about you. You are every bit as beautiful and desirable as you ever were."

"You can't mean that, Chase." Kally was losing her battle against the tears. "You couldn't really care about a woman who . . . who . . ."

"I could and I do. I've never said this to another woman in my life, Kally. I love you. I'll always love you." Now that he'd said it, Chase wasn't sure what to do. Kally was standing looking up at him with a stunned look on her face and tears running down her cheeks.

"Chase—I don't know what to say—I was so sure. . . ." Kally dissolved into tears as Chase reached out for her and drew her to him. He held her close and she sobbed into his chest for almost an hour. Neither of them spoke.

Finally Kally's body began to relax in his arms and the sobbing stopped, but she didn't try to pull away from him. Chase was the first to speak.

"I know I'm just a gunman and you could have any man you wanted, but do you think you could ever love a man like me?"

Kally pulled back and looked up into his face for a moment. "Oh, Chase, I do love you, but I don't know if I could ever . . ." Pain filled her voice and face as she turned and ran back into the darkness, toward camp.

"Kally—wait," Chase called after her, but he knew he was wasting his voice. He wanted to run after her, but he understood what she was trying to say. He remembered Seth's advice about being patient, so he decided she probably needed some time to work through what he had told her. But she had said she loved him, so he could wait. He would give her all the time she needed.

Kally crawled into her bedroll, confused and bewildered at all Chase had said to her. She realized now she did love him—she probably had from the beginning, but had tried so hard to convince herself otherwise. Now the pain deep in her chest was almost more than she could bear. It had been easier to pretend that he hated her. She had felt so warm and safe and loved in his arms. If only that could be all he would ever want from her, but she knew what men wanted. What Pieter had wanted. She cried herself to sleep.

✳

Two days later they rode out of the canyon onto the lower desert. It was even hotter than the canyon had been. They camped wherever sundown caught them. It was smooth and flat almost everywhere. There were patches of sun-bleached grass for the stock, but not nearly enough. Cactus and a few ocotillo scattered here and there were the only growth, and wood for fires was hard to come by. They crossed two long stretches of dunes where the horses and mules had to struggle to walk in the loose sand. They didn't have enough water to give the stock a drink the last morning. The lack of water and graze was beginning to show on them.

Kally had been quiet and withdrawn since Chase had told her of his love. He watched her constantly, looking for any sign of response from her, but the few times he had caught her looking at him, she looked away as soon as their eyes met. He would wait.

They rode through dinner that afternoon, too tired to be hungry. A couple of hours before sundown, the stock found the strength to pick up their pace. They could smell water. In a little while they saw the Salt River ahead of them. Its banks were lined with small trees and green grass. It was a small river but plenty big enough for their needs. They let the stock move out and they were soon at the river. The animals were allowed a long drink before the wranglers moved them back to the bank long enough to pull their packs and saddles.

Kally pulled off her boots, threw her hat on the bank, and ran out into the water with all her clothes on. Chase and Seth laughed at her, and she looked back at them with the first smile they had seen in days. It was as if coming out of the hot, dry desert into this little oasis of grass and water had brought a renewed sense of hope to all of them.

Chase and Seth walked up the river a short way to where there were some rocks for a fire. They gathered armloads of firewood and set their saddles and bedrolls on the grass. They would stay here an extra day to rest themselves and the stock. The next week of travel would be easy riding along the river.

When Kally finally came dripping from the river,

Chase stood in awe at her incredible beauty. Her face shone with a refreshing glow, and her wet clothes clung to her body showing every curve. His whole body pulsed in response to hers, and he had to turn away for a moment before he could speak.

"Why don't you get some soap and clean clothes, and do that right?" He pointed to a place up the river a short way where there were some big rocks out in the water. "You'll have all the privacy you need up there."

Kally nodded, and did as he said. When she returned and sat on a rock to brush her hair dry, he took his clean clothes and had a bath himself. It was a relief to all of them to get into the shade and to have all the water they wanted. Seth and the wranglers walked up and took their baths before supper. Chase was glad for the opportunity to have a little time alone with Kally. She was busy digging dirty clothes out of her saddlebags to be washed the next day.

Chase walked up behind her. "Kally, can we talk?"

She responded without looking up. "I don't know what to say to you, Chase. The fact that I love you doesn't change how I feel or what's happened to me. I don't think I could ever be the woman you want and need. It wouldn't be fair."

"You let me be the judge of that. I can be a very patient man if you're what I'm waiting for. I don't know a lot about this kind of thing, but Seth told me time and love can heal almost anything. I believe him, and I'm not going to let you go until we do everything we can to beat this thing."

Kally was looking up at Chase now, and he

reached his hand out to her. Slowly she got to her feet. The love in his eyes drew her to him and she reached out for his hand. He pulled her to him and leaned his head down close to hers. He gently touched her lips with his, and as she started to respond he kissed her with such passion it took her breath away. In that moment, her whole body tingled with a delight she had never known before. He kissed her over and over again until she had to pull away from him to catch her breath.

"Oh, Chase, I want to be everything you need, but I'm frightened, so frightened."

Chase didn't say anything. He just reached out and drew her back into his arms and held her for a long time. He stroked her hair gently as she cried softly in his arms. He didn't let her go until Seth and the wranglers returned.

10

*T*hey had an early supper that night. Seth and Kally pooled their cooking talents and came up with better fare than they had become used to with the shortage of water. They sat around the fire a long time after supper and talked about what lay ahead. They were all looking forward to the easier ride along the river for the next week. The trip through Death Canyon and across the desert were the worst they would see, at least until they discovered what lay behind Pike City when they got into the canyon on the map. There would be a long, hot stretch of desert to cross when they left the river, but not as bad as what they had just come through. The water holes would be closer together, though pretty nasty-tasting in some places.

They were still splitting the watches into five. The danger of followers was past, but although they hadn't seen any, the Apaches were out there somewhere. It was wise to always have someone on watch. The moon was filling again and lit up the open country where they were. The one on watch only had to find a big rock and keep his eyes open.

That night Kally moved her bedroll closer to Chase's than it had ever been. After they had crawled into their bedrolls, Chase leaned over and kissed her good night. He lingered as long as he dared. The warmth of her body next to his was almost more than he could stand. As he rolled back onto his blankets and got comfortable, Kally reached out for his hand and held it as she fell asleep. It was a deeper and easier sleep than she had had for many weeks.

Early the next morning, Kally gathered up her pile of dirty clothes and headed for the river to wash. The others took advantage of the time and water to do the same. Chase brought his near to where Kally was working. She volunteered to do his too, but they were so dirty he wouldn't let her.

"You look right at home washing those clothes," Kally teased. "Maybe I should have let you do mine." Chase scooped a handful of water and threw it in her direction. By the time the water fight was over, they were both laughing and rolling on the grass.

Chase stopped suddenly, propped himself up on one elbow, and looked over at Kally. "I love you," he said. With that he got up and started laying the clean clothes out on the rocks to dry. Kally helped him, a look of deep contentment on her face.

The remainder of the day they rested, taking short catnaps in the shade of some small willows as the stock filled up on fresh, green grass.

The next morning they were up and on their way again as the sun broke. The riding was as easy and uneventful as Seth had predicted. They came to the Verde River and followed it almost due north. A few days later they sighted the trading post at River

Bend just before dinner. They didn't ride right in, but scouted around to be sure no one was there except the trader who ran the place. When they were sure the only horses around belonged to him, they all rode up to the front of the long, sun-bleached building and dismounted.

A tall, dirty man with long, greasy hair stood behind a board counter as they entered. The inside of the trading post was stifling hot and smelled of sweat and spoiled food. Kally put her hand over her nose and tried not to breathe. They saw a lot of Indian trade goods hanging and lying about, but the man did have a good stock of canned and dried goods on the shelves.

"Howdy, folks," the man behind the counter greeted them with a smile that was missing one front tooth. "What kin I do fer you?"

"We need quite a few supplies, and from the looks of your shelves, you should be able to accommodate us," Chase said as he looked around the store.

The dirty storekeeper was eyeing Kally as Chase spoke.

"Tell you what, mister," the man said, "I'll trade you all the supplies you need fer that Chinee woman. I had me a good squaw before, but she runned off. Ain't never had me no Chinee woman before. You jest leave her with me an' y'all kin take whatcha want." The man smiled at Kally with the same toothless grin.

Chase's arm shot out and gripped the man's greasy shirt collar and yanked him halfway over the counter so his feet were off the floor. Chase twisted his hand and tightened the collar around the man's neck. The man struggled, but in vain. Chase twisted all the harder. The man's face was turning purple and his eyes were starting to bulge as he gasped for air.

"The lady you're talking about happens to be my wife, and I'd kill you if you as much as breathed your filthy breath on her. Now let's hear a nice apology out of you." Chase's jaw was set hard as he spoke.

The man tried to speak, but his wind was cut off. Chase loosened his grip a little, and the man sucked in a lungful of air. "I beg your pardon, ma'am. I made a mistake, an' I'm right sorry." The color was draining from his face.

Kally couldn't even stand to look at the man, and didn't acknowledge his apology.

Chase shoved him back off the counter and he crumpled to the floor.

"Since you like to trade so much, I'll make you a deal you can't refuse. We have too many horses and saddles. I'm sure you'd like to take them off our hands in exchange for the supplies we need. You must have people coming through here all the time who need fresh mounts. If that doesn't suit you, just say so. I'd like nothing better than to set fire to this whole stinking rat's nest and watch you roast with the rest of the rats." The man nodded weakly in agreement.

They all started pulling the things they needed off the shelves and carrying them out. In a short while the mules were fully loaded again. Chase led the extra horses and packhorses back to the man's pole corral and let them loose inside. He pulled off their saddles and left them outside the gate.

Seth led the way back to the river and they followed it north until they were well out of sight of the trading post. Then he led them into the river, and they stayed in the water for more than two miles before coming out on the other side. They filled all their canteens and let the stock drink their fill while they ate a hasty dinner out of tins. Seth looked at the sun and set a course northwest as he and the wranglers headed out.

Chase and Kally stayed behind to watch their back trail for a while. They wanted to be sure the trader didn't have any friends who might want to get revenge for him, or who were curious about where they were going.

Chase and Kally rode up the river a short way to some willows, and dismounted. They stood in the shade, hidden from down river, and watched as they talked.

"That's twice," Kally said.

"Twice?"

"That you've defended my honor. But what was that about my being your wife? I don't remember that part," she said, grinning.

"I just wanted to put that rat in his place. I'm sorry if that offended you, but I wish it were true," Chase said seriously.

The smile faded from Kally's face. "I'm flattered, Mr. Wade, but I don't know if that will ever be true." Kally turned her back and walked a few steps away from him as she continued, "The last few days have been the happiest of my life. I wish they would never come to an end. But someday you'll need more than a touch, or a hug, or a few stolen kisses. I'm still not sure I can ever give you more."

"I'm not pushing you, Kally. I've told you that. And you're wrong about someday wanting more. I

want more right now, but I'm going to wait until
you're ready—until you offer it freely. I'll never push
for it." He reached out and took her by the shoulder,
turning her to face him. "You believe that, don't you?"

"Of course I believe you, it's just that it's all so
unfair. You deserve better...."

"I want you to know something, Kally," said
Chase as he tipped her chin up and looked directly
into her eyes. "I will never want anyone but you.
Even if there never is more than what we have right
now."

Tears ran down Kally's cheeks. "I'll try, Chase.
I'll never stop trying." Kally slipped her arms around
him and he held her close as he watched the river
behind her for the next few minutes. When it was
time to leave, he moved her away from him far enough
to lean down and kiss her deeply. She responded as
fully as she had ever been able to.

Chase gave her a leg up as she mounted Pacer.
It had been a long time coming, but she was finally
willing to accept help. The flying vaults she'd been
using had become increasingly difficult the more tired
she had gotten on the trail.

✳

Every day on the trail became a repeat of the day
before; long hot hours in the saddle. They made a
couple of dry camps, then camped on a water hole.
The water was terrible to drink and, as Chase had
said in the beginning, only a little better than dying
of thirst. A couple of weeks out they spotted a small
band of Indians, but they were moving fast and didn't
even stop to watch the mule train. An hour later, a

large detachment of soldiers came along behind them. They only waved as they passed in pursuit of the Indians.

Each day Chase and Kally grew closer. They talked as much as they could while they rode, or caught time away from the others in the evenings just to be together. Chase never pushed the relationship any further, and Kally thrived on their closeness and warmth.

By the end of the fourth week since they had left the river, the country began to change. Large rock monoliths rose up against cobalt skies, and it got hotter the longer they traveled. Seth figured they were no more than a day out of Pike City by then.

The next morning, Seth sat on Maude and examined the surrounding country for a long time before he led off. He turned more to the north. After a couple of hours, he led the group down into a wide, shallow wash.

"If I ain't forgot this country," Seth said, "this wash should take us right up to what's left of Pike City. I reckon about noon tomorrow."

They rode on up the wash. About the time they started looking for a place to stop for dinner, they smelled smoke. Stopping quickly, they dismounted and handed their reins to the wranglers.

"Stay put until we come back," Chase cautioned the wranglers as he motioned for Kally to follow him. "Bring your rifle, but stay behind me and hit the dirt fast if I give you the word."

The three of them eased up the wash, hugging its shallow bank, using rocks and mesquite to cover their movements. When they came around a little bend in the wash, they could see two older men sitting around a small fire, eating.

Chase loosened his gun in its holster and took the lead. He stepped out into the wash and called out to the men.

"Hello there. I smelled your smoke, but didn't want to barge in until I saw who you were. I've got some friends with me, but we're not looking for trouble, just a place to stop for dinner."

"Come on in then," said one of the men. "You can share our fire, but you'll have to bring your own grub. Ours is all but gone. There's a little seep over yonder. Ain't much, but we dug it out an' it keeps fillin'. You can water your animals an' fill your canteens, but it'll take a spell. The name's Jake. Me an' Joe here could use some company."

Chase nodded at them as Seth stepped out from the bank, and Kally went back for the wranglers. Soon Kally was back and Joe and Jake fell all over themselves trying to please her. They hadn't seen a woman in months, and were surprised to see such a beautiful one in that desolate country. They talked continuously while Seth and Kally fixed dinner.

As Roberto and Carlos watered the stock and moved them out to the sparse grass along the wash next to the old prospectors' two burros, Chase looked around. From the number of holes that had been dug, it was obvious Joe and Jake had been in the area for some time.

While they ate, they learned that there was plenty of water at Pike City. The two men described a small stream that flowed from the rocks at the end of the box canyon, north of the old town.

"A couple years ago we heard about a strike around Pike City," Jake said, "so we came to try our luck. Me an' Joe an' our friend Elmer. There weren't no one there when we come, but we could see sign someone'd been there not too long before."

"We looked everywhere around Pike City," Joe added, "but didn't find no color. Leastwise not before that young ox an' his five men rode in an' told us to git out."

"Elmer didn't cotton to them movin' in on us an' put up a ruckus. The big one pulled a gun an' shot him. Joe an' me jest hightailed it outta there. After about six months of workin' this dadburn wash, we snuck back to take a peek at Pike City. Weren't nobody there no more, so we started lookin' again."

"Did you have any luck?" Seth asked.

"Nope," Joe went on, "but that pole cat an' his men came back. Lucky for us we spotted them before they spotted us. We ain't been back since an' there's no gold around here near as we can tell. We're pullin' out." Joe and Jake looked tired, and from the bad luck they told about, it was no wonder.

"What did that big feller look like?" Chase asked.

"Mean-lookin' cuss, dark hair, lots bigger than you," Jake said.

Chase watched Kally as she listened to the description. From the look on her face, he didn't have to ask if it fit Pieter. Every muscle in her body tensed as Jake spoke. Chase reached over, took her hand, and nodded reassuringly.

From the prospectors' story, it sounded like Pieter and his men had likely run off anyone else who had come looking for the gold. Obviously they had only left long enough to go out for supplies when they needed them. If they had been able to decipher the map, they wouldn't still be in Pike City. They had to be waiting for Kally to come with the real map.

Chase had never wanted to kill a man as badly as he wanted Pieter. He didn't have much stomach for killing anymore, but this time it would be a pleasure. Chase hoped that killing Pieter would release Kally from some of her fears about their future together. Now he knew he would have to take five others, too, but Chase figured that at least he and the others would have the canyon to themselves. He was sure Pieter had seen to that.

By the time they finished dinner and their conversation, the wranglers had managed to fill the canteens from the slow seep.

"Thank you for your hospitality, and the warning about Pike City," said Chase as he and Seth shook hands with the old prospectors. "We're heading up into Nevada, so we'll steer clear of Pike City," Chase lied, so as not to arouse their curiosity.

They pushed on up the wash for the rest of the afternoon and then led the mules up out of it and on to the desert to graze before they stopped to make camp. After supper, Seth, Chase, and Kally had a chance to talk about the day's events.

"Sounds like your cousin is working the area around Pike City alright," Chase said, "but you must be right about him not having much money. I'm guessing when they run low on supplies they're going out to rob a stagecoach or bank so they can buy more."

"The description they gave fits Pieter alright," Kally said, "but how do we know he'll still be there?

Maybe he's given up by now." Kally wanted him dead, but she knew they would be outnumbered. And if Pieter should kill Chase, she would no longer have a reason to live.

Chase knew what she was thinking. "You heard what Joe and Jake said about the canyon," Chase reminded her. "It's a box canyon, like I remembered it. It may take us several days to figure out the map. No, Kally, you'd better hope that Pieter is there waiting so we can end this thing once and for all."

Seth suggested they turn in so they could get an early start in the morning. If they pushed, they could be in Pike City by late tomorrow afternoon. Neither Chase nor Kally slept very well. Kally couldn't get Pieter out of her mind and Chase couldn't get him out of his gun sight.

They followed the wash again the next day and made better time than they had expected. Shortly after they had stopped for dinner, Seth pulled up. He smelled smoke again. Now they all smelled it.

"How far you figure?" asked Chase, wanting to confirm his own estimate.

"Maybe a mile."

"You suppose they got guards out?"

"I doubt it," Seth said. "From what Joe said, they probably run everybody else off long ago. It's likely they're all packin' iron an' figure they can handle any regular prospectors what wander in. I think we'll be safe to ride on 'til the smoke gets stronger."

Seth led off again slowly. After a little while, he stopped and dismounted. "Reckon we better go on foot an' take a look see. No sense ridin' up on 'em 'til we know how many for sure."

They left their horses with the wranglers again and walked cautiously up the wash. Kally had her rifle. As the wash turned into the start of the canyon, and the rock walls got higher as they went, they came to a pile of tattered canvas and trash from an old tent cabin. They crawled up behind it and looked over. Pieter was easy to spot. He was a big man, but Chase could see he was all fat. His thick hair was long and shaggy, and he hadn't shaved in several days. The five men with him were dirty and unshaven too. It was obvious from looking at them that they'd have no qualms about robbing and killing for money.

The six of them were sitting in a hastily made lean-to, built from pieces of what had been a short-lived mining town. The lean-to sat close to a small trickle of a stream that ran along the west canyon wall.

Kally's heart started beating wildly and she had trouble breathing when she caught sight of Pieter for the first time. All the horrible things she had tried so hard to forget about that night came charging back in a barrage she couldn't stop. She felt sick to her stomach and leaned against Chase as the three of them ducked back down behind the pile of rubble.

Chase steadied her as they slid down. "Are you alright, Kally?" he whispered. The terror was still evident in Kally's eyes as she nodded her head. She took a deep breath and let it out slowly.

"I'm ready to take him now," Chase whispered again, to Seth this time. "I think we'll all sleep better tonight if that scum is out of this canyon." Chase looked at Kally now. "Maybe you'd better stay here. Seth and I would consider it a pleasure to take care of this for you. As soon as Pieter is dead, the past can die with him."

Kally's eyes flashed with fear, but also with determination. "No, Chase," she whispered hoarsely, "I've waited too long for this moment. I'm going with you. I want to be sure he sees me before he dies. I want him to know...." She put her hand over her mouth as she composed herself. She knew she had to pull herself together if she was going to go through with this.

"I'm ready," she said, finally.

11

*C*hase motioned for each of them to take a side and stay a little behind him. As he came over the top of the rubbish, one of Pieter's men spotted him. Almost instantly they were on their feet and out of the lean-to. Pieter was in front as they came a few feet toward Chase and waited in a group.

Not too smart, Chase thought to himself, stopping a scant thirty feet from them. He and Pieter looked each other over for only a second before Seth and Kally came over the pile of junk to back him up. The surprised look on Pieter's face showed that he recognized Kally instantly. She stood her ground, holding her rifle trained on him.

Pieter was everything Kally had described, only a few years older than when she had seen him last. He was big, but soft and flabby. His ill-fitting clothes were worn and dirty. It was plain he hadn't changed much since coming west. The only things that gave him the resemblance of a cowboy were the twin six-guns hanging at his sides. Chase had to figure if Pieter had done anything since he had come west, it might

146

have been to learn how to use those guns.

The other five men were of the same cut as Pieter. Flotsam of the West, floating from one place to another. Never working for their money and willing to do anything but work. It was easy to see how Pieter had wooed them with stories of easy gold, and kept them here waiting for Kally to come with the real map.

It was hard to tell how many men they might have killed to keep intruders out of Pike City. Chase would have despised a man like Pieter even if he hadn't known what he'd done to Kally. Now he couldn't wait to put an end to this gutless excuse for a man. He had already lived too long.

"Well, Pieter," Chase began, his icy voice tightening as he spoke. "Looks like Kally's description was dead right. You're a no-good thief and claim-jumper. I see the map you stole didn't do you much good, or you were just too damn lazy to look for the gold."

"You're right about that, mister, but I knew I could count on that freeloading little slant-eye to bring the real map if I waited long enough. Now me and my friends can get the gold," Pieter hissed.

"You're mistaken about that," said Chase, his voice cutting the desert air like a sharp knife. "You're not going to get your greasy hands on the map or the gold. I've got the map now."

"Doesn't matter. We can take it off your body as easy as that little Chink's. On second thought, might be more fun killing you and your friend there, then having a little fun with that slant-eyed slut. As I remember she was a right nice piece of…"

Chase's gun bucked and roared. Pieter's hat and

most of the top of his head flew behind him as he went over backward. Chase had been wrong; Pieter hadn't learned anything about how to use his six-guns, or about the threat of men like Chase. He reached, but neither gun cleared leather before Chase's bullet found its mark.

The other five drew, and Chase's gun roared three more times, so fast the roar was as one shot. He heard shots from both sides of him, and all five went down. Chase thumbed fresh cartridges into his gun as he walked forward and turned a couple of them over with the toe of his boot and checked the others. They were all dead. He circled the area of the old town before holstering his gun. His job was finished for now.

He hadn't looked at Kally until now. She had dropped to her knees and her rifle was lying in the dust. Her face was colorless and she appeared to be almost in a state of shock. "I had to kill him—I had to...." she mumbled, looking up at Chase. "He was going to kill you."

"It's alright, Kally," said Chase tenderly. "Pieter is dead. They're all dead. Pieter was too slow to ever get me."

"No—no—the other man. He would have killed you, I had to kill him—I had to." Suddenly color filled Kally's face again as her hand went to her mouth and she stumbled over behind some rocks and threw up.

"Guess I wouldn't make much of a gunman," Kally said as she returned, trying to manage a smile. "I had thought a lot about killing Pieter one day, but I'd never even seen that man before. Chase, I can see now why you're tired of killing men you don't even know. Men you have no grudge against. If your life hadn't been in danger, I'm not sure I could have pulled that trigger."

Chase took Kally in his arms. "I know how you feel, Kally. We all killed our first man once. We never forget him. I'm not sure any of us ever get over that sick feeling in the stomach after we have to kill someone. Except when it's someone like Pieter. That was almost a pleasure."

"I can hardly believe he's really dead, Chase. A few weeks ago, I'm not sure I would have been able to stand there so close to him and not let him intimidate me. I knew you would kill him, and because of the way I know you feel about me, the things he said weren't important. I knew they were lies. I didn't always know that; there was a time I believed all the terrible things he said about me."

Chase held her closely. "That's all over, Kally. He will never say those things again," he assured her. "Now, you can start fresh—all that happened in the past is dead and buried."

"I want to believe that, Chase," said Kally as she looked up at him. "I already feel a greater sense of freedom. He's dead and I'll never have to worry about seeing him again. We've accomplished at least one of the things I set out to do."

"I hope we're not far from doin' the other," said Seth as he returned from getting the wranglers and mules. "This is Pike City, Kally. Why don't you an' Chase have a look see, while the boys an' I unload the mules an' drag this garbage off out of sight."

"Thank you, Seth. I'd like that." Kally slipped her hand into Chase's as they started up the canyon. "It's hard for me to believe my father was in this canyon. He probably walked right here where we're walking." They went on in silence as Kally relived some of her favorite memories of her father. She compared the canyon with the way she had visualized it for so many years.

They followed the tiny rivulet of a stream. Chase was looking for a hole deep enough for bathing. They might be here for some time before they figured out their way beyond the canyon wall. He wondered how many others had tried to unlock that secret, and failed. They walked all the way to the end of the canyon. Their way was blocked by a high wall of giant rocks, as high as the side walls of the canyon. The water flowed under two large slabs of rock at its base. Chase had seen no deep holes. They would have to settle for dishpan baths, but he was thankful they at least had the water.

They circled and followed the wall of rocks toward the other side of the canyon. This wall wasn't as solid as the side walls of the canyon, but proved to be just as much of a barrier. It was a box canyon. It was obvious the wall had been formed long after the canyon itself, perhaps the result of huge rocks— some as big as houses—falling from a giant pinnacle or tall upthrust of rock from above the canyon's rim. Chase could see it was impenetrable. Yet the map told them different.

As he and Kally neared the west wall, they found heavy thickets of mesquite. It was not worth fighting their way through them, so they headed back to camp.

Kally gripped Chase's hand more tightly. "Do you really think this is where the map starts? I don't see how we could possibly get beyond that wall. Maybe we read it wrong."

"This is the only Pike City I know of. It matches the map. I have no idea how we're going to get beyond that wall, but we'll get the map out tonight and start studying it. If your father found a way around the wall, or if we're in the wrong canyon, we'll find that out."

By the time they returned to the others, all the packs were stacked near the lean-to, and Pieter's fire had been rebuilt. The dead men were nowhere in sight. Seth and the wranglers had finished their work and were sitting on rocks drinking coffee.

"You two love birds just have a nice walk, or did you discover a way through that wall?" Seth asked with a chuckle.

"Just did a little scouting," Chase returned. "The trickle of water doesn't get any bigger. Not even any spots deep enough for a bath. But at least it's clear and cool. I'm just afraid if it gets much hotter, it will dry up altogether."

"We could be in a heap of trouble if it does," Seth agreed.

"It's a box canyon alright," Chase said, "but I'm sure the map shows this canyon going on north. That wall was here long before Kally's father got here. As far as I can see, there's no way over it or through it. Otherwise, I think Pieter and his bunch, or Joe and Jake, or someone would have found it. I think he must have meant another canyon near here. This looks like a dead end to me."

"Y'all may be right," Seth agreed. "Let's get supper over with an' take a look around. Won't take much to see all that's left of Pike City. Looks like this lean-to is the only thin' still standin'. Less y'all count that pole out there with the crosspiece an' bucket hangin' from it. The bucket's rusted plumb through an' it looks like someone's taken a few potshots at it. Rest of the old town's lyin' down. Most wood left from the buildin's was pretty much burned up a long time ago."

"I'd expect there were quite a few men through here when the word of gold got out," Chase said.

"Was this once a regular town," Kally asked, "with buildings and everything?".

"Best I remember," said Seth, scratching his head, "there was only two or three all-wood cabins. The rest was just wooden frames with canvas stretched over 'em. See, there's still a little piece of the canvas flappin' in the breeze from the crosspiece on the pole out there. It's probably an old piece of tent frame. As slow as Pieter an' his friends were with their guns, they probably used the bucket for target practice—once."

"I'm not sure they ever practiced." Chase shook his head. "If they'd ever come up against anyone but prospectors, someone would have killed them long before we got here."

" 'Pears to me, they was too dumb to find the gold anyhow. I reckon with the real map an' Kally's help—an' a little lookin'—we'll find a way into that canyon. Kally's daddy made that map. The gold he sent Kally proves he found a way in, an' we don't know but that all he had was word of mouth as to how to find it. Iffen he was able to find it without a map, we shouldn't have any trouble with one." The old adventuresome twinkle was back in Seth's eyes as he talked about the gold.

It didn't take Seth and Kally long to put supper together. Afterward, Carlos walked out to the mouth of the canyon to start the first watch. Roberto checked the stock and then came back and spread his blankets between two rocks and lay down. Seth lit a lantern as Chase pulled the map from its hiding place in his bedroll. He spread it out on a flat rock as Seth and Kally moved in close to look at it. They all studied the map for a long time before Chase spoke.

"After looking at the map again, I'm sure this is the canyon your father meant, Kally. He doesn't show the piles of rubbish left from the old town, but there's an X right here, and he took the time to print out 'Pike City.' The only problem is he doesn't show the rock wall blocking the canyon. His map goes right on from there. Unless he was a bird and could fly, or some kind of spirit that walked through rock, he must have found another way."

"This map is no good to us unless we can figure out how he did it," said Kally. "All the other Xs on the map are beyond the wall, including the spot where the gold is supposed to be. See, it shows two forks here, marked by Xs, and four forks farther on." As Kally pointed out the spots on the map, she realized the map gave no clue as to which fork they were to take in each place. "I sure hope he left more clues on the trail."

Seth and Chase had come to the same conclusion. "We could use some more clues," Chase agreed, "but for now let's concentrate on this first one. The rest won't matter unless we get by that wall. We've got to be missing something. He made this map for you, Kally. Do you see anything here your father would have believed you would recognize? Something you'd know about that we wouldn't?" Chase rubbed Kally's shoulders as they talked.

"No—not a thing. But I've got to believe there's something here I'm not seeing. I know my father found the gold and he made this map so I could find it. From all we've seen so far, I don't think anyone else has been able to. I have to believe it's still there. We have to find it."

Chase agreed, "None of us is ready to give up yet, Kally. We've come too far. We still have plenty of supplies, and as long as that little trickle keeps coming, we're alright for water. Now, all we have to do is start thinking like your father. What kind of clue would he have left for his little girl? You were still a little girl when he saw you last and that's who the clues would be for. Not the woman you are now. This may take us some time, but I'm for staying until we run out of supplies, or find the gold."

Seth and Kally were in full agreement.

"Looks like I've got some work to do," Kally said. "It's been a long time since my father and I were together. I'm sure I've forgotten a lot of things I'm going to have to remember before we're through with this."

"Y'all have done enough for one day, little lady," said Seth, patting her on the shoulder. "I reckon we ought to all get some sleep an' start over in the mornin' when we're rested up."

Kally smiled and nodded. "I am awfully tired, now that you mention it. I'm ready to turn in." She looked over at Chase. "Are you coming?" As they walked to where the bedrolls were already laid out, Chase noticed theirs were some distance from Seth's, and so close to each other they were almost touching.

Kally looked at him as they both sat down to pull off their boots. "Am I too close?" she asked softly. "I thought if the past was really dead after today, then it was time to start working on a new tomorrow."

Chase didn't say anything. He just smiled, reached over, and pulled her down on the blankets under him where he could look into her eyes. He searched her face for a moment, then kissed her. Very tenderly at first. Then with all the passion that rushed through him as their lips met. At that moment, he would have liked nothing more than to show her how very much he loved her, but it was not the time nor the place. He could wait.

As they stretched out on their blankets, Kally snuggled up against his side with her head resting in the crook of his arm. Chase looked down at her face, radiant in the moonlight. "I love you," he whispered softly, but Kally was already asleep.

Neither of them had moved when Roberto came to wake Kally for the next watch. He smiled and said, "*Amor*," under his breath as he touched Kally's foot with the butt of his rifle. She pulled her foot up and snuggled closer to Chase, still fast asleep. Chase nodded at Roberto who left them alone and went to his own bedroll.

Chase carefully slipped his arm out from under Kally. He knew she was exhausted. Tonight he would take both of their watches. He slipped back into his boots, buckled on his gun belt, and walked quietly out to the edge of the old town site. They would have to be more quiet and alert on watch again. As long as they remained in Pike City, there was the chance someone would jump them. Although Chase was quite sure Pieter and his gang had run off any interested prospectors, he couldn't be sure there weren't others like Joe and Jake, waiting just out of sight until Pieter and his men were gone. Chase wouldn't relax until they had deciphered the first clue and found their way beyond the canyon wall.

As Chase walked softly around within the shadow of a big rock, he thought of Kally. For a man who had been a loner all his life, the relationship he had with her was a new experience. She seemed to know what he was thinking, even feeling, a lot of the time. That had been unnerving at first, but he was getting used to it. And he liked it.

As much as he loved Kally, and wanted to be with her, there was still a deep fear, and he was having more and more trouble keeping it below the level of consciousness. He was a gunfighter, not a cowboy or a rancher or a businessman. Sure, he had talked of working the Colorado ranch and hanging up his gun. But could he really? Even if he was willing to give up the only life he knew, with his reputation, would others let him walk away so easily? And how much jeopardy would Kally be in if she was at his side? These were questions he didn't have answers for. Questions his happiness kept pushing out of sight and mind.

Chase was thankful Kally was sleeping. Between seeing her cousin killed and killing her first man, it had been an eventful day for her. He couldn't help hoping Pieter's death would start to put an end to her fears. As Chase grew closer to Kally and fell more deeply in love, he was finding it more difficult to stop after a few kisses. In the past, making love to a woman had been no more than a means of physical release. With Kally it would be so much different. It would be the path to total fulfillment—for both of them.

12

*S*eth had taken the last watch, and when he came to wake them the next morning, he found Chase and Kally lying as Roberto had seen them. "Come on you two love birds," he teased. "This is the big day. We're gonna figure out what kind of magic is gonna get us through that wall yonder."

Carlos and Roberto, who usually said little, talked quietly between themselves all through breakfast and morning chores. Chase thought they might be confused about what was going on, so he called them aside.

"I just wanted you boys to know we'll probably be spending a few days here. Your work will be easier until we move on. Just keep the stock moved to fresh graze as needed, keep the canteens filled, and gather wood for the cook fires."

The boys nodded.

"You will need to keep your rifles handy, though," cautioned Chase. "If you see anyone coming, come get Seth or me, or fire a shot."

The two nodded again, and Carlos spoke as Chase

turned away. "Señor Chase, are we perhaps going north from here?"

"Probably," Chase answered. "Why?"

"No reason, señor. My brother and I only wondered."

"I'm not sure how long it might take, but you won't have to do much to earn your wages until we're ready to head back. Even then we'll probably ride the main trail, so it'll be a lot easier than it was coming."

"Gracias, Señor Chase. That is all we wished to know."

As Chase walked away, he heard Roberto utter under his breath, *"Tierra de lo gente vieja."*

"Tierra fantasma," Carlos whispered back.

When Chase got back to the camp, he found Seth and Kally looking over the map again. He sat down next to Kally and poured himself a cup of coffee.

"Seth, you know the Mexicans better than I do. Are they as superstitious as the Indians?"

"Not usually, but there's a heap of Injun in some of 'em. They're all mighty superstitious, I reckon. Why do you ask?"

"Carlos just asked if we planned to go north. I thought they were just curious about our plans, but evidently they didn't realize I understood Spanish."

"What did they say?" Kally asked.

"As I was walking away, Roberto said, 'Land of the old people,' and Carlos said, 'Land of the spirits.' Sounds to me like they're a little spooked."

"They've heard the Injuns' stories alright," Seth agreed. "They'll bear watchin' from now on, but chances are the stories ain't gonna mean as much to 'em as the money they're makin'. Besides, they're a long way from home."

"You're probably right. Have you two figured out anything more about that map this morning?" Chase looked over Kally's shoulder at the map.

"Just that Kally's pa did a right good job of makin' this here map. Look at how closely the outlines on the map fit the shape of this canyon. I'm sure we're right where we're supposed to be."

Chase nodded. "The little wavy line is in the right place for the stream too."

"That's right," Seth said, "but what gets me is his first X is right here in the middle of Pike City. There ain't nothin' out there but that crazy pole an' bucket Pieter was usin' for target practice. If it had been here when he made the map, he would have showed it. I can't see any connection between that X an' our gettin' beyond the wall." Seth was scratching his head.

"Maybe our first move is to find out if there is actually anything beyond that wall. I say we should start where the water comes out under the rocks."

"Wasn't you an' Kally up there yesterday?"

"We didn't look very closely," Kally offered.

"The mesquite grows pretty heavy in that section," Chase said. "We didn't try to walk back into it. Reckon now we should. We won't be the first ones to check it out, though. There's got to be a lot of men who have looked for a way through."

"Joe an' Jake said they spent two years diggin' around this area. You'd think they'd have found it if there was a way." Seth thought a moment. " 'Pears to me, lookin's not gonna help. We can check it out, but Kally's got to be the key into that canyon. Her pa told her to bring twenty mules, so there has to be a way to get 'em over or through that wall." Seth looked at Kally. "I reckon the answer to the puzzle's in your daddy's map. Y'all are gonna have to figure it out, honey."

Chase squeezed Kally's hand. "Come on, let's go check on where the water's coming from first."

The three walked up the little trickle of a creek to where it came under the rock wall. They stood and studied it for several minutes. Then Seth lay down and put his ear to the big slab of rock the water flowed from. After a few minutes, he stood up.

"That water don't start in them rocks. She's comin' under 'em. I say the map's right an' them wiggly lines are showin' this same stream comin' down the canyon yonder. Accordin' to the map it could be bigger in some spots than it is here. I have to believe the canyon goes right on from here, but how in the hell do we get past this wall?"

Chase stepped back, looking up. "We sure can't climb it. Those bigger rocks up near the top have sheer faces and there isn't even a place to toss a loop around so you could climb up on a rope. Even if we could get over, how would we get the mules over?" No one had an answer.

They walked slowly toward the other side of the canyon, exploring every little crack or crevasse in the rock. When they found big rocks jutting out above the floor of the canyon, they crawled up to look from there. They found nothing.

When they reached the thick mesquite, Seth moved along close to the wall, while Chase and Kally circled around the outside of the mesquite patch.

Seth's call brought them running back. They found him standing in an opening about six feet across and six or seven feet high. He was smiling broadly. Excitedly, Chase and Kally followed him into the opening.

Their excitement was short-lived. Less than twenty feet into the narrow, dark corridor, they could see their path was blocked by a giant slab of rock at the end of the passageway. They were forced to return the way they had come. Outside in the sunshine again, Seth studied the ground.

"Reckon I should have been smarter than that. Look at all the boot prints in the dirt out here. Probably every man what's looked for a way through tried that one. It was too easy anyhow." Seth looked disappointed just the same.

"Let's keep looking," Chase suggested. "We'll check the rest of this wall. There may be a hidden tunnel or something." They didn't find one.

They saddled up and rode back down the wash to where the canyon began. On both sides were high, smooth walls, honed to a glasslike finish by centuries of blowing wind and sand. They provided no way around or into the canyon beyond. By the time they returned, it was dinnertime. After they had eaten and the wranglers had gone to move the stock to new graze, Chase got out the map again. They finished off the pot of coffee as they talked and studied the map. None of the three could find anything different to give them any clues. That afternoon they walked both canyon walls and the blocking wall again, but found nothing new.

After supper, a feeling of frustration and discouragement filled the camp. Seth sat close to the fire, still studying the map, long after Chase and Kally were sick of looking at it. Chase sat on the ground, leaning against a rock. Kally sat between his upraised knees, leaning back against his chest. They both enjoyed the warmth of the closeness, even though it wasn't much cooler out than it had been during the day.

Kally was thinking about the map and her sense of frustration. The more they looked without success, the more she realized it was going to be up to her to discover a secret. A secret her father had hidden in the map. A secret only she would recognize. It had been many years since she had been on the ship, or had seen her father. Maybe she would no longer be able to remember things her father had counted on her to recognize. They had come this far; she couldn't bear the thought that she would fail them now.

Chase wrapped his arms around her shoulders and drew her back more tightly against his body. She turned her head to the side and kissed him over her shoulder. "I'm sorry we didn't find anything today," she began. "I feel like I've let you down—not being able to figure out the map."

"Nonsense. We knew this wasn't going to be easy. If it had been, Pieter or someone else would have found a way through long before we ever got here. It will all come together in time. We expected to have to spend a few days here before moving on. Just relax. I know you'll do it when you've had time to put it all together." Chase nibbled on Kally's ear affectionately as he finished talking.

"I appreciate the vote of confidence, Chase. I'll do my best to live up to it. I've got to keep believing

I can do it." Kally snuggled back against Chase and sat quietly for a few moments before she spoke again.

"You know something?"

"Uh-uh."

"I just realized that when you mentioned Pieter's name a few moments ago, it didn't bother me. Now that I think about it, Seth mentioned him this afternoon too. Before you killed him, every time I even thought his name, and especially if someone said it out loud, my chest would tighten with fear and I would feel sick to my stomach. But that's not happening anymore." Kally turned sideways so she could look at Chase.

"You've done that for me, my darling, and I thank you." She pulled him to her and kissed him passionately as he wrapped his arms around her and held her. After several more kisses, Kally relaxed with the side of her head against Chase's chest. His arms encircled her small body as he spoke.

"I hope that's just the beginning for you, Kally. You are free of Pieter. Free, I hope, to come to me. But you're a better judge of that than I am."

"I want to believe that more than I've ever believed anything. You, and Seth too, have taught me I don't have to be afraid of all men. There are good, decent men in this world I can trust. I'm sure that's something my father would have helped me learn if he'd been able to. I've always thought Pieter had destroyed my chances of ever having a man really love me. And that somehow it was my fault."

"Oh, Kally. What am I going to do with you?"

"I know now that's ridiculous, Chase." Kally moved to look at him again. "You have done so much to restore my belief in myself as a woman. You have awakened feelings I never thought I'd even want to have. But I do want them and I do want to be a woman. A complete woman for you."

"Not for me, Kally. I love you and I know you love me, but from now on, I don't want you to do anything to show your love just to please me. Making love—in a complete physical way—should never be done just for my pleasure. I want it to always be an expression of our love for each other. You should want it and enjoy it as much as I do. Because of what happened with Pieter, you may not want or be ready for that as soon as some women would be. I don't want you to push things. When you're ready to go further, you'll know, and you'll let me know. In the meantime, I'll still be the happiest man alive." Chase held her close and kissed her over and over again. Their love was quickly dissolving the dark cloak of loneliness that they had each wrapped themselves in for so many years.

Seth rolled up the map he had been studying all this time and got up, stretching. "I'm gonna be deciperin' this map in my sleep," he said as he walked toward them. "Reckon I'll have nightmares about bein' stuck here forever. Or flyin' over walls all night." He chuckled and laid out his bedroll. "Reckon we should give the boys the early watches from now on. I don't want them out there for the late night or early mornin' watches if they're likely to get spooked."

As soon as they had decided who would stand watch when, they all went to bed. Because the men felt there was a good chance they could have more company before they left Pike City, Chase decided he and Kally should stand their watches together. He got no argument from Kally. Tomorrow would be another day of searching.

The search went on, one day after another, turning up no new clues. On the afternoon of the fifth day, Chase sat propped against his saddle, scanning the rim of the canyon with his army field glasses. Seth was sitting on a rock studying the map for the thousandth time. Kally had slipped away to a secluded spot for a bath.

Chase lowered his glasses and sat thinking. Kally came back with a towel wrapped around her hair. She sat down with her back to Chase and handed him her comb. He carefully combed her long black hair until it was dry and glistening. He pushed it to one side and kissed the back of her neck as he got up.

Chase walked to Seth's side and looked over his shoulder at the map. Neither spoke. They agreed riding around wasn't going to help, and they had already inspected the walls so many times that they knew every crack and bump by heart.

Kally stared vacantly out at the post with the crosspiece and old rusty bucket hanging from it. After a few moments, her eyes no longer held a vacant look. She looked more closely at the post and bucket. This time it was more than a target for shooting practice. In another moment she was up and walking toward it. Chase and Seth exchanged baffled glances; Seth shrugged his shoulders.

Kally stood looking at the contraption for a long time, then walked around it. She moved in closer and pushed on the post with her hand. It was deeply imbedded in the rocky ground. She pushed hard again. The post stood steadfast. She gently fingered the old battered piece of canvas on the crosspiece, then walked back to the lean-to where the men were standing, watching her every move.

She bent over the map in silence, studying it once again. Finally she straightened up and spoke. "Father left the first clue right where he marked the *X* on the map. It's been right there all this time."

"Right where?" Seth looked skeptical.

"Standing right there." Kally smiled, pointing at the post. "You said yourself that post was right where the *X* was on the map. You saw me try to push it over. I couldn't budge it. I don't think anyone would have gone to the trouble to dig up this hard, rocky ground just to put up a post for target practice."

"I can't argue with that," Chase said. "Have you got something?"

"Not all of it yet, but the post has to be the first clue. I'm sure of it. That crosspiece isn't just part of an old tent frame. Father put it there for a reason. The post has been notched, and the crosspiece tied on with leather thongs. They are tied with knots sailors call clove hitches. My father had me tying those by the time I was four, but I've never seen either of you use that particular knot since we've been on the trail."

Kally had their full attention as she went on. "As I was sitting there looking at that thing a while ago, I remembered what Seth said when we first saw it."

"I don't remember sayin' nothin' important," said Seth, shaking his head. "What was it?"

"You said something about that tattered piece of canvas flapping in the wind."

"So?"

"They use canvas for sails on a ship," Kally said. "That started me thinking about ships and my life at sea. I believe Father set that post to represent a ship's main mast. The old board with the piece of canvas was meant to be a sail yardarm. The bucket could be a crow's nest. That's where the lookout stands, especially on a whaling vessel. The crow's nest looks like a bucket or barrel, and the lookout stands inside it."

"Everything you say makes sense, Kally." Chase was looking at the post, a bewildered expression on his face. "But I still don't understand what all that has to do with getting us beyond the wall. While you were talking, I thought maybe the crosspiece was going to point us in the right direction, but one end of it points at the east wall, the other end points out of the canyon, and the post itself points straight up. We've covered every inch of that wall a thousand times, without any luck, and we still don't know how to fly."

"Maybe we can't fly," said Kally as a look of understanding began to spread over her face, "but we can go high. I think that's what Father was trying to tell me. The crow's nest and the top of the main mast are the highest parts of a ship. He's telling us to look high," finished Kally, her voice rising with excitement.

"You could be right," Chase said, glancing back and forth between the map and the place on the wall where the crosspiece was pointing. He walked to where he had been sitting earlier, and picked up his field glasses. Now he studied the same spot more closely with the glasses. He saw a ten-foot-high pile of rocks on the canyon rim. It was the highest spot. He took the glasses down, then looked again. Suddenly he hurried back and dropped the glasses by his saddle.

"Come on, Kally." Chase took off toward the eastern wall of the canyon, moving so fast Kally had to trot to keep up with him. Seth stood watching the two of them with his hands on his hips.

When they reached the heavy growth of mesquite, Chase worked his way through it to the canyon wall. He walked down the wall a ways, then turned and walked back toward the cross-wall. After a few feet, he stopped. He stood studying the wall. Up a few feet, a fissure opened and some desert growth protruded from it, with several long limbs hanging down within his reach. For a moment, his eyes followed the fissure up the wall.

Without taking his eyes off the wall, he called to Kally. "Run get my moccasins—and bring Seth."

Kally moved across the canyon floor like a young deer, and before long she had returned with Seth at her heels. She helped Chase out of his boots and into his moccasins.

"What'd you find, boy?" Seth asked excitedly.

"I'm not sure yet. I think I saw something glittering in that pile of rocks up there. Could be it's just quartz, or a heavy deposit of silica. But the more I study those rocks, the more convinced I am some of them weren't put there by Mother Nature. That's why I was looking at the map again. It shows the pile of rock, and if you look real close, you'll see a tiny mark sticking out to the side, like a pointer."

"I saw that a million times," Seth said, "but I

figured it was just where he slipped a might when he was drawin' it."

"So did I, but when I saw that glitter, it sure fit with what Kally said about looking high. I may be wrong, but I think Kally's father was too careful to have slipped with that short line off to the side of those rocks. This was too important for him to have allowed himself any slips. That's got to be the rest of his clue about how to get in the canyon."

"But how will you get up to the pile of rocks?" Kally's head was thrown back as she looked up at them.

"I think it has something to do with that fissure up there. We've walked by it a dozen times, but it's the only place on either side of the canyon a man might be able to get up part way. The crosspiece points right to it. My guess is it'll take me to the pile of rocks."

Kally held her breath as Chase caught one of the limbs hanging down and hoisted himself up until he was able to grab the edge of the fissure. As soon as he had pulled his feet up and into grooves in the fissure, he slipped out of sight. They waited, almost afraid to breathe. Seth couldn't stand it any longer, and began to pick his way back between the mesquite. Kally followed. They had to walk quite far back into the clearing before they could see Chase standing at the base of the big rock pile, looking up.

He changed his position at the base of the rock pile several times until he apparently found what he was looking for up among the rocks. He now stood with his back against the rock pile, looking up over his head and then out at the blocking wall, adjusting his position slightly each time until he seemed satisfied. Then he directed his attention to the wall blocking the canyon. He walked along the edge of the canyon wall until he reached the high, narrow ledge where the cross-wall joined it. Carefully he walked the ledge as Kally watched, terrified, from below. When he reached the end of the rock slab, he looked down into the wall itself, then, shading his eyes, looked at whatever lay beyond it.

Moments later, Seth and Kally watched him inch his way back along the ledge. Kally didn't start breathing normally until he stepped safely back onto the solid rim of the canyon wall. He glanced at the pile of rocks, then moved quickly back to its base. He jumped several times, trying to retrieve something, before he was successful.

Waving to them, he started down. Seth and Kally hurried back to the bottom of the fissure. In a few minutes they heard Chase sliding down the rock before he came into sight. When he reached the bottom of the fissure, he jumped to the ground where Seth and Kally waited.

Reaching into his shirt, Chase handed Kally a gold ingot. "Here's another message from your father, Kally," he said with a smile.

"Did you find out how to get through?" asked Seth impatiently.

"Actually, you found it, but I reckon you were getting too old and blind to see it. Maybe you should plan to spend part of your share on some new spectacles." Chase was laughing as he slipped back into his boots.

"Come on, you two. Time's a wastin'." Chase led

off toward the cross-wall at a trot. Soon he arrived at the large opening Seth had discovered the first day; one they had been in several times since. He ran right into it with Seth and Kally at his heels. When Chase reached the big rock slab that blocked the passage, he turned left and followed along the face of it for thirty or forty feet to where it apparently butted against another solid rock at its end. There was barely enough light to see, but as Chase reached the rock wall at the end, he suddenly turned right and disappeared from sight.

Kally leaped ahead to catch up and Seth was close behind, muttering, "I'll be damned," as they reached the place where they had last seen Chase. As they turned the end of the rock slab, they found a narrow opening so low Seth had to duck to keep from bumping his head. The narrow passage was dark until they turned a bend and then they could see light at the end where the opening led out into the daylight. Chase was standing on a rocky place looking out into the large, wide canyon they had been seeking for so long. The little creek ran along the far side, and it was surrounded by abundant, dry grass.

"How did you know...?" Kally started to ask, still in a state of disbelief.

"I could see the opening on this side of the wall from up on top. I just had to work my way back from there. The only answer had to be an opening at the end of that slab somewhere. I saw something else from up there," said Chase, looking back at a rock that protruded above the opening where they had just come out. "From up there it looked like someone had put a piece of paper on that ledge and held it down with a rock." Chase couldn't see anything from where he was standing, but reached up to find a rock on the ledge. As he lifted it, an envelope fluttered to the ground.

Chase picked it up and looked at it a moment before handing it to Kally. "It has your name on it," he said solemnly.

13

*K*ally stood staring at the envelope in her hand, almost afraid to breathe as the impact of its significance began to sink in. Chase had been right. The name on the front, now barely visible, was her own. She recognized her father's distinctive handwriting.

Her hands began to shake as she turned the envelope over and carefully removed a single sheet of paper. She looked up at Chase before she unfolded it. He nodded his encouragement as she spread out the yellowed sheet of writing paper and her eyes slowly scanned its contents. Seth and Chase waited in silence as Kally read and the tears began to run down her cheeks. She had to blink hard so she could finish reading.

She was sobbing quietly as she handed the letter to Chase and walked slowly toward the creek. Chase watched her for a moment before turning his attention back to the paper in his hand. He looked at it a moment before reading it aloud to Seth.

" 'My dear Kally,' " it started. " 'If you have found this letter, it will tell you two things: You are on your

174

way to finding the gold, and I am dead. I wanted to send you more gold, but I knew I wouldn't survive another trip out of this canyon. The risks are too great.

" 'I've made sure the trail to the gold is one only you can follow, but it will mean remembering all you learned on the ship as a child. I know you can do it. Take out only twenty mule-loads of gold, and never return. There is something evil and mysterious about this place. I fear it will kill me. I don't want it to kill you.

" 'I'm sorry I had to leave you. My one prayer is that I might see you once more before I die. I hope the gold will make up in some way for what I was never able to give you. I love you more than life itself. Your loving father.'

"Well, now she knows for sure," said Chase in a quiet voice, looking out to where Kally stood staring down into the stream. "We'll give her a few minutes alone, then I'll go get her."

"Her daddy loved her alright," Seth said. "It's a cryin' shame he never come back for her. I reckon that would have meant more to her than the gold ever will. But it makes me a might skittish—all this talk about the gold bein' evil and mysterious. I'm surprised her daddy was that superstitious."

Chase shook his head. "My guess is he wore himself out before the gold had a chance to kill him. At least four feet of that rock pile was put there by hand so it could be seen from below. That gold ingot was set just right so it pointed to the right spot in the ledge I walked out on. It showed exactly where to go. I never would have found the opening or the note on the ledge without that clue. I can't imagine a man carrying all that rock and piling it by himself. Even if the mate was helping him, it was a lot of work. It's easy to see how much he loved her and wanted her to have his treasure."

Seth was looking at Kally now. "Well, all I can say is if he sets up the rest of the clues like he did this one, we could be quite a spell gettin' to that dadburn gold. I sure hope Kally can remember all that sea stuff. I'm startin' to get some big ideas about what we can do with a fortune like that."

"No sense worrying about what we're going to do with the gold yet. We've got to find it first." Chase was beginning to realize their work had just begun.

"I'm going to get Kally. It's going to take us most of the day to get the animals and gear in here. Looks like we'll have to bring the animals through without the packs or saddles and carry everything else in by hand."

"It'll be a tight squeeze even then," Seth agreed, "but I'll go get the boys started." He disappeared into the narrow opening in the wall.

Chase walked out to where Kally was sitting on a rock near the stream. In his hand, he carried her father's letter in its tattered envelope. Chase wasn't sure what to say as he sat down next to her. She was staring, without tears, into the water slowly flowing past her, and for a moment she didn't seem to realize he was there. In a few moments, she turned to Chase and reached out for him. He folded her into his arms and held her close. Neither of them spoke for several minutes.

"I'm alright now, Chase," Kally whispered when she finally spoke. "I guess I believed he was gone a long time ago, but now—to know it for sure—it's just hard." Kally buried her face in Chase's shoulder.

"I can still remember how I felt when my father was killed." Chase gently stroked her hair. "It always hurts. But just remember, you're doing what he wanted you to do. What he died for. Here's his letter. I know you'll want to keep it. We may find other things, but at least now you have something more to remember him by." He took hold of Kally's hand. "He loved you a great deal." Chase went on to tell Kally about the rock pile and the gold ingot.

"I just can't help thinking I might have been here in time to see him again if I'd come sooner." Kally looked up at Chase.

"You came as soon as you could, Kally," Chase assured her. "From the looks of the clues we've found so far, it's been a lot of years since he was here. There isn't any way you could have come soon enough to help him."

"I know you're right." Kally let out a deep sigh. "It's just so hard to let go." She turned her face toward his, and he kissed her tenderly.

"Thank you for being here with me. For understanding so well how I feel. It helps a lot." She kissed him again. "Now, just let me wash my face and I'll be ready to go. We have a lot of work to do." Kally looked back toward the wall, but Seth was nowhere in sight.

Chase caught her arm as she started to get up and go to the stream. "Seth and the boys and I can get the gear in. You can have some more time here by yourself if you like. You don't need to help."

"But I want to." Kally pulled away and knelt down beside the stream to wash her face. "It will help to do something besides sitting here thinking about what might have been. This was my father's canyon; now it's ours. It's time to push on. I'm going to help."

Kally dried her face on her neckerchief before she and Chase headed back toward the wall and slipped through the opening to the other side. By the time they reached camp, Seth and the wranglers had the mules and horses loaded. Seth was kicking the ashes of their fire out into the sand. Chase helped him easily push over the lean-to, but both had to put all their strength into breaking the pole out of the ground and kicking off the crosspiece and bucket. They spent the next few minutes trying to erase any evidence that they had been there.

Seth covered their tracks as they led the animals toward the opening in the wall. When they reached it, they unsaddled the horses and dropped the packs from the mules. Seth held Maude's bridle up close and led the way into the opening. It was a short, tight turn for the horses. They rubbed on both sides as they turned the end of the long slab of rock. After they had gone back and carried the saddles through, Seth and Chase left Kally with the horses and went back to help the wranglers with the mules. It took them more than an hour to bring all the animals through the passageway. Some of the mules didn't like the dim light or close confines and had to be coaxed and prodded through. They also brought through the six horses and two pack mules left by Pieter and his gang.

It was a long and tiring job to carry the packs in one at a time, and the men were hot and exhausted when the last one was finally through. Seth broke off several branches of mesquite and carried them with one of the burlap sacks back into the opening. By the time he backed out, sweeping the dust smooth with the sack and branches, Chase and the wranglers had the packs on the mules and the horses saddled. Seth tucked the sack into one of the packs and stepped up on Maude.

"Reckon we've got a couple hours before dark," he said. "We may as well get on up the canyon far enough so our smoke won't show in Pike City. Don't reckon anybody'd be there to see it nohow. Long as we got water, we can camp anywhere now. Don't got no idea how far we'll have to go 'til the next clue, seein' the map don't give us the miles. If I remember right, we have to go to where the canyon splits into two forks."

Just before dark they came to a widening of the canyon. It was a beautiful spot with lots of grass and a tiny falls in the little creek. The water was so low it made no sound as it cascaded over the rock into the pool below it. They dropped the packs by some rocks next to the east canyon wall, and unsaddled their horses. The stock was watered and left to graze where the grass grew the thickest.

As they began to prepare supper, Seth commented, "I've never been in a canyon quite like this one. Most of the ones I've seen were full of rock an' hot as blue blazes. This one's got more grass an' trees than I've ever seen in these canyons. There's even a slight breeze blowin' down it."

"Beats me," Chase said. "The way the walls are getting higher, and from the pictures of cave dwellings on the map, I'd bet there were people living here because of that cool breeze. I think that little stream was a lot bigger in those days too. With all the earthquakes and falling rock this isn't the same country it was years ago."

"I sure wouldn't argue with you," Seth replied.

"I still think there was once a village or a mission up ahead," Kally added. "My guess is that it's where Father put those bells on the map."

"I can't explain any of it," Chase confessed, "but I'll take this canyon over plenty of others I've been in. I could stand a few cool breezes and that running water over there. Soon as we eat I'm going to sit in that little pool. I worked up a good sweat carrying those packs today."

"Reckon I'll follow suit," Seth said. "No tellin' when that stream might peter out. I know the waves continue on the map, but we don't know but what it might have been drawn some other time of year."

Later, after the men had taken their baths, they came back to the fire for a cup of coffee, and Kally had the pool to herself. There were no rocks for privacy, but the men kept their backs to her as she bathed.

Carlos and Roberto took their coffee and moved off by themselves and talked quietly as Chase and Seth discussed the events of the day.

"Have you noticed those two today?" asked Chase, motioning toward the wranglers. "They've been acting real strange since we came through the wall."

"I'm thinkin' they're a heap more superstitious than we figured. I wouldn't worry too much about them, though. I doubt anyone else will find the way into this canyon, so it won't hurt none to have them standin' watch, even if they are a little skittish."

"It's been quite a day for Kally," said Chase, changing the subject. "She's holding up pretty good, though. I know how hard this has all been for her, but she won't give up. It's hard for me to believe she's the same woman I met in that hotel room in Albuquerque." Chase shook his head.

"She's quite a gal," Seth agreed.

"I love her. I guess you know that." Chase looked into the fire as he spoke. "She's the best thing that's ever happened to me, but sometimes she sure makes it hard for me to keep my hands to myself. She wants to sleep close to me, and there's nothing I'd like better, but she's still battling the old thing with Pieter. I told her I'd wait until she was ready before we went any further, but having her body right next to mine is driving me crazy."

"I wondered how you was handlin' that." Seth grinned as he spoke. "We're both used to spendin' months on the trail without a woman anywhere around, but havin' to sleep next to one, an' one as pretty as Kally, must be a real test of your willpower. How's she doin' with the Pieter thing? Gettin' any better?"

"She seems to be comfortable with me. Lots more than in the beginning. But all we've done is kiss and hug. I don't dare go any further until she asks for it. I'm just afraid she may never want to go any further. She seems content with just the closeness. After what Pieter did to her, do you think she will ever be ready to have a man? Even one who loves her as much as I do?"

The old twinkle was back in Seth's eyes again. "Don't you worry none about that, boy. Kally's been through a lot, but we've seen what she's made of. She's a tough gal, but I reckon she's all woman too. I've been watchin' the two of you for weeks now. She loves you like few women could. I'm bettin' when the time's right she'll give herself to you."

"I hope you're right. I know she's fighting the fears in her mind, so there's nothing I can do but fight my battle too. If you see me sitting in that stream over there more often than normal, you'll know why," said Chase with a grin.

"That felt so good, I could have stayed in all night," said Kally as she rejoined them for a last cup of coffee before bed.

"I've been thinking about the extra horses and mules we picked up back at Pike City," said Chase, changing the subject again. "What would you think about leaving them right here? There's plenty of water and graze, and we can pick them up on the way back."

"Sounds good to me," Seth agreed. "We can use the extra animals on the ranch if we don't find the gold."

"Won't they wander off?" Kally asked.

"Well, they won't go back through the wall by themselves, and as long as there's water and graze right here, they aren't likely to leave it. Even if they wandered on up the canyon, we'd find them on our way back," Chase explained.

Seth soon moved off to his bedroll as Chase and Kally prepared to turn in. Kally had dressed in clean clothes and her skin still felt fresh and cool to Chase's touch as he held her close and kissed her. They were both tired, but Kally seemed to welcome his attention. He kissed her face and eyes, then lifted each of her hands and began kissing all of her fingers. As he moved back to her lips and kissed her deeply, his hands ran the length of her body in a deep desire to explore every inch of her.

By the time he lowered his head and began to kiss her throat, she was breathing heavily. He kissed up and down as she clung to him. The first three buttons on her shirt were unbuttoned and Chase slowly kissed down. When he could go no farther, he moved his lips around, gently widening the opening of her shirt. He kissed back and forth across the top of her breasts. Her body quivered under the touch of his lips, and he started to pull away. Kally rested her hand on the back of his neck and pulled him back to her bosom.

"Don't stop," she whispered softly. "I love the feel of your lips on my body—I'm just afraid."

Chase moved back to where he could look in her eyes. "You don't ever have to be afraid of me, Kally. I promise I'll never hurt you. I'll never do anything you don't want."

Kally reached up and stroked the side of his face with her fingertips. "It's not you. You know that. I'm just so afraid I'll never be the woman you want and need." Kally pulled Chase to her. "Can you be patient with me a little longer?"

Chase rolled to the side and pulled her up close to him, with his arm under her head. "Little lady," he said, touching the tip of her nose, "I can wait forever if I have to, but I'll bet you my share of the gold that

I won't have to wait that long." Chase kissed her long and hard, and then settled back with Kally in his arms to go to sleep. It had been a long and eventful day, and tomorrow was still a question mark.

14

*T*hey slept a little later the next morning, then rode up the canyon. It was easy traveling alongside the little creek. Just before sunset, the canyon began to narrow. Before long, the canyon floor was covered with loose rock of all sizes. A short way farther, they came to a spot where one of the tall pinnacles of rock had plunged to the canyon floor generations before. It formed a rocky barrier across the canyon floor. A narrow, twisting trail snaked its way up and over the wall of rock.

Near the beginning of the trail were two ancient, carved totem poles, about six feet high. The riders dismounted to inspect them more closely.

"It looks like they were painted at one time," Kally observed.

"They probably used some of the colorful clay deposits from this canyon," Seth speculated. "The weather's pretty much worn off any color they might have had once," he said as he ran his finger over the splintering wood. "My guess is they mark a burial ground. I've seen totems like 'em before."

185

"Who would be buried here?" asked Kally as she looked around nervously.

"Reckon it would be whoever it was lived in this canyon before the Injuns we know about. Injuns believe the spirits of their ancestors live here."

Kally shuddered. "Should we be just standing here? I don't feel real comfortable standing on someone's grave."

"Well, if we was Injuns, we wouldn't be standin' here. They never crossed a burial ground without a real good reason. An' then not without havin' the medicine man say a few extry prayers or concoctin' some strong medicine to protect 'em from any roamin' spirits they might run into."

"Spirits?" Kally took hold of Chase's arm.

Chase laughed as he looked down at the expression on her face. "Don't let him spook you, Kally. He doesn't believe in all that mumbo jumbo about spirits."

"I'm not too worried about spirits, but I'd much rather take that narrow, rocky trail in good light, especially if I have to fight off any of them spirits on the way." Seth winked at Kally as he reined Maude around and headed back the way they had come. They had to ride a mile or so before they found a good place to set up camp for the night.

Carlos and Roberto were jumpy all the way back to the campsite, and were talking so fast to each other in Spanish that Chase could understand little of what they were saying. All he caught were the words he had heard back at Pike City; words about this being spirit land.

They said nothing to the others, but went about

their business unloading the mules and leading them out to good graze. Carlos took the first watch after supper, and the others turned in.

Chase was so used to waking at about the same time every night, he woke abruptly and realized by the position of the moon that it was past time for him and Kally to relieve Roberto on watch. He kissed Kally awake, slipped into his boots, and strapped on his gun as she got ready.

They walked out to where Carlos and Roberto had spread their blankets.

The blankets and saddles were gone.

When Chase and Kally hurried to the stock, they found the Mexicans' horses and four mules missing.

"I'll get Seth," said Kally as she turned to leave.

Chase grabbed her arm. "No. It's hard telling how long they've been gone. No sense trying to follow them until daylight. First we'll see how many supplies they made off with."

He put his arm around Kally's shoulders as they made their way around the stock and back to a rock where they sat down to wait.

"Chances are they lit out as soon as they were sure we were all asleep so they could make it out of here by moonlight. They won't stop until they're well past Pike City." Chase slapped his thigh in frustration. "I should have known better than to let them stand watch. I knew they got really spooked back at those totem poles. It's my own damn fault for not telling them the truth from the beginning."

"You had no way of knowing they were that superstitious."

"We'll check when it gets lighter, but if they

haven't taken too many of the supplies, I'd just as soon let them go. They won't be any use to us now anyhow."

"You know I can help more than I have been. I'm sure we can get along fine without them," Kally encouraged.

"When Seth gets up, I'll talk to him about not keeping watches while we're in this canyon. We haven't seen any fresh tracks since we came through the wall. We've been doing it from habit, but I don't think we need to for now, at least until we have the gold."

"Do you really think we'll find the gold, Chase? It's taken us so long to get this far, sometimes I feel like it will never happen."

"We've come this far, and you've already figured out the first clue. I have to believe we'll make it the rest of the way."

"What's going to happen after we find it? We'll be rich. Do you still plan to go to your cabin up in Colorado?" Kally asked as she snuggled closer to him.

"I've been thinking a lot about that, but I'm not sure I've decided anything. It's beautiful country up there. The cabin sits up high among towering pine trees, on the slope of a valley of grass. There's a beautiful view of the wide valley and the little river that twists its way through the bottom. The cabin probably gets snowed-in in the winter."

"It sounds wonderful. Will Seth be living in the cabin with you?" asked Kally with a mischievous grin.

"Seth's a good friend, but I'd much rather be snowed in with you. It won't take us long to build another cabin for Seth and Carmen." Chase took her in his arms and kissed her.

"Is that a proposal?" she whispered in his ear.

"Do you want it to be?" Chase asked cautiously as he moved her away from him so he could look in her eyes.

She looked at him more seriously now. "Chase, there's part of me that wants that more than anything I've ever wanted in my life, but...."

"But what?" Chase wasn't aware he was holding his breath as he waited for her to finish.

"I love you more than I ever dreamed I could love anyone. I can't imagine not having you by my side for the rest of my life, but it's not fair for me to offer you only half a woman."

"Kally, you're not..."

Kally put her fingers on his lips to stop him. "If you can hold that offer open for a while longer, I'll answer you when I know there's a real woman in here to be your wife." She waited now for his response.

"It's getting harder and harder for me to be patient, Kally VanDerVeer, but that's an offer I can't refuse. You're the only woman I will ever want, if I never get to do more than hold you on this rock for the rest of our lives." Chase kissed her tenderly and then sat holding her close to him.

"What's goin' on out here?" asked Seth as he walked toward them, stretching. "I figured you two would be standin' guard?"

Chase and Kally got up and explained to Seth about the wranglers running off.

"Dadburnit, I knew we should have kept our eyes

on them two. They've been as skittish as a couple of spooked calves since we got close to this canyon. How much did they take with 'em?"

"We were just about to go check. They got four mules, but we had to wait for a little light to check on the supplies," said Chase as he started toward the packs. A quick check found that they had taken only enough food to get them back to Albuquerque. They hadn't even taken extra ammunition.

"Might as well let 'em go," Seth said, "it's not worth the time it'd take to bring 'em back, an' they sure ain't gonna be any good to us now."

"We can handle the mules between the three of us, and we were thinking we really didn't need to stand guard while we're in the canyon, unless we run into some fresh tracks," Chase added.

"I just thought of something," said Kally, putting her hand to her mouth. "Roberto and Carlos know how to get into the canyon. Do you think they'll tell anyone?"

"My guess is that those two will be too scared to talk to anyone before they get back to Albuquerque, and by the time anyone could get an outfit together we'll have the gold and be on our way home."

"I'm sure you're right, Chase."

"I'll have to agree about standin' guard," Seth said. "It'll take some of the load off us if we don't have to be losin' sleep at night. I'll keep an extry sharp eye out for any signs of company, but I reckon I best go back to the wall an' wipe out their tracks. They'd be a dead giveaway to anybody snoopin' around."

"I'm afraid you're right, Seth. It'll take you the better part of the day to get there and back, but I think we'd all sleep better if you did," Chase agreed.

Chase looked up at the sky. "Speaking of sleep. Kally and I have been up quite a while. I think we'll take a nap while you ride back. We'll plan to stay right here and wait supper until you get back."

Seth had a quick breakfast out of tins, and Chase and Kally helped him get ready to go before they slipped back onto their blankets and were soon asleep. It was late morning before they awoke again. They had a leisurely breakfast and spent the rest of the day relaxing and sharing long-hidden memories from their pasts. Before they realized it, Seth was riding back into camp.

Chase took Maude's reins from Seth and unsaddled her as Kally handed him a fresh cup of coffee. "Did you catch up with the boys?" asked Chase, as he joined them.

"Never saw hide nor hair of either of 'em. They must have been movin' mighty fast to get out of here. Left plenty of tracks at the wall, so it was worth the time it took to go back. They took the extry horses an' mules we left back at the park too. I was thinkin' about 'em on the way back. If they've got any smarts at all, they ain't likely to go back to Albuquerque. They'd have to figure Chase would come lookin' for 'em after we got back."

"They'd be right about that," Chase agreed. "They're probably planning to sell the extra animals to give them a start somewhere else. Reckon we can't worry about them now."

Kally was busying herself with supper preparations. "Supper will be ready in a minute, Seth. You've more than earned it today." They all turned in early so they could get an early start in the morning after losing a whole day.

After breakfast the next morning, they rode back to the totems and Seth led the way up the rock slide. The footing in the loose rock was treacherous in some places, but overall the trail wasn't as bad as they had suspected. When they finally reached the other side, the trail returned to normal. Seth rode the point, Kally was close behind leading the mules, and Chase brought up the rear. The riding was growing monotonous again, but losing the wranglers had cost them very little time.

The next day the walls of the canyon rose even higher. It was midafternoon when they first spotted a large cluster of cave dwellings high up on the eastern wall of the canyon. They were just as they had been marked on the map. The three of them rode by in silence, watching for any sign of life—or maybe spirits.

That night after supper, Kally asked Seth if he knew anything more about the cave people.

"Reckon nobody knows much of anythin' about 'em. I've been told they lived here long before the Injuns of today. Ain't never heared from anybody exactly how long ago that was. Besides that, there ain't no tellin' where they went. They just disappeared. Ain't a skeleton or bone left to give a clue as to what happened to 'em. They just vanished off the face of the earth."

"This whole place gives me the spooks," said Kally with a shiver. "Maybe Carlos and Roberto were the smart ones."

✳

The days were endless hours of riding as they got farther and farther north. The canyon walls rose higher above them and were dotted with giant sentinels and pinnacles of rock. Some of the larger and more distinctive landmarks were shown on the map that Seth still studied by the fire every night.

Two days later, they reached their next destination. The forks marked with an *X* on the map. It was early afternoon when the forks came into view. In a little bend in the stream, a long, hollowed slab of rock made a catch basin. The water was deep enough to fill a bucket. The wall of the canyon above the basin was smooth rock.

The three of them hurried and pulled the packs and saddles. They turned the animals loose to graze and then walked up to where the canyon forked. The question now was which fork they should take.

"There goes that theory," said Chase as they reached the fork.

"What was that?" asked Kally, turning to look at him.

"I was hoping we'd be able to follow the water into the right canyon," Chase explained.

"I see what you mean. There's a small stream coming from both canyons and running into the one we've been following. I guess we should know by now it would never be that easy."

They walked up each fork a short way, picking up wood here and there on the way back, but they could find no clue as to which they were to take. They were almost identical. Neither of them had a distinctive landmark they could identify on the map.

They returned to their campsite and started a fire. They had hardly finished eating when the sun dropped behind the western wall of the canyon leaving them in darkness much sooner than they would have been on the open desert. The walls were so high now that it took longer for the moon to rise above them too. Full summer was upon them and the moon was bright when it did come up.

Seth lit a lantern so they could study the map. They set the lamp on a rock and spread the map out where the glow of the light illuminated it. Although they all practically knew it by heart by this time, they each concentrated on the spot where it showed the two forks. Finally Seth spoke.

"Your daddy sure made another mystery out of which fork to take, Kally. All he shows is enough of the forks to tell us they are forks, then the map goes on as if there was just one canyon again."

"The six mules pictured here have got to have something to do with it, but I sure can't figure what," Kally said. "It's even more frustrating to realize it's going to be my job to figure it out."

"We'll do all we can to help. You know that, Kally. Now that we're here, it's plain to see that the X is on the smooth canyon wall above the stream, if that helps at all. Maybe we can see something more on that wall when it gets light." Chase slipped his arm around Kally's shoulders.

"I surely hope this clue don't take as long to decipher as the last one. It's a might cooler in this canyon with its cool breeze than it was out on the desert, but this time of year no tellin' when that little stream might dry up. We'll be in a heap of trouble without water, besides, I'm gettin' plumb anxious to find that gold an' get back to spend it before I get too old to enjoy it." Seth continued studying the map long after Chase and Kally had given up for the night. Little could be done until daylight.

They had dropped the nightly watches, sure that the "spirits" would probably keep any Indians away, and it wasn't likely a white man could ever find his way into the canyon. Besides, Seth was such a light sleeper that any unfamiliar sound he heard during the night would bring him to a full sitting position.

Chase and Kally took a walk in the moonlight to stretch their legs before going to bed, while Seth finished the coffee and stayed glued to the map until his eyes grew too tired.

Soon they went to their blankets, and Chase drew Kally close to him. After he had kissed her, she asked, "Does this canyon make you feel weird or—I don't know—spooky?"

"No, I don't think so. Why?"

"I don't know. I've been feeling strange ever since we left the burial grounds. When we rode by the cave dwellings I felt like we were being watched. I don't mean I thought someone was there, not some-one following us. I felt like it was . . ." Kally hesitated.

"It was what?"

"Like the spirits were watching. Like they didn't want us here." Having said the words, Kally realized how silly they must have sounded.

Chase laughed. "Are you sure you're not part Indian or Mexican? I think you've been listening to too many of Seth's old wives' tales."

"Don't make fun of me." Kally pushed him away playfully. "I'm really serious about this, Chase," she said, lowering her voice. "I can't explain why, but I just have this strange feeling of uneasiness a lot of the time lately."

"I'm sorry. I didn't mean to make fun of you." Chase put his arms around her and held her for a moment. "I'll take good care of you, I promise. I've never run into a spirit before, but if I do, I'm sure I can handle him." Chase kissed Kally on the forehead, and she curled up next to him. Silly or not, she did feel safer being this close to Chase. Suddenly she felt as if there was nothing that could ever hurt them or come between them.

"I love you, Chase Wade," Kally whispered into the darkness. Chase tipped her chin up and kissed her in response to her declaration of love. During the next few minutes, they didn't need any more words to express the depth of love and passion that filled them both. Chase could feel his heart beating and his blood pumping in every inch of his body. He had never wanted to express his love more than he did right now. Kally responded fully to his every touch as he ran his hand over her softly rounded hips and up the front of her shirt until he cupped it under her breast and began to kiss down the opening of her shirt and across the top of what was exposed of her breasts.

"Chase," Kally said in a soft, breathless voice. "Your love and your touch are beginning to change a lot of my old feelings. You have taught me so much about the feelings of real love. Maybe I'm ready to go a little further. I want so much to be what you need."

Chase raised his head and paused for a moment before he spoke. "Oh, Kally, my darling, darling Kally. You don't have to worry about being what I need. I've never needed or wanted anyone so much. That's my problem. I'm only human, so I'm going to have to turn down your offer to go a little further. I'm afraid if we go any further than we already have, I won't be able to keep my promise to you. All the time you've been battling your old feelings, I've had to fight a big battle of my own. I want to show you how very much I love you, but until you're ready for that— all of it—we'd better stick with what we know we can handle."

"Oh, Chase, I'm so sorry." Kally buried her head in his neck. "I have been so wrapped up in my own feelings I didn't even stop to think about what all this was doing to you. Can you ever forgive me for being so selfish?"

"You know you don't even have to ask that."

"You are beginning to arouse the exciting feelings of a woman within me, and from what I have heard about men, those kinds of feelings must be so much stronger in you. No wonder it's been hard for you." Kally kissed him on the cheek. "I don't want you to have to wait any longer, but I'm afraid of what might happen if I'm not ready. I couldn't do that to you."

"I understand, Kally. That's why we'd better leave things as they are for now. I don't want to take a chance of losing all we've gained."

"I promise you it will be worth the wait. When I'm sure I'm ready, you'll be the first to know. I won't care about some fancy words from a parson, or a little piece of paper to keep in my diary. When I'm ready, you'll have the answer to your proposal too. Are you sure you don't want to take that back? You could be stuck with a nagging Mrs. Wade for the rest of your life, you know."

"Threats, all idle threats." Chase pinched the end of her nose teasingly. "Now, you'd better get some sleep. You're going to have to dig up your sea legs for tomorrow, if we're ever going to find that gold."

Kally's attempt to find her sea legs didn't help the next day, or the next, or the next. They had walked along both walls of the canyon several times. They had searched every inch of the smooth rock wall where the *X* showed up on the map. All they found was a smooth rock wall. They had walked up the center of both canyons, watching carefully for any clue. Seth had crawled along the edge of the stream on his hands and knees up to the place where the dished-out rock held the most water, but had found nothing.

Chase was obsessed with the six mules pictured on the map, sure that was part of the clue. He roped six mules together and walked them up and down the side of the stream and out into each canyon. Nothing they did gave them any clues to which fork of the canyon they should take.

They studied the map again. They were in exactly the right spot. The *X* was plainly marked over the hollowed-out rock in the stream, and putting the six mules where they belonged hadn't helped a bit.

"This thing is driving me crazy," Kally said in exasperation. "I know it's got to be right in front of me, and I'm not seeing it. I've spent so much time trying to remember my time on the ship with Father that I'm getting seasick."

"It'll come to you, I'm sure of it," Chase assured her. "All this running around is getting us nowhere. Let's take some time and try to think this through. It worked last time. Maybe something will come to you." The three lay down in the shade as Kally ran over all the clues in her mind, then went through as many recollections of her life at sea as she could. Nothing seemed to fit together.

They had been at the fork for six days when one morning after breakfast Kally suddenly reached for the map again. She studied it for a moment and then set it back on the rock.

"I think I have the answer," she said as both men turned to her. "I've remembered a lot about my time at sea, and I may need some of that knowledge up ahead, but I don't think this clue has anything to do with ships. In all that remembering, I've also recalled a lot of things I had forgotten about Father, and I think this clue has to do with those things."

"What kind of things?" asked Chase, moving closer.

"He was not a man to make jokes, and he was serious about everything he did. I don't think there's any doubt that he was very serious when he made this map. He was precise in every detail."

"We ain't gonna argue with you there, but what has that got to do with the clue?" Seth was looking more bewildered than he had since they'd started.

Kally continued, "Nothing we have found on the map so far has been symbolic, it's all been exactly as it has appeared. Even though we haven't always recognized it. The first *X* marked the crosspiece and bucket, but we ignored it for days. Now, I have to believe that this clue must be just as he put it on the map. He shows the *X* is on the wall over the water hole, and the six mules are standing right in front of it. I think I've figured it out. I may be crazy, but you'll just have to humor me." Kally started walking out to where the stock was grazing.

"I want you to hobble six of the largest mules, and keep the rest of the stock away from the basin. They can drink below it if they want. Then I think I can show you which fork to take."

"I don't understand what keeping the stock from the water could possibly have to do with this, but I'm ready to try anything," said Chase as he and Seth began to follow her orders.

In a few minutes they had hobbled the stock out on the grass where they could not reach the little stream. Then Kally called them back to look at the map with her.

"See where the buckskin is lightly burned in the area around the stream and the *X*? At first I thought it was just where the buckskin had been damaged, but after looking more closely, I could see it had been burned just lightly. Using a hot knife point or nail would have made it hard to do any shading on the map, but I think that's what Father was trying to do. My guess is that he's trying to tell me that it should be nearly dark to find this clue. Now all we can do is wait. Remember, this is a wild guess."

It was a long day. The fact that they had already had plenty of rest, coupled with the excitement of being this close to a possible answer, made it impossible to nap. They spent the day cleaning their weapons and checking over their gear in hopes of moving on the next day. Kally walked down the stream a bit, out of sight of the men, to take a bath, wash her hair, and wash out a few clothes. They drew all their water from the creek, and avoided the water trough all day.

After what seemed more like a week than a day, the sun finally started dropping. For once, they were thankful it happened sooner in the canyon than it would have out on the desert. Kally sent Chase to get the six mules and rope them close together, side by side, just as they were pictured on the map. Chase led the mules back to where Seth and Kally were waiting at the edge of the long, hollowed-out rock that formed the cistern. Kally held the map in her hand and was checking the location of the X.

"The map shows the X right about in the center of the long hollowed rock," Kally said, almost to herself, then looked at Chase. "Center the mules right here, and I think you'll find the six mules, side by side, will be about as wide as the rock is long."

"Do you know what you're doing, Kally?" Chase asked with a note of skepticism in his voice. "This doesn't make any sense to me."

"I was afraid you were going to ask that," Kally answered a little sheepishly. "Actually I don't, but I've decided we have to take all these clues literally, just as they appear on the map. Father was very logical, and I'm trying to be too. We have the right time of day—I hope—and the six mules next to the X. Now it's up to the mules to do the rest."

"Now what do we do?" Seth asked.

"Let the mules drink all they want," Kally commanded. "We'll just have to see what happens."

The mules were thirsty after a hot day with no water; they plunged their muzzles into the cistern rock and drank deeply. The trickle of water that ran in to fill the cistern was so slight that it couldn't refill the cistern as fast as they were drinking. The water level dropped immediately as they started to drink. They continued to drink their fill and the water dropped another two inches. In another moment or two Kally let out a shriek.

"There it is!" she said, pointing at the part of the rock wall that was exposed as the water level dropped.

"Well, I'll be damned," Seth said. "It was right there all the time."

Chiseled into the rock, six inches below the usual water line, was an arrow pointing to the right. The mules finished drinking, and slowly the cistern began to refill, eventually covering the arrow again.

"You did it!" Chase scooped Kally up in his arms and swung her around. "I don't know how you figured it out, but at daybreak we'll be ready to take the right-hand fork. We've been here too long—I'm ready to go find that gold."

*T*he next three days were easy riding. The stream had not dried up completely, as Seth had feared, but it was down to a very small trickle. They were forced to find natural cisterns or holes, or dig them, in order to water the stock. They had not come onto any narrow ledges or dangerous places. By now the mules just doggedly followed along and were no trouble at all. Chase or Kally had to drop back only once in a while to hurry up the stragglers that fell behind.

By the time they started looking for a campsite for the night, at the end of the third day, they came to where the canyon forked again. This time it was the four forks that appeared on the map with the next *X*. They found a place where the little stream provided the most water, and settled in for another stay. The stock was turned out to graze. The animals preferred the grass next to the stream, so they were content to stay nearby.

The three hurried through supper, but as usual, Seth had to light the lantern before they finished. The walls climbed higher and higher the farther north they traveled.

After supper Seth got out the map. Kally would have been content to wait awhile. She was already getting tired of trying to figure out clues. Now it would be up to her again to discover the secret that would take them into the right canyon.

The map was drawn as it had been before, with the four forks clearly marked, but with only one canyon continuing beyond that point. This time her father had drawn in a sun almost directly overhead, seemingly indicating some time between 10 A.M. and 2 P.M. Since he had made rays around the small circle, they were sure it was a sun and not a moon.

One of the rays extended down farther than the rest and ended at an *X*. By the *X* was the number 1200, but they had no indication as to what the number might mean. With no colon between the 12 and the zeros, and no A.M. or P.M. following it, it didn't seem to indicate time.

"Sometimes I wish he would have just put the *X*s in front of the right fork. Sure would have made it a heap easier for us to find," Seth said, shaking his head.

"Yeah, easier for us and anyone else who got their hands on the map," Chase reminded him.

"Well, this *X* is marked right in the middle of the canyon where we are now," Kally noted. "It appears to be equal distance from the entrances to each of the four forks. The more I look at this clue, the more I wish I had brought a sextant with me. I remember Father plotting our course on the sea by looking at the sun through the sextant. Maybe that's what we're supposed to do here. That number could be the number of degrees that would indicate one of the canyons."

"I don't know nothin' about sextants or degrees," said Seth, scratching his head. "I couldn't work one if you had brought it. Could either of you?"

They both admitted they couldn't. "If it had ever occurred to me we might need it, I would have learned how and brought it along," Kally added.

Chase looked at her thoughtfully. "You could be right, but from what I know of your father already, I doubt he would have expected you to go out and learn something you didn't already know. So far the clues have been based on things he was sure you could figure out. Were you pretty smart as a little girl?"

"Yes, I think so," Kally reflected. "My father spent a lot of time with me, teaching me my ABCs and how to count, while I was still quite small. The sailors on the ship were always teaching me songs, nursery rhymes, or riddles. They taught me how to tie knots and to make things from rope. I still remember a lot of those things. Father often remarked about how quickly I learned."

"You may have to recall some of those things you learned before we're through here," Chase said as he looked back at the map.

"This here number's really got me stumped," said Seth as he pointed to the 1200 on the map.

Kally scanned the map again. "There are some other numbers up here at the end of the map, but there are slashes between those. Besides, they don't mean any more to me than this one does."

"We know by now this won't be easy," reminded Chase, "so we might as well get some sleep and try it when our minds are fresh in the morning." He didn't get any argument from the others.

Kally and Chase lay on their blankets after Seth had gone off to sleep. Kally's head was cradled in the bend of Chase's arm, and she was enjoying the closeness, but her mind was still on the map and the clues.

"You *are* in there somewhere I hope?" said Chase, rolling toward her so he could look in her eyes.

"I'm sorry, Chase. I'm having a hard time getting my mind to turn off. Those clues just keep running through over and over again. I didn't mean to ignore you." Kally reached up and kissed him. "Let's talk about something else. Maybe that will help get my mind off it."

"We haven't remodeled the ranch house yet tonight," offered Chase with a grin. Most nights now they talked about the big house they were going to build on the ranch in Colorado after they got the gold. Each night they rearranged the location of the corrals and barns, or the furnishings in the house. Building and rebuilding, or adding something new. It was a pastime they both enjoyed, and one that served to draw them closer together as they each discovered the other's likes and dislikes, even their private dreams for the future.

All this talk, of course, had more than one purpose. They were learning a lot about each other, but it also tended to dampen the intensity of their physical contact. Kally was still not ready to go any further, and she was much more aware of how important it was not to excite Chase beyond what he would be able to control. Although they had never spoken of it to each other, they each knew it would be better, at least for now, to keep a little more distance between them. The result was that their relationship was deepening day by day. Much more than it might have if they had been free to express their love physically. They were exploring each other in other, deeper ways. Chase's hope was that by the time they reached the ranch, Kally would be ready to become his—totally. Soon they both slept, to dream.

After breakfast the next morning, the three of them saddled up and rode a short way up each of the four canyons. From their past experience, none of them felt too confident they would find anything, but there was always a chance there would be a clue, something they could start working on. As before, each of the canyons had water. They found no clues.

All they discovered was that the structure of the canyon walls was beginning to change in each of the canyons. The rocks had more vivid coloring, and the walls showed the signs of great upheavals in days long past. Great slabs of rock, some as large as a two-story house, were piled in random fashion to make up the high canyon walls. Some of the openings between the rocks were big enough for a horse and rider to ride into. Seth checked out many of them, but most went in only a short way before more rock blocked them. Besides, the map was clear. It didn't show them taking any detours.

Kally was awed at the different colors of rock—almost every color of the rainbow. They ranged from the yellow clay that matched what they had seen on the ingots, to deep reds, blues, pinks, and oranges. At one time, these rocks had been subjected to tremendous heat.

Chase and Seth disagreed about how far they had come since leaving Albuquerque. "I reckon we're about plumb in the middle of the canyon country—or the spirit country as the Injuns call it. My guess is we're out of Arizona now an' somewhere in Utah," Seth speculated.

"No, I don't think we've come that far yet," said Chase, shaking his head. "It just seems like it because we've lost so much time looking for clues, or traveling slower so we could watch for landmarks."

Kally had no idea which one was right, but Seth's mention of spirits made her shiver again.

"I wish I'd never heard of those spirits," Kally said aloud, even though the men were still discussing their location. They both stopped and looked at her.

"Are those old superstitions still bothering you, Kally?" Chase asked. "I thought you got over that."

"I can't help it. It started out as funny feelings; I was just uncomfortable somehow, but now it's more a feeling of apprehension, like something's going to happen. I can't explain it. I know it sounds silly."

"Not silly at all," Seth broke in. "I didn't say nothin' earlier 'cause I didn't want to spook you no more, but I've had a funny itch on my neck ever since we passed the old cave dwellings. It's not like when I feel someone's around, don't know how to explain it." Seth rubbed the back of his neck as he spoke.

"You two make a fine pair." Chase laughed. "If you keep this up, you're bound to scare the boots off each other."

"Chase's right, I reckon," Seth said, giving Kally a reassuring pat on the shoulder. "I never yet heared of a spirit killin' no one. I'm not likely to let one keep me away from that gold either. We're too close now."

They turned back and rode to where they could sit their horses and see the openings to each of the four canyons. Chase pulled the map from his saddle-bag, and compared it to the scene in front of them. The sun was overhead, but there was nothing where the X appeared on the map except perhaps one of the large rocks that dotted the area.

"I figure the ray coming down to the X is only to tell us the sun is connected to the clue in some way." They sat on their horses in the same spot until two in the afternoon, enduring the intense heat of the sun, in hopes something would appear as the sun changed positions. As the sun started its drop to the west, they hurried back to camp to find a spot where they could cool off. The waiting and watching had been in vain.

The rest of the afternoon, they were all lost in their own thoughts, trying to fit the clues into any-thing they had seen since they had been there. Noth-ing much was said until after supper.

Chase broke the silence. "I think we're wasting our time and a lot of energy by running back and forth out there. We know from the last clue that Kal-ly's father was very exact about what he put on the map. If we'd used our heads, we could have found the arrow a lot sooner."

"Got any ideas?" asked Seth as he poured another cup of coffee.

"The X appears to be out in the center, an equal

distance from all four canyons, right about where we were waiting this afternoon. We didn't see anything there, but we probably weren't in exactly the right place. The number on the map may mean that we should be twelve hundred feet or yards back this way from the entrances to the canyons. Tomorrow I'm going to step off twelve hundred feet and then we'll watch all four canyons from there as long as the sun is in the right position. If that doesn't work, the next day we'll try it with yards."

"I reckon that makes as much sense as anythin', Chase," Seth interrupted. "I sure ain't come up with nothin' better."

"I'm willing to try anything," Kally agreed, "but I can't help but think that number has something to do with whatever I'm supposed to remember about the sea."

"I don't know. I just feel certain the sun and the position of the X tie together somehow. All we've got to do is figure out how." Chase poured Kally and himself more coffee.

"Your idea is all we have to work on for now," Kally said, "but I wish there was some shade. I had about all of that sun I wanted today. I don't think it's fair to make the horses stand out there too. We probably had better do it on foot tomorrow. Now I'm going to bed, before it's time to go out there and cook in that sun some more."

The next morning they were in no hurry to get up, and sat longer than usual over breakfast. The sun had fully cleared the eastern canyon wall before they walked out into the middle of the canyon. Chase walked around the area several times, standing behind one rock and then another, looking out into each of the canyons in turn.

"What are you doing, Chase?" Kally asked, when she could stand it no longer.

"I got to thinking, after we went to bed last night. That *X* could be indicating one of these rocks."

"Is it?" she asked, looking around at them.

"Well, I figured if it was, it would have to be one that was located in a spot right in the middle of the four canyons, and in plain sight of each. I've checked them all, and this is the only one that fits," Chase said, slapping the top of a large boulder.

"What does that mean?" asked Seth, looking the rock over more carefully.

"I'm not sure," Chase confessed. "I reckon we should check over the rock itself first to see if there's a clue on it. If not, maybe this is the point where we should start measuring the twelve hundred feet or yards." Chase began to look closely at every inch of the rock that was exposed, but found no unusual markings. Then, he and Seth put their backs to it to see if it might move, in hopes a clue might be hidden under it.

"That one's not gonna move with sixteen mules tied to it," said Seth, trying to catch his breath after the exertion of pushing. "I reckon it's buried deep, or only part of a bigger rock formation sticking out of the ground."

"Before it gets any later, I think we should try some measuring," said Chase as he straightened up. "The more I think about it, the more I realize the measuring could be done in any four directions from the rock. Help me, Seth, and we'll step off twelve hundred feet north, south, east, and west. If we're lucky, we'll find something at one of those points."

Kally watched as they walked out each way and marked the spots with the heels of their boots. As they left their marks and went on, she started to check around the marked spots for any clues. She found nothing but dry ground, not even a rock. By now, the sun was in the proper position according to the map. For the next four hours they moved back and forth between the four spots checking the view of all four canyons, at least what they could see from each vantage point, including the high canyon walls and any of the open spaces between the rocks. They weren't sure what they were even looking for, but Chase had brought along his field glasses and began to search every inch of the walls for something out of the ordinary. He especially watched for a glint of gold like the one he had found in the rock pile at Pike City.

The hours dragged by slowly as the heat became more intense and Chase found nothing. As the sun dropped past the 2:00 position, the three trudged back to the camp, hot and discouraged. Kally was the first to head for the stream for a cool bath. When she finished, the men did the same.

The next morning Chase and Seth stepped off 1200 yards in long paces and repeated the same process. This time they could see more of the canyons, at least from the three most distant points. The day was simply a repeat of the day before, and just as fruitless.

That evening, Chase and Seth sat near the lamp studying the map again. Kally sat off by herself, thinking. The men realized she was reaching back to her childhood for something that would help, so they left her alone. Chase had obviously been wrong about the number 1200 standing for a measurement, and he hadn't been able to come up with any other ideas. He was about to express his frustration to Seth again when Kally suddenly got up and walked over to them.

"Hate to do this to you, old scouts, but I think I may have the answer again," she began.

"Don't worry about hurting our feelings, if you've got even the hint of an idea, I'll kiss you," Chase replied.

Kally laughed. "You've got a deal, but I was only kidding, I may be completely wrong. I've really been working my way back, and I'm amazed myself at how much I've been able to remember. Some of it has been about things I learned as a child, but a lot has been about the time I spent with my father.

"Until just now, I had forgotten about how he had taught me to tell time. On a ship they use a twenty-four-hour clock, so twelve hundred hours would be twelve o'clock noon, and midnight would be twenty-four hundred hours."

Chase looked at Kally in amazement. "I think it's time we made you head scout around here. Your brain sure is working better than ours. They use that kind of time in the army, too, but that never occurred to me. So now we know the 1200 stands for twelve noon, but I'm not sure that's going to be a lot of help."

"That's not all I remember," Kally went on. "On the ship, they rang a small bell every half hour. Father spent a lot of time trying to teach me how to tell time by the bells. I don't remember a lot of it now, but after my mother died, my father was often busy with his duties on the ship, so he wasn't free to eat the noon meal with me. Since I had the run of the ship, and he wouldn't always know where I was, he devised a plan where he would leave my dinner in a low cupboard where I could come and get it when I heard the eight bells they rang at noon. I would have to stop and count the bells each time they rang so I'd know when it was time to eat. Since I was still quite small at that time, he had trouble finding a cupboard low enough for me to reach. I think he knew I would remember that. Obviously there wouldn't be a cupboard out here, but I'm sure the clue will be low— low enough for me to reach it." Kally stopped to catch her breath after letting her ideas spill freely.

"Low enough for you to reach?" Chase said slowly as he thought through what she had said. "I never thought about looking low. Since the first clue was high on the top of a wall, I have been looking up on the walls here too."

"Well, 'pears to me we'd best hightail it out there at noon tomorrow an' see what shows up down low," Seth said with a look of amazement. "Y'all are some scout, little lady. I don't know about you two, but now that we have a clue to work on tomorrow, I'm ready to get some sleep."

16

*T*hey waited until 11:00 the next morning before they saddled up and rode out to the rock that stood in front of the four canyons. The spot they hoped was where the *X* was marked on the map.

Even though Seth and Chase knew better, and had warned Kally about it, they all started looking too soon. By the time Seth pulled out his watch to check the time, and squinted up at the sun, all of their eyes were playing tricks on them.

"Well, she's high as she's gonna get, but my eyes must be stickin' out a mile, I've been lookin' so hard."

Chase didn't answer, and Kally didn't stop looking. Chase stepped down off Ranger and got his field glasses, moving in front of the rock. Holding the glasses to his eyes, he swept the mouths of the four canyons, but nothing caught his eye. The next time he moved and stopped, moved and stopped, until he had moved across the four entrances again. Each time he looked and found nothing, he lowered his range. He knew distances could be deceiving and it was hard to tell what would be low enough for Kally to reach.

He swung the glasses to the farthest canyon on the right and slowly worked his way across it. He kept dropping down as he looked. He began picking up some of the bigger rocks on the ground as he started his last sweep of that canyon. He stopped with his glasses focused on a large, low rock of hard yellow clay. It sat against the wall of the canyon, just inside its entrance. He moved on to the center of the canyon and caught sight of another rock. Suddenly he swung back to the yellow rock. Chase held on it for several seconds.

Then he lowered the glasses and held his hand over his eyes for a moment, blinking hard. Seth and Kally were watching his every movement by now. Chase raised the glasses and again focused on the clay boulder, then swung away. He swung right back and held steady. He returned his glasses to their case and dropped it in his saddlebag.

Swinging into his saddle, Chase finally spoke to the others. "It's over there in the last canyon to the east. I nearly missed it. It's not too clear, but there's something there." With that, Chase led off with the other two right behind him.

He stopped Ranger in front of the yellow clay boulder. They all saw what Chase had seen before they were off their horses. There were three gold ingots buried in the face of the rock. Time and the blowing sand had dulled their color. They had been set at just the right angle in the rounded front of the rock so they would be almost impossible to see except at noon, and from the spot where the *X* was marked on the map. They had also been placed so they formed the letter *K*.

"Here's another message from your father, Kally," said Chase as he and Seth pried the ingots from the clay with their belt knives. They brushed them off and handed them to her. She dropped them into her saddlebag with the one from the rock pile at the wall.

The three of them talked as they rode back to camp. "Your father never ceases to amaze me," Chase said, shaking his head. "And neither do you. You must surely be your father's daughter. Between the two of you I'm beginning to believe we really will find that gold. I think this one was a little harder than he had planned, though. He must not have realized how dull gold can get when it's exposed to the elements. I almost missed it."

Seth joined in. "He surely knew what he was doin' alright. Hidin' somethin' right out in plain sight. If Kally hadn't remembered the low cupboard, we would've missed it too."

Kally smiled. "Just one more clue to go."

"From the map, it don't look to be more'n two or three days from here. We'll get an early start in the mornin' an' maybe before we know it we'll be lookin' at the gold. There sure must be a heap of it for him to use the ingots so freely for markers. I'm dyin' to see how much there really is." Seth's eyes sparkled with anticipation.

Things were a little livelier around the camp that night. Success had a way of erasing the tiredness that had left them dragging for the last few days. Now they realized how close they had come to the gold. None of them knew yet how to interpret the final clues on the map, but so far Kally had been able to figure them out. Their thoughts were beginning to focus on what they would do with the gold when they got back to civilization.

Kally wrapped the gold bars they had found in one of the burlap bags so they wouldn't rattle around in her saddlebag, and tucked them carefully back inside.

Chase stopped her as she started back toward the fire. "I'm so proud of you, Kally," he said as he took her in his arms. "There's no way Seth and I would ever have gotten this far if you hadn't figured out those clues. You're quite a woman, Kally VanDerVeer. And you're mine—all mine." Chase looked into her eyes a moment before kissing her. He had to again push down his feelings of love and deep need for her. He wasn't sure how much longer he could wait to have her, totally. They walked back to the fire hand in hand.

Seth was so excited and wound up that he hardly stopped talking for the rest of the evening. It was obvious he missed his little Carmen and envied the closeness Chase and Kally were able to share. He talked at length about what he was going to do with his gold when he got it. Chase and Kally were so wrapped up in their feelings for each other they heard little of what Seth was saying. Seth didn't notice. His thoughts were only of the gold and the new life it would buy him. When he finally ran down, they all turned in.

They moved out of camp as the first rays of the sun started lighting the eastern rim of the canyon. It was almost noon before Seth relaxed and smiled. They saw two big, square rocks standing on the western rim of the canyon that matched a marking on the

map. Now there was no doubt this was the right canyon. It provided the easiest riding they had found yet.
Seth was sure wagons had once traveled the floor of
this canyon. It was worn smooth. Only an occasional
rock that had fallen from the cliffs lay here and there
in their way. The walls of the canyon were made up
of rocks of many colors that were cracked and broken.
They saw many side canyons and openings between
the rocks as they rode, but none important enough
to draw them away from the path the map laid out
for them.

They camped that night on the floor of the valley.
The stream was so narrow and shallow by now that
Seth and Chase had to dig a hole so the stock could
drink and they could fill their buckets.

The next day they made good time as the valley
floor remained smooth and almost flat. Seth kept them
moving at a pace faster than the others really cared
to go. They stopped for dinner below the biggest
cluster of cave dwellings Chase or Seth had ever seen.
They were set back in a deep hollow of the cliff and
showed little sign of deterioration.

Kally was curious about their structure, and
couldn't help looking at them as they ate, but they
still filled her with a strange uneasiness. She was more
than ready to ride by the time they had finished their
dinner. Seth didn't say anything, but Chase noticed
he had rubbed the back of his neck several times. He
smiled to himself, thinking old Seth just might have
heard too many of those Indian stories.

They camped in the middle of the valley again
that evening, next to a natural hole in the tiny stream
where they could easily draw water.

When they got up the next morning, Seth was the first to notice that twelve of their mules were gone. "Now where do you s'pose them knot-heads wandered off to?" he said, mostly to himself. No sign of them could be seen in any direction. He circled the camp and soon found their tracks. They had started back the way they had come. Seth walked back down the canyon in search of them as Kally started breakfast. Chase helped her and they both expected Seth to come driving the mules back any minute. They had never wandered off before and they assumed they had only strayed a short way around the last bend in search of better graze. Seth returned by the time breakfast was ready, but the mules weren't with him.

"They must have kept right on going," said Seth as Kally handed him a plate. "Don't know what got into 'em. There's good graze along the stream, but the tracks show they wasn't grazin'. Sure beats me. Y'all get camp cleaned up an' the packs ready. Soon as I eat, I'll saddle up Maude an' go after 'em."

Chase and Kally had things ready to go a short time after Seth left. Chase walked around to where the other mules and their horses were still contentedly cropping the short grass. He examined the tracks. It appeared as if the stock that remained had just wandered in a large circle during the night. The twelve had simply left the others, as a group, and headed back down the valley. It was obvious that they had not wandered. They had moved down the trail without stopping to graze at all.

Kally stood beside Chase as he looked down the valley in the direction Seth had ridden. He had kidded Kally about her goose bumps, and laughed to himself about Seth's itchy neck, but now the hairs on the back of his neck were standing straight out. He wasn't about to say anything to Kally, but something didn't feel right. He bent over and studied the ground around the mule tracks. When Kally wasn't looking, he loosened his gun in its holster.

Chase and Kally walked back quite a ways, then returned to camp. Chase was looking for tracks of men, but the only ones he could find were Seth's. All they could do was sit down and wait. Kally fixed dinner and Seth still wasn't back. After she and Chase had finished eating, she shoved the skillet over to the edge of the coals with Seth's dinner still waiting.

It was midafternoon before Seth returned—without the mules. He dismounted and took the plate Kally handed him. He rubbed the back of his neck before picking up his fork.

"Durndest thing I ever seen," Seth said, between bites. "I've been trackin' since I was a youngun', an' I never seen any animal fly. But I reckon them mules did." Seth took two more big mouthfuls of food before handing his plate back to Kally.

Then he continued, "I followed their tracks straight back to them cave dwellin's. They stayed right in the middle of the valley an' didn't stop nowhere. Right in front of the cave dwellin's the tracks stopped, or I should say, just plumb disappeared."

Chase and Kally exchanged bewildered looks. "What do you mean, they disappeared?" Chase asked.

Kally shook her head. "You're not making sense, Seth. Tracks don't just disappear."

"Well, these did!" Seth said, shaking his head. "I rode on a couple miles an' never saw another track except for ours comin' in. I rode back to the caves an' right up to the face of that cliff. No sign of a track. I looked for man tracks agoin' an' acomin'. There ain't any. I made a dozen circles of the area an' there ain't no other tracks or nothin'."

"Maybe they went through one of those cracks in the wall," Kally ventured.

"I thought of that. I spent all afternoon pokin' into every crack or openin' in the canyon between here an' there. There's no place they could have gone through, especially without leavin' tracks. I checked the place where the tracks stopped a dozen times, an' that's what they did—they stopped."

"How do you figure it then?" Chase asked with concern.

"That's the worst of it," Seth admitted, rubbing the back of his neck again. "I ain't got no more ideas. It's like the earth just opened up an' swallowed them twelve mules. There weren't no shakin' last night; I'd have felt it. Nothin's disturbed an' I sure didn't find no cracks in the ground where the tracks disappeared. Them durn mules just up an' vanished."

"You're scaring me, Seth," Kally admitted. "I knew I didn't like those caves, but how could they have just disappeared?"

"Durned if I know, Kally. I never believed in spirits, an' I ain't about to admit to anythin' now, but this itchy neck's drivin' me crazy. It feels real funny. Ain't felt quite like this ever before."

Chase questioned Seth. "What do you want us to do? Stay here and keep looking?"

"No, sir! Let's leave the tools here an' repack. Some of the packs are empty anyhow. I think we can get most of the supplies what are left on the four mules an' my packhorse. We can come back for the tools if we need 'em."

"Do you want to ride out now?" Chase asked.

"We've got a couple hours of light left. We're this close; I'm not about to let an itchy neck keep us from gettin' to that gold. I say we pack up an' get out of this place."

*T*he four remaining mules and the packhorse were heavily loaded by the time they set out on the trail again. They had left the mining tools behind, but managed to get everything else, including a case of dynamite on the animals. They weren't able to move as fast, but they rode steadily until dark. None of them was anxious to spend another night where the mules had disappeared.

They found a place to stop for the night, unloaded the packs, and hobbled the animals. They decided to stand watch again, if just to keep an eye on the stock. Kally wouldn't admit she didn't want to stand watch alone, but made it clear she would take her watch with Chase. She didn't leave much room between them as they slept either.

The next day they rode in close formation. None of them had much to say as they each thought about the missing mules, but since no one could come up with any feasible explanation, the mules were never mentioned again.

That night, they again hobbled the stock and

stood watch. By the next afternoon, they came to a place that, from a distance, looked like the end of the canyon. Much like Pike City, it had a high rock wall that seemed to block their way. However, as they drew closer to the wall, they could see a steep, narrow trail going up and over it.

Chase and Kally waited with the stock while Seth climbed the trail to take a look. Shortly he returned.

"We can take the horses and mules over the top, but it'll have to be one at a time. There's lots of loose rock on the trail and it's pretty treacherous at the top."

Kally asked, "What's on the other side?"

"Looks like a big canyon, shaped like a bowl. 'Pears as if the canyon comes to a natural end, right there on the north side," said Seth as he pointed in that direction.

Kally stayed with the horses while Chase and Seth took the mules and packhorse over the trail one by one. They then rode their horses up carefully and very slowly. When they reached the top they paused for a moment before starting down. The canyon widened and was bowl-shaped as Seth had described. They eased their animals down the steep trail to where the stock waited on the floor of the giant bowl.

They all dismounted as the men surveyed the new canyon. At the east side was a long, smooth, benchlike strip of land. The north end of the bench was covered with piles of rock that had fallen from the high cliffs above it. The rest of the cliffs, surrounding the bowl, were all rock-covered and very steep. The only possible place to camp was at the south end of the wide, smooth bench.

They remounted and made their way across the rock-strewn floor of the bowl, then up a narrow trail that led them to the bench. The trail was steep, but clear of loose rock. After they reached the top, the men went back and led the pack animals up.

As they looked around the bench, they were surprised to find it much larger than it had looked from down below. They all spotted the lean-to at the same time. As they walked toward it, they could see it had been made from cedar poles and was once thatched with cedar boughs. The needles on the limbs had long since dried up and fallen off. Still, with a tarp stretched over the top of it, it would provide them shade from the afternoon sun. There were old, rusted tin plates and cups scattered around the campsite, but they were unable to tell how many men might have camped there earlier.

It was an ideal place for their camp. Dried grass for the stock was in abundance at both sides of the lean-to. A small trickle of water seeped from a crack in the canyon wall, providing all the water they would need. It ran for a short distance and then disappeared into the broken jumble of rocks that formed the high cross-wall. Seth felt sure this was the beginning of the stream they had followed from Pike City.

As they looked more closely, they discovered that a hole had been dug to collect water for the stock and to fill a bucket.

Seth was the first to speak. "Well, Kally, I'd say this was your daddy's camp. I reckon he was the one what dug that hole. The cedar poles for the lean-to would have to have been carried in here by somebody too." Seth looked around the high rim of the canyon.

"And as much as I've looked at that map, I'm sure those sentinel rocks up there are the ones marked on it. As soon as we get things squared away here, we can walk back down to the bottom an' check everythin' against the map."

"I can't believe we're finally here." Kally stood looking around her, as wide-eyed as a child. She reached out and gave Chase a big hug, then walked around gently fingering the poles of the lean-to and letting the water run over her hands. "Knowing my father probably spent years right here in this place makes me feel very safe and comfortable."

Chase had been studying the grazing area for the stock. "What do you think of me going back to the trail over the wall and rolling some rocks across it, Seth? If we have to hobble the stock, we'll just have to keep moving them."

"Alright with me," Seth agreed. "As steep an' rocky as this whole canyon is, they're not likely to wander very far anyhow. I feel like Kally. My neck's feelin' a lot less itchy since we got into this canyon. Help me pull the packs before you go an' then Kally and I'll get a good camp set up. No tellin' how long we might be here. The other clues sure wasn't easy, an' I figure this one's gonna be even harder."

By the time Chase returned to the floor of the big bowl, Seth and Kally had walked down to meet him. They had brought the map and were looking up at the cliffs. Chase looked over their shoulders at the map and then at the landmarks Kally's father had marked.

"It all matches," he said. "There's no mistaking those two big pinnacles up there above our camp.

They're too big and squared off to miss. And see, there's one lying across the biggest one, just like it shows on the map."

"Kally's daddy showed the moon right above 'em, an' those numbers alongside. The five bells are right along the edge of the map, not in a place what looks like it's markin' anythin' in particular."

Kally was looking more closely now too. "There's a heavy *X* burned into that big cross. From its size, it reminds me of the big ones they use on churches or missions. That makes me think these bells still have something to do with a mission. But the map shows the cross on the west side of the bowl, almost directly across from our camp."

Seth looked up from the map. " 'Pears to me iffen it was that big we could see it even from here, but that side of the canyon is a real rock patch. Rocks have likely been tumblin' off those cliffs for a long spell. But some of 'em..." Seth looked more closely at the rocks across the canyon before he finished. "Some of 'em are awfully square. I'm wonderin' if they all fell. You notice anythin' familiar out there, Chase?"

"I don't know what you're getting at, Seth. I've never been here before, if that's what you mean."

"I know y'all ain't been here before, but does the shape of them rocks remind you of anythin'? See how much lower the floor of this canyon is than on the other side of that wall we just came over?"

Chase stood silently a moment, surveying the floor of the bowl. "You're right, Seth. It looks like a quarry. All those smooth, square rocks scattered around out there couldn't be natural. It's like some of the other places we've seen where the old Indians used to cut stone." Chase could hardly believe what he was seeing. "It all fits," he continued. "The floor of this bowl, under all that scattered rock, was once real flat and smooth. That fits with Kally's idea too— that this was once a small town or a large mission."

Kally had been listening to every word, trying to grasp the meaning of what they were saying. Now she spoke. "I can see what you're talking about. My theory about the mission does fit, and so does Seth's about there being a road out there on the floor of that last canyon."

Seth spoke quickly, in an excited voice. "We don't know what this country might have looked like three hundred years ago. This could be the place where they melted down gold from this whole area. That road could have led straight to Mexico. Whoever was here then could have still been cuttin' rock an' buildin'."

"You could be right," Chase agreed.

Seth stopped only long enough to catch his breath. "That wall of rock we climbed over back there is like the one back at Pike City. It fell a long time after this quarry was abandoned. There might be a mission or some kind of building under all that rock on the west wall, or even up there at the end of the big bench where we set up camp."

Chase had been looking around as Seth spoke. "It all seems to fit. What do you think, Kally?"

"Everything Seth says makes sense, but I'm still trying to fit it all into where the gold is and how we're going to find it. This place is so full of my father, I'm as anxious to find out more about what happened to him as I am to find the gold. But I suspect the answers to all my questions may be in the same place." Kally looked at the map again.

"I agree with you, though," she went on. "From the size of this cross he made, I would think we could see it lying over there."

Seth turned and started walking back toward the bench. "I don't know about you two, but I'm hot an' tired. Let's get settled in up there an' get some rest. We can't do nothin' 'til we figure out the map nohow. I say we have an early supper an' get to bed early. We've got time to study that map some too."

Chase and Kally were right behind him. "I don't see any reason to stand watch either," Chase added. "By the time somebody got over that rock wall and up to the bench, we'd hear them."

The three of them climbed the trail to the bench and put the finishing touches on their camp. They stretched a tarp across the top of the lean-to so they could rest out of the sun. The men spread out the map and concentrated on the final clue, while Kally went exploring the rest of the bench.

Before long she returned with a rusty, old pick and a broken-handled shovel, and a dark blue coat. The coat had brass buttons that had turned almost black from age.

Kally was breathless with excitement. "I found these in a little cave down there where the rocks start. There are some other old tools, but this is the captain's coat my father wore on the ship. There's nothing in the pockets, but I know it was his." She had let the old tools drop to the ground, but she held the coat lovingly in her arms. "This and the letter are more than I ever hoped I would be able to find of him. I know we've come a long way to find the gold, but these things mean more to me than the gold ever will. Can you understand that?" She looked at Chase, wanting him to understand and share in some of what she was feeling.

Chase reached out and pulled her to him, putting his arms around her and the old coat. He held her closely, loving her more deeply than he had ever thought possible.

That night after supper, when Chase and Kally lay side by side on their blankets, they watched the moon come over the rim of the deep bowl and light the western wall. The moon was not quite full yet, but it threw a lot of light against the darkness. Chase lay watching Kally's face in the moonlight. She was far away, lost in her thoughts.

Finally he spoke. "Thinking about your father?"

Slowly she returned to the present and smiled at him. "I can't help but think about what his life was like here—and what might have happened to him. It seems so strange, after all these years, to finally be where he spent his final days doing everything he could to get the gold to me. I still think about what it would have been like if I had been able to get here while he was still alive. I could have been hugging him today, instead of his old coat." The tears welled up in her eyes, but she kept talking.

"I guess what I think about most is that he did all this to make me happy. The strange thing is that even if we never find the gold, he's done that. The happiness has come in the journey, not in the destination. I spent a whole year looking for you, having no idea you would bring me the happiness I expected to find with the gold." She turned to face him with tears running down her face. "I love you so much it hurts sometimes."

"Oh, Kally...." Chase kissed her softly, then held her in his arms as they shared the mutual pain and total joy of their love for each other. The quiet darkness of this canyon swallowed up the sound of two hearts that now beat as one, and they slept.

After breakfast the next morning, Chase and Kally stood looking across the canyon at the west wall, trying to visualize the spot where her father had marked the large cross on the map. After deciding on a spot and fixing it firmly in their minds, they set off across the bowl. Seth was going to walk the bottom of the bowl and look over the north wall, hoping to find the bells.

Chase and Kally found it fairly easy climbing up to the spot where they thought the cross should be. "It looks like some of these rocks have been rolled to one side," Chase remarked as they stopped to look around.

In the place where they thought they might find the cross, they found only a slab of rock, about the size of a house door, but much thicker. It lay on an angle on the side of the hill as if it had come to rest there during one of the slides. Like many of the other rocks in the quarry, it appeared to have been cut in an almost perfect rectangle. Above it was another much larger and taller rock, standing straight up. It, too, looked like it had been cut by hand.

"That one up there has got to weigh tons," said Chase, pointing to the one above them. "Can you imagine the force it would have taken to move it down the canyon wall and into an upright position? I think this all may prove your theory is right. This very likely was a mission or small city that's been buried under all this rock. Most of these rocks could have come from a main wall that fell all at once, burying everything in its path. That would explain why the place was abandoned, and the gold never taken out."

Kally had been looking around as she listened to Chase's conclusions. "I don't see anything here that looks like a cross or an *X*," she said as they started to search every inch of the area they had pinpointed from the map. They climbed over rock after rock, eventually covering the whole south end of the giant slide. At noon they all returned to camp, hot and tired.

Seth hadn't had any more luck than they had. They rested for a while after dinner and exchanged what few thoughts they had left about the situation. After getting their second wind, they all three crossed the floor of the canyon and climbed the rock slide. They spent until nearly sundown crawling over rocks and looking behind every big one they came to. There was not a cross, an *X*, or a bell to be found anywhere.

They returned to camp that evening, tired and disappointed. They had hoped to at least find the bells or something that resembled a cross. After an early supper, Kally walked down to the other end of the bench while the men used buckets to take a quick bath. When they had dressed, they gave Kally some privacy for her bath.

"What do you think now, Seth?" Chase asked as they both stood staring across the bowl.

"Damned if I know what to think. As hard as the

other clues have been, you'd think Kally's daddy would have knowed no one but her would get this far. Seems to me he could have made this clue the easiest one, but so far nothin's like it looks on the map."

"Well, I'm totally stumped. I haven't any idea what to do next. Maybe it's going to be up to Kally to figure it out again. I don't know where to start."

"Me either," Seth agreed. "But as long as we've still got grub, I'm for stayin' here an' lookin'. We've seen enough of them gold ingots to know there's gold here somewhere, an' plenty of it. This is closer to bein' rich than I've ever been before. I'm not about to give up now."

"I didn't say I was ready to give up. Only that I was stumped. We've been stumped before, and Kally has always come through with the answers. Even if we have to eat one of the mules, I'm for staying until she can figure it out. I still plan to build that big, fancy house for her and one close by for you and Carmen."

After three more days of scouring every inch of the bowl with no luck, they had practically worn the soles off their boots. Every time they went to the map, it took them back to the original spot where they had found the two rock slabs. But they appeared to be where the force of the slide had taken them. They were much too heavy for anyone to have placed them there deliberately. The three had searched every inch of them and everything nearby. They found no crevasse or hole behind either of them, nor any cracks or depressions on them.

The next morning Chase carried the map across the bowl again, and up the side of the rock slide. All three of them studied it and the rim of the canyon above their camp, where the moon was drawn on the map.

"There's no doubt in my mind we have to be standing almost right on top of that gold," Chase said in desperation. "The whole rim of this bowl fits the map exactly. Kally's father drew in the two square spires, and the fallen one, perfectly. I think it's time we quit frying our brains out here in the sun and find a shady place to put them to better use. Especially you, Kally."

"I have been thinking," Kally protested. "I don't know what else I could possibly remember."

Chase draped his arm around Kally's shoulders. "I don't know either, but you'd think we would have learned by now that all this running around and looking isn't going to help. We've done the same thing with all the other clues and it never got us anywhere. You're the one who always figures it out, so let's go sit in the lean-to and do some thinking."

The three walked back to camp and made themselves comfortable in the lean-to, out of the sun. No one spoke for a long time as they rested and ran what information they had over and over through their minds.

Finally, Chase picked up the map again. "I just can't make heads or tails of these markings. The circle has got to be a moon. There's no rays coming from it like the sun in the last clue. So, since it's a round moon, understanding your father's logic, it must indicate a full moon. Can we agree on that?"

"Makes sense to me," Seth agreed. "The moon's

almost full now, so at least we won't have to wait for that."

Kally nodded.

"Okay," Chase went on. "The rocks on the rim are exact; we've already agreed on that. My guess is they're only to tell us we're in the right place, or that this is where we were to camp."

Kally interrupted, "On the map, the moon is right over the two rocks up there on the ledge. Understanding my father's logic, as I certainly am beginning to, I would say he means for us to stand under those rocks during a full moon. But that still doesn't tell us what the numbers mean or what the mission bells or cross have to do with anything."

"We've already determined the cross and the *X* aren't on the other side of the bowl, so that part doesn't make any sense. But it's these numbers off to the side here that really throw me," Chase admitted. "It's obvious from the way they're written they have nothing to do with time."

"My father wouldn't have written them if they hadn't meant something," Kally interrupted again. "We can't dismiss anything as being unimportant now."

"I didn't mean they were unimportant. I just haven't a clue to what they mean. At first, the way they were written, I thought they might mean a date, but nothing seems to fit. This 8–9–10/7/188, just doesn't fit for a date. If the first three numbers with the dashes between them stand for months, we're a month too soon. By my reckoning, this has to be July—the seventh month. Eight, nine, and ten would be August, September, and October. The seven could mean the seventh day of any of those months, but one-eighty-eight certainly doesn't work for the year. That ruins any logic as far as a date goes."

Seth had been quiet and listening up until now. "You've done a heap of talkin', boy, but I don't see that we know a bit more. Is all this gonna take us any closer to the gold?"

"I don't know if we're getting anywhere," Kally said, "but it does help me when the two of you talk through some of this with me. If those numbers aren't a date, I don't have any idea what they could mean. And if there were five bells left from the mission, it seems like Father would have used them to mark something or to give us some sort of clue. Otherwise, why would they be on the map? Surely he wouldn't have buried them with the gold?"

"Unless they were made of gold," Chase ventured. "That doesn't make any sense either. I'm sure gold is too soft to make into a church bell, and if it wouldn't ring, why bother to go to the trouble to make it in the shape of a bell?" Chase shook his head. "I think I'm beginning to talk in circles."

Kally was still thinking out loud. "What if the bells come later? After we find the cross? Maybe the bells are going to mark a right passageway or something. That would make sense, since we haven't been able to find them anywhere around here."

Seth got up and walked toward his blankets. "All this talkin' an' thinkin's givin' me a headache. I'm gonna take a nap. I don't need no dinner. Besides, if we're gonna have to be here until October, we'd better start goin' light on the grub."

Seth got a drink of water, moved his blankets

into the shade, and stretched out. Chase and Kally sat a while longer looking at the map and thinking before they moved to their blankets too. The last few days had been more tiring than riding the trail had been. The hot sun and climbing over the rocks all day had taken its toll on their strength and their spirits. They all enjoyed a long nap.

It was two o'clock in the afternoon before they woke again. Seth got up and moved his blankets back by his saddle while Chase and Kally were still stretching. Then he walked over to the water hole and sloshed water on his face, drying it with his neckerchief.

Chase and Kally were just getting to their feet when Seth called in an excited voice, "Chase—Kally—come here, quick."

They ran to where Seth stood looking out where the stock was grazing.

"How many mules do you see?" he asked in a strange voice.

"One," they said in unison.

"What happened to the other three?" asked Kally, before Chase had a chance.

"I don't know, but I'm sure gonna find out," Seth said angrily. He pulled his six-gun and checked its loads.

Chase checked his gun and they walked out to where the one mule, the packhorse, and their saddle horses remained. Kally stayed close behind Chase as he eased over to where he could look down the trail coming up to the bench, and out over the bowl. Seth crept along the canyon wall. The only tracks were their own. Seth came back down the rock wall rubbing the back of his neck.

"I'm saddlin' up an' goin' after 'em, Chase. Y'all stay here with Kally. This looks like an Injun horse-stealin' trick to me, but I can't believe either of us could have slept that hard. Even if the Injuns could've sneaked in here without us hearin' 'em, we'd have heard the mules' hooves on the rocks. I sure didn't see no tracks, but I'm goin' lookin'. I'll hurry; they couldn't have gotten far."

Seth quickly saddled Maude and rode down off the bench. He walked her up the steep trail and rolled away the two big rocks Chase had put in the trail earlier. No one had moved them. When he reached the top, he mounted and disappeared over the wall.

Chase and Kally walked down to the floor of the bowl and searched everywhere for tracks. The only fresh tracks were Seth's. They walked slowly back up to the bench and stood where they could watch the whole canyon and the trail coming over the high rock wall. Neither had anything to say.

18

*I*t was nearly dark when Seth reappeared at the top of the wall. He dismounted and led Maude down to where the rocks had blocked the narrow trail. He rolled the two he had moved back into place and added several more to them.

He led Maude across the trail and up to the reservoir on the bench. She had been ridden hard. Seth pulled her saddle and bridle as she drank. He dropped the saddle near his blankets and picked up a burlap sack. Walking back to where Maude was still drinking, he gave her a good rubdown. When he finished, he threw the bag back on the pile and picked up some hobbles.

Without speaking, Chase grabbed some of the others and followed Seth out to where they hobbled the rest of the animals. Seth didn't speak until they got back to the lean-to.

"I ain't said nothin' 'cause I don't know what to say. I pushed Maude hard. I figured if some Injuns had managed to get them mules out of here without us hearin', they didn't have time to get 'em far. Y'all know I'm a good tracker, Chase. About as good as any man in this country. My eyes an' my hearin's as good as they ever was."

Chase nodded.

"If there'd been any tracks, I'd have found 'em. I found nothin'. Weren't nothin' at all out there." It was obvious Seth was confused and disappointed, as well as downright mad.

"I ain't offerin' no guesses as to what happened to 'em, but the rest of them animals is stayin' hobbled 'til we get out of here, an' we're goin' back on watch."

"Don't blame yourself, Seth," Chase said. "I figured we were pretty safe in here too. I know if there'd been any tracks you'd have found them. I don't believe in spirits, and I keep telling myself those mules just found a way out of here we don't know about. I know they should have left some tracks, but there's something strange about this canyon. Kally's father felt it too; he said so in his letter."

Kally had been listening to every word. "I wish you two would stop it. You're giving me goose bumps again." She shivered. "Now what are we going to do? Do you think we should get out of here while we still have enough pack animals left to get us back? We could use the ingots we have to outfit again and come back later."

"Not this year we couldn't," Seth said. "It'd be winter by the time we could get back. Between the rains an' storms an' possible flash floods, we could get into some real trouble. Besides, we'd have to deal with followers all over again. Next time we might not be so lucky."

"Then what can we do?" Kally was looking at Chase.

Seth was quick with an answer before Chase could speak. "I say we stay an' look for the gold as long as we got food. If we find it, we can take out enough to hold us 'til next year. If we cash in the gold when we get back an' stay put all winter, we'll throw off a lot of would-be followers. Me an' Chase could sneak off once in a while to three or four different towns for a few mules an' supplies. Then when we was ready to head back, we might just ride over here all by our lonesome."

Chase and Kally exchanged glances and nodded their heads in agreement. "But what about that itchy neck?" Chase asked. "You're not going to go Indian on me, are you?"

"No, but I am goin' to start actin' like a whole bunch of fellers was after us, an' stay on my guard. We've stood here jawin' 'til we're gonna have to fix supper by lantern light. Let's get at it. I'm plumb tuckered out. I'll hit my blankets as soon as we eat. You two can take the first watch, an' I'll be rested when my turn comes."

The night was uneventful, and Seth woke Chase and Kally at sunup. They washed up and Kally started breakfast while Seth walked out and moved the stock to fresh graze.

After breakfast, they laid the map out and sat around it in what had almost become a daily ritual. After a few minutes, Kally got up and kneeled by it, studying it more carefully.

"I think I've figured out part of it," she said, finally. "Last night I went to sleep thinking about all the things you had said yesterday, Chase. The numbers particularly had me baffled. I went over and over what you

had said about how you thought it was a date, but it
didn't fit. You said it would be the seventh day of the
eighth, ninth, or tenth month, and in America it would
be. But in any other part of the world—like where
my father spent most of his life—they write the day
first and then the month."

Kally hurried over to her saddlebag and returned
with a small calendar she had been using to mark off
each day to keep track of the date. She looked at it a
moment before she spoke.

"The moon is never full on the first of the month.
It can vary two or three days. Some years even more.
Tomorrow is the ninth of July. The calendar shows a
full moon then. My father had to guess that the moon
would be full on the eighth, ninth, or tenth of July."

Chase interrupted, "But what about the year? I
still don't understand the one-eighty-eight."

"Now that we know the rest is a date, the one-
eighty-eight can only mean eighteen hundred and
eighty-something. He wouldn't have known what year
I might come, but he could have made the map about
1879 and I'm sure he would have assumed I would
get here sometime during the eighties."

Chase looked at her in astonishment. "I don't
know how you figured all that out, but I'm sure glad
you did. So what you're saying is that something is
going to happen tomorrow night when the moon is
full? Have you figured out what?"

"I have no idea, but we also know we're supposed
to stand under those square rocks up on that ridge
over the camp. Beyond that, it's all going to be guess-
work."

"At least that gives us something to work on,"

said Chase as he gave Kally a hug. "That's a lot more than we had a few minutes ago."

Kally kissed him and turned back to the map. "Now I'm going to concentrate on these bells. Maybe somehow I can work them into what we already know. I can't see how some old mission bells lying around this canyon can help us, unless they were marking an entrance or something. Since we haven't found any sign of them since we've been here, I have to think they have a different meaning. Just give me some time. I'll figure it out."

"Is there anything we can do to help?" Chase asked.

"I don't think so. I'm going to stretch out on my blankets and close my eyes. There has to be some little thing I'm forgetting that Father thought I would remember."

For the next few minutes, Chase and Seth sat studying the map and looking at the calendar Kally had brought along. Everything she said made sense to both of them.

Kally still hadn't come up with anything more by suppertime. At bedtime, she kissed Chase good night and for the first time since they had been sleeping close together, she turned away from him. He knew she was still reaching far into her past for any clue that would help unlock the secret of the gold.

Kally looked haggard the next morning. She hadn't slept well. They would find the gold tonight, but only if she was able to put the rest of the clues together by then.

Chase put his arms around her after she'd gotten up and splashed water on her face. "You were doing a lot of tossing and turning last night. Did you get any sleep?"

"Not much," Kally said as she turned toward the fire to start breakfast. "I've got to come up with something, and soon."

Seth returned from moving the stock. "Sit down, little lady, I'll fix breakfast. Y'all look like you've been fightin' coyotes all night."

"Thanks, Seth. I think I'll take a little walk before breakfast. Call me when the coffee's ready." Kally gave Chase a peck on the cheek and walked out to where Pacer was grazing. She stood stroking his neck, deep in thought.

"I wish there was some way we could help her," Chase said as he leveled out the coals for Seth's frying pan. "I think she's trying too hard, but she knows she only has until tonight to find the answer."

Seth checked the coffee before turning back toward Chase. "I know she can do it. She's pulled us out every time so far, ain't she? Maybe we can run over everythin' again like we done yesterday. Looks like the coffee's ready. Why don't you call her."

Chase called and Kally walked slowly back to where the men waited. After breakfast, Chase suggested they take another look at all the clues.

Chase spread the map out where they could all see it, and started to review what they had already learned. "If you figured it right, Kally, we're to stand under the two square pinnacles with the fallen rock, during a full moon, which will be tonight. The only other clues are the cross with the *X* on it, we're assuming we'll see by the full moon, and the five bells."

"It's the five bells I'm trying to figure out. I've tried every way I know to tie those mission bells into something. Since there was no mission on the ship, I've tried to remember if we had anything to do with a mission in San Francisco during the time I was there with Father. There's nothing I can remember. It's driving me crazy."

Chase reached out and took her hand. "It's alright, Kally. We're going to figure it out. We know your father was logical, so let's look at this as logically as we can. What is it that the five bells will tell us? What do we still need to know?"

Kally and Seth sat looking blankly at Chase as they thought about his question. Seth spoke first. "Well, we know where to stand. We know it's tonight. We know it's durin' the full moon. And we know what to look for. What else is there?"

"That's right," Chase said, "but are you planning to stand out there all night? That moon's out a long time."

"The time!" Kally shouted. "How could I have been so stupid? I threw us off from the beginning. I was so sure those were mission bells, I couldn't even think of anything else."

Seth sat looking at her like he thought she *had* gone crazy. "What in tarnation are you talkin' about, girl?"

"Five bells. Don't you remember back at the four canyons. I told you about the bell they rang on the ship to tell time. This time the five bells do stand for the time of day."

Chase joined in. "That still doesn't make sense. There's no full moon out at five o'clock in the evening, and it's too light to see much of the moon at five in the morning. How does that help?"

"No, Chase, the bells don't work like the chime on a clock. That's why I had such a hard time learning them as a child. We left the ship before I got real good at telling time by them, so I'm not sure what time five bells would be. It'll take some time to figure that out."

"Can you do it?" Chase asked, studying her face.

"I think so. At least I've got all day to try."

"It's just that your father has been so precise about each of the clues. I feel certain the time must be important if we're going to see what he wants us to see. Is there any way we can help?"

"I don't think so. I'll just need some time to think this through and see if I can remember what Father tried so hard to teach me as a child. It's back there somewhere, I've just got to dig it out." Kally put down her empty cup and walked to the other end of the bench, toward the cave where she had found her father's coat and the old tools. She felt closer to her father there than anywhere. She hoped that feeling of closeness would help her remember. Inside the cave, Kally sat down with her knees up and leaned her head back against a rock. She was so tired it was hard to think anymore. Within five minutes she had lost the battle; she slept.

When she hadn't returned by the time Seth had dinner ready, Chase came looking for her. The crunch of his boots in the loose rock woke her as he bent down to enter the cave.

"Chase?" She looked at him blurry-eyed for a moment as she tried to figure out where she was.

"Oh, no! The bells. I fell asleep. I don't know what happened. I just came here to think." Kally jumped to her feet as she realized how much precious time she had lost.

"It's alright, Kally. It's only dinnertime, and I know how much you needed to rest."

"Dinnertime! That's it."

"That's what?" Chase looked at her closely, not sure she was really awake.

"Dinnertime. Remember I told you that when I was on the ship they rang eight bells at dinnertime? They never rang more than eight bells, and the bells rang every half hour. I can figure it out from there. There would have been five bells rung six different times of the day, but, I hope, only once while the moon was out." Kally was leading the way out of the cave by now. She hurried back to camp where Seth was waiting dinner.

Kally rushed past him to her saddlebags and pulled out a sheet of paper and a pencil.

"What's goin' on?" Seth asked as Chase caught up with her. She sat on a rock and started figuring.

"She remembered how the bells worked," said Chase with a big smile. "Now she just has to figure out what time five bells would be."

Dinner was forgotten as the two men stood waiting for her to finish writing. Finally she looked up at them with a smile bigger than Chase's.

"Five bells could be ten-thirty, two-thirty, or six-thirty. I think our best bet is ten-thirty; while the moon is still rising. It's too light at six-thirty, morning or evening, and if we don't find anything at ten-thirty, we can always try again at two-thirty."

Chase grabbed her and hugged her so tightly she could hardly breathe. "I knew you'd do it. Your father was a pretty smart man to have put all those clues together, but he wasn't a bit smarter than you. I'm so proud of you, Kally."

"That goes double for me," Seth agreed, fairly dancing for joy.

"Well, that's all the thinking I'm going to do for today. Where's dinner? I'm starved!" Kally took Chase's hand as she walked over to the fire. They were all ready to eat.

19

The three of them spent the rest of the afternoon discussing their plans for that night, and what they hoped to find.

Chase asked Kally, "What exactly do you think we're going to see tonight? It seems strange that we'd see a cross at night that we haven't been able to find in the daytime."

"I'm really not sure," she admitted, "but I do think we're supposed to mark the cross with an X when we see it. The map shows that X burned deeply into the buckskin, more than the other Xs were. I hope it's going to show us the way to the gold."

"It's still a mystery to me, but if you're right, we'd better get another lantern ready, and pull a couple big sticks of charcoal out of the fire so we can mark the X on the cross when we see it."

They made their preparations, and checked them over and over as the afternoon dragged slowly by. No one was hungry at suppertime. They were too excited to eat. They lay down to rest awhile after supper, knowing they wouldn't have to worry about falling asleep. Seth got tired of pulling his watch out every few minutes to check the time, and set it on a rock next to his bedroll where he could watch the minutes tick past.

At ten o'clock, all three were standing at the edge of the bench waiting for the moon to lift above the western cliffs. At 10:15, Seth lit the second lantern and they waited impatiently for fifteen minutes to pass. At twenty-five after, Kally pointed across the bowl.

"Look."

The moon's bright light was beginning to creep up the rock slide. It took the men a second to see what Kally had. A shadow about a foot long was starting to show on the big rock slab that looked like a door. The shadow was square at the bottom like a large timber or the base of a cross. As they watched, it grew longer.

"I'll be damned," Chase said, without moving. "Those rock sentinels were more than a landmark. They're going to cast the shadow of a cross on that rock. Let's get over there. It should be a full cross by the time we can reach it. The map shows the *X* marked right where the two pieces cross in the center. If we wait too long we won't know where to mark it."

Seth was already leading the way across the bowl, moving as quickly as he could through the rocks. The shadow was starting to form the crosspiece as they reached the other side. They moved up the path where it looked like rocks had been rolled away, and found the complete shadow of a large cross on the slab of rock that lay in the rubble. Chase quickly marked the *X* where the two shadows crossed.

They stood watching in silence as the moon continued to climb in the sky. In less than fifteen minutes, the cross had disappeared and only the charcoal *X* remained in the center of the slab.

"Now what?" Kally asked, looking at Chase.

"I'm not sure, but there's nothing we can do until daylight. We might as well go back to camp and start over in the morning."

They made their way back to camp. It was Chase and Kally's turn to stand first watch, but it would be a short night. It was already eleven o'clock.

Seth headed for his blankets. "Give me a tap on the foot when you're ready to go to bed. I don't reckon I'll sleep much anyhow—not 'til I've got that gold in my hands."

Seth woke Chase and Kally the next morning an hour earlier than usual. The coffee was already made, and he handed them each a cup as soon as they had washed their faces.

"What's your hurry this morning, Seth?" asked Chase with a laugh as Seth started breakfast. "That gold's not going anywhere. And it's sure not going anywhere until we figure out how to move that big slab. It must have come down after Kally's father was here. I don't see how he could possibly have moved it, even if his mate had been here to help. I'm as eager as you to get the gold, but I'm in no hurry to get out in that sun and start digging."

"That's why I got you up early. We can get out there an' get started before the sun gets too hot. I can't wait to get ahold of that gold an' get out of here. I'd use the dynamite if I thought we could keep the whole cliff from comin' down on top of the slab an' buryin' it for good. Problem is we don't have many tools to work with. I may have to go back to where we left 'em an' pick up what we need."

"We've all had more of this trip than we wanted, so if you'll dish up that breakfast, we'll go see what we can do with the old tools Kally's father left in the cave. I don't want you to have to make that trip back there unless you really have to."

"I'll get the lanterns," Kally volunteered. "If we do find the cave or whatever is hidden under that slab, we'll probably need some light."

They hurried through breakfast and grabbed the lanterns and tools before starting across the bowl. Seth ran back at the last minute and picked up a couple of the burlap sacks. Chase and Kally laughed as they all crossed the bowl and walked up to the big slab.

"Hold up a minute before you start digging, Seth," Chase said. "Kally's father has been teaching me a lot about logic. If there's some way to move this thing without ruining our backs, I'd just as soon find it out first. Besides, I'm not too sure how steady that big upright slab is. I wouldn't want it to fall on us while we're trying to move this one—it's a heavy one."

Kally stepped back out of the way as the men climbed up to where the tall rock slab stood upright. They rolled some of the smaller stones away from it. Chase shoveled away more of the gravel around its base. It seemed to be buried deeply. To be sure, Chase and Seth put their shoulders against it and pushed as hard as they could. The rock didn't budge.

"I guess it's safe enough," Chase conceded. "Now

let's see what we can do to move the other one. At least we won't have to worry about this one falling on us while we work. Seems to me the easiest way to move it will be to get it to slide on down the pile out of the way. We're sure not going to be able to lift it or push it off. Let's move everything we can out from under it first."

Seth and Chase spent the next few minutes rolling away everything that would move. All the loose rocks rolled easily down the hill, except for one that was stuck tight under one edge of the slab. It was a square, smooth stone that stood out from one bottom corner.

"This one's buried deep," said Seth as he caught his breath. "She ain't gonna move without a lot of diggin'. If it wasn't for this one, now that all the other rock is cleared, we could likely slide the slab right on down." Seth looked it over again. "'Pears to me this rock was cut too. Maybe it was put here to keep the slab from slidin'."

Chase walked around to where Seth was and looked closely at the square rock before speaking. "It's hard to tell," he said as he walked around the big slab again. "Darned if this slab doesn't look like a door. Now that we've cleared away the loose rocks, the rock underneath is really smooth." Chase bent down and tried to look under the edges. "If it was a door it would have to have hinges, and some kind of a handle. I don't see anything here." He stood up.

"Hand me that pick." He motioned to Seth. "Maybe I can get it to start sliding without moving that corner stone. It's worth a try."

Seth handed the old, rusty pick to Chase as he

and Kally moved back out of the way. Chase swung the point of the pick up under the edge of the slab. The slab didn't slide. It swung out sideways. Chase dropped the pick and pushed the slab door with his hand. It swung open even farther with little effort on his part. He pushed it until it came to rest on top of the square, smooth rock Seth had been unable to move.

"Well, I'll be damned. It is a door," Seth exclaimed.

"And what a door," Chase agreed. "I never met an Indian smart enough to rig something like this. That slab has to be perfectly balanced to move like that. And look at that round rock it pivots on. I've never seen stone like that around here."

"Whew!" Kally put her hand over her nose as she and Seth moved over to the opening. "It doesn't smell too good in there."

Seth was still looking at the stone. "It sure didn't come from this quarry. Everything here is sandstone or limestone. That one's black granite. It's hard rock that had to be hauled in here."

"Let's light the lanterns and see what we've found," Chase said, turning to Kally. "The smell seems to have cleared up some."

The opening was cut into solid rock. It was like a door opening, only narrow. The big slab that had covered it was double the width of the opening. Even in the sunlight, they could see in only a couple of feet. Seth lit the lanterns and handed one to Chase as he stooped and entered the passageway. Chase started in behind him with Kally at his heels. Before they were inside, Seth's voice stopped them from up ahead.

"Hold up there a minute, Chase, an' don't let Kally come in. I'm comin' out."

Chase and Kally stepped back outside and Seth joined them a minute later. The smile was gone from his face, and he looked at Kally for a moment before he spoke. "I don't know no easy way to say it, Kally. The gold's in there alright, but I found this an' some bones right where the short tunnel opens into a big room."

He handed Kally a silver ring with a setting of jade carved in the image of a dragon. It was her father's. Tears ran down her cheeks as she stood staring at it. Chase gathered her into his arms and held her while she cried. The men could have said little to ease her grief. They gave her those few moments to come to terms with her loss.

Finally she pulled away from Chase and dried her tears. The pain still showed in her eyes as she spoke to Chase. "I thought the letter and his coat would be all I'd ever have. Now I have the ring Mother gave him, and we can give him a decent burial. That way I'll always know where he is. I'm ready to see him. Take me in, Chase."

"Are you sure, Kally? It's not going to be pretty. Seth and I can bring him out and bury him for you over on the bench."

"I've seen a lot of unpleasant sights since I started this trip," Kally said in a low voice. "I want to see my father's remains. Then you can bury him for me."

Chase took Kally's hand, and extending the lantern in front of them, he led her into the dark tunnel. After a few feet, the narrow tunnel opened into a wide room with a low ceiling. On the dusty floor, at one side of the tunnel, lay the bones of a man, still covered with the rough clothes of a miner. Kally knelt in the dust and looked in silence.

Seth eased by Chase and Kally and moved into the room.

Kally reached out her hand tentatively a couple times before she could bring herself to touch the back of the shirt that covered her father's skeleton. She only touched him for a moment. At last, she stood and dried her tears again. She took Chase's hand as they followed Seth into a room filled with gold.

The ingots were piled almost to the low ceiling from the outside walls to where a narrow passageway ran through the middle of the room. Seth followed the passageway for another ten feet before turning back. The passageway and ingots kept on going.

Seth's eyes were wide in amazement as he spoke. "Your daddy was right about twenty mules not bein' enough to carry all this out. I'm not sure two hundred would do it. I don't know how far back this room goes, but way more'n my lantern light'll reach.

"I reckon we can take out all we can carry this trip an' then come back twice a year for years. We ain't gonna have to put out no sweat to build that ranch, Chase. With all this gold you can build a mansion an' hire all the servants you need to take care of it. We ain't gonna have to work another day in our lives." The usual twinkle in Seth's eyes had been replaced by a strange shining as he fingered the ingots of gold.

"There's plenty of gold here, alright, but aren't you forgetting something?"

Seth didn't seem to hear him.

"Seth, listen to me. I'm not about to forget what's been happening to us since we got into this canyon, or what happened to Kally's father over there. He wasn't crushed by rocks, and there's no bullet or knife holes in his clothing. He warned us not to take more than twenty mule-loads of gold out of here, and I don't think we should."

"I'm not forgettin' nothin'." Seth whirled around suddenly and faced Chase. "I ain't had no money to speak of my whole life. Now I see more gold than I ever dreamed there could be. I don't know what happened to Kally's daddy or his first mate, or the mules, an' I don't give a damn. I'm gonna live good the rest of my days, an' no spirit's gonna stop me." Seth turned back to the gold.

"I'm gonna fill these sacks, boy, an' then bring over the mule an' my packhorse. Sooner we get this gold loaded, the sooner we can get out of here an' come back for more." The tone of Seth's laugh now matched the wild look in his eyes.

Chase realized there was nothing he could say to change Seth's mind for now. He hoped only to divert him. "Alright, we can get the gold, but first come help me bury Kally's father. I know she'll feel a lot better when he's in a proper grave."

Seth was carefully filling his bags with gold ingots. "You two go on ahead an' start sewin' up a tarp to put him in. I'll be there as soon as I get these bags filled up." His strange laugh echoed through the room as Chase and Kally eased past her father's remains and followed the short passage out into the sunlight.

"I don't know what's come over Seth," said Chase

as he blew out the lantern and set it down. "I've never seen him like this."

"It's like the gold has made him crazy or something." Kally shuddered.

"I've heard lots of strange tales of men getting gold fever. About how they do go almost crazy when they realize they're going to be rich. But I can't believe that would happen to Seth. Maybe after he gets a few of those bars over to camp he'll settle down. He's probably just excited. But, are you alright?" He looked into Kally's eyes as he spoke.

"It's been a hard day already, but with you in my life I'm going to be just fine. I never dreamed we would actually find Father's body. I wasn't prepared for that, but I'm glad now we did. At least that puts a final ending to all this. It will help to know that he's buried, and this ring will be something I will always have of his to treasure. It's strange, but right now that gold doesn't mean very much to me." Chase held her for a few moments before they started across the bowl.

"We'll stitch up one of the tarps to put his remains in, then we can bury him up on the bench. You can pick any spot you like. It won't make much difference to us. The ground here is all pretty hard, so it's going to take some digging. As soon as Seth gets back we'll start. We can wait until morning to load the gold if we need to, and then leave after that."

"Thank you, Chase. I would like to spend a little time by Father's grave after he's buried. While you and Seth are digging, maybe you can talk to him about not trying to take out all of the gold. He may be able to shrug off all that's happened, but I can't. Father wouldn't have been so insistent about taking only twenty mule-loads if there hadn't been a good reason. With all the strange things that have happened, I don't feel good about stretching our luck any further."

"I agree with you, so I'll talk to Seth. I'm sure he'll be back to his old self if we give him a little time. He's always been one of the most levelheaded men I've ever known. I don't think the gold could change that."

As Chase and Kally began stitching up the tarp, Seth climbed up on the bench with a sack of gold in each hand. He took them over to his bedroll and dumped them out on his blankets. Chase and Kally watched as he carefully stacked them on a flat rock before turning to speak to them in a voice they didn't recognize.

"I could only carry twenty ingots in each sack. They got mighty heavy carryin' 'em over here. Reckon I'll throw a pack on my packhorse an' go get me a real load this time." Seth started toward the horse.

"Seth, " Chase called after him. "We need to get that grave dug first."

He stopped and looked back at Chase. "You go ahead with the tarp. I'll be back soon enough." He stood looking back at his stack of gold ingots for a moment, and then turned back to Chase and Kally. "Remember, that stack's mine," he said in an almost threatening tone.

Chase and Kally watched him in silence as he saddled his packhorse, jabbering to him in a strange tone as he led him down off the bench and toward the cave.

"I can hardly believe that was Seth," Kally said

as she watched him move away. "I've never seen him act like that. And what did he mean? That's *his* gold? It belongs to all of us. That was the deal from the beginning."

"I don't know what to tell you. I don't understand this any more than you do. He sounds almost hysterical. I may have to slap him hard to bring him back to his senses. I'll talk with him as soon as he gets back, I promise. Now let's get the bottom of this sewed up and I'll go have Seth help me put your father's remains in it."

They finished pushing the big sack needle through the tarp, and Kally tied off the heavy cord. As they started to roll it up, they heard a low rumble from across the bowl. They turned quickly to look across at the other side. Just as they looked, the giant slab of rock that had stood upright above the opening to the cave came crashing down with such force Chase and Kally could feel the earth shudder beneath their feet.

20

"**O**h, my God!" Chase cried. He and Kally came down off the bench and ran as quickly as they could across the bowl to the rock pile. Chase reached it ahead of Kally.

"Stay there, Kally," he commanded, putting his hand back as he reached the bottom of the pile. "We don't know if Seth was inside the cave or on his way in."

Kally stopped where she was with her hand over her mouth, a look of shock and disbelief in her eyes. She couldn't speak.

Chase worked his way carefully up the rock pile, keeping a close lookout for loose rock that might fall down on him. He circled what was left of the large slab, pushing loose rock out of the way as he looked for any sign of Seth and the packhorse. He wasn't sure what he might find. If Seth had been in the cave, he might still be alive, but Chase wasn't sure if they could ever get him out. Only dynamite would be able to move this mass of rock now, and even one charge could bring the whole cliff down on top of them.

As Chase climbed over a big boulder that blocked

his way, he didn't have to wonder any longer. It was several moments before he could say anything to Kally. "Go on back to camp and wait for me there, Kally," he said in a tight voice. "Seth's out of his misery, but the horse is all broken up. I'll have to shoot him." Chase didn't want Kally to see what was left of their friend. He wished he hadn't.

He shot the horse in the head to end his pain quickly. Then Chase sat down on the rocks with his head in his hands. He had not been prepared to say good-bye to the only real friend he had ever known before Kally came into his life. A deep sadness welled up within him as he sat quietly beside his old friend.

Kally climbed up to the bench with the gunshot still ringing in her ears. She walked slowly into camp with tears running down her cheeks. She needed the warmth of Chase's arms around her, but she knew he wanted some time alone with Seth. He had loved Seth like a father.

Kally slipped to the ground next to a rock and sobbed out her grief for the two special men the gold cave had claimed. She had expected her father to be dead, but she wasn't prepared to lose Seth too. She sobbed uncontrollably for the next few minutes.

When Chase returned, he found her slumped against the rock like a weak kitten. She hadn't realized he was there until he reached down and lifted her into his arms. Without a word he carried her over to their blankets.

"Oh, Chase, was it terrible?" she asked as he laid her down on his bedroll and stretched out beside her.

"That's a hard way to lose a friend, Kally. I can't

believe he's really gone." Chase's voice quavered as he spoke.

Kally wiped her own tears and looked over at Chase. His eyes were red and the pain of his loss was etched deeply into the lines of his face. She curled up next to him. There were no more words for either of them. They both closed their eyes and slept.

It was well past noon before they stirred.

Chase turned to look at Kally as she woke up. "Are you alright?"

"I am as long as I'm close to you. I can't believe we slept so long, but I guess it was the best thing we could do. So much has happened in the last few hours."

Chase nodded as he sat up. They both got up and went to wash their faces in the stream.

"I'm going to miss Seth," Kally said as she dried her face on her neckerchief.

Chase nodded. "I learned a lot from that old coot. I was still pretty wild when I first met him. If it wasn't for him I could very well have ended up on the other side of the law. In some ways he was like a father to me, but at the same time he was a true friend, and the best man I ever rode with. I'll miss him too."

Kally looked at Chase a moment before she spoke again. "I know what Seth meant to you, Chase, and nothing will ever replace that, but I'd like to help fill his place if I can. You're different from any man I've ever known and I love you more than I ever dreamed I could love anyone. I want to spend the rest of my life making you happy, and when the time comes, I'll be a complete wife to you. I have no doubts about that anymore."

Chase took her in his arms and held her as he spoke. "If that's a proposal, I accept. Seth told me everything would be alright in time. Wherever he is I'm sure he has that old twinkle in his eyes and he's saying, 'I told you so.' You've made me the happiest man alive, Kally."

Chase kissed her tenderly and then held her close for several moments.

"If you build a fire, I'll fix a pot of coffee," Kally offered as she turned around. "I'm not hungry, but I'll fix you something if you'd like."

"Maybe later. But I will take you up on that cup of coffee. We have some decisions to make." Chase started the fire.

"About what we're going to do?" Kally asked as she made a pot of coffee. "I don't know what choices we have now."

"Well, the gold is still over there. We might be able to get to it if we can blow the rock away from the entrance without bringing the cliffs down on top of it. We can try it if you want."

Kally looked surprised. "Is that what you want?"

"This was your trip to begin with, Kally. I'll do whatever you want, but I think you need to decide. You can have some time to think it through if you want."

"I know what I want. I don't need any time." Kally looked over at the pile of gold ingots Seth had left behind. "I don't know how much of a ranch we can build with those forty ingots, plus the four I have, but I'm willing to settle for it, whatever it is. I have no desire to go after any more gold."

"Are you sure?"

"Would you be disappointed if I was?"

"Of course not. I feel the same way you do about the gold. I'm not willing to risk any more to get it. You're what's important to me now. Besides, I still have enough money in the bank to start the ranch, and there's more than two thousand dollars in my pocket of your money left from the supplies, plus what a few bushwhackers contributed back there on the trail. All that, along with the gold, will be more than we need to get a good start."

"All my father ever wanted was for me to be happy. He thought it was the gold that would do that, and in a way it was. If it hadn't been for the gold I never would have met you. What he didn't know was that you would be my treasure. The gold is pretty dull compared to that. All the gold in the world would never replace a full, happy life as Mrs. Chase Wade."

"I think you're plumb loco, woman, but nothing you could say would make me happier." Chase pulled Kally into his arms and kissed her over and over again.

"That's enough, Mr. Wade," Kally said finally. "Your coffee's ready and we still need to make some plans." She poured them each a cup and they sat down next to each other as they talked.

"Can you be ready to pull out first thing in the morning?" Chase asked as he sipped his coffee.

"In the morning? I was hoping . . . I mean . . . could we leave now? It wouldn't take us long to pack things up and we could ride until dark. The sooner we're away from this canyon, the happier I'll be."

"I was hoping that was how you felt too. I have some unfinished business across the bowl, but if you'll start wrapping the gold in empty flour, salt, and coffee sacks, we can hide it among the other supplies—just in case someone gets nosy on the trip back."

"You don't mind then?"

"Mind? I would leave right this minute if we could, but we have some things to do. We'll have to use Maude for a packhorse, but with her and the one mule, we'll make it just fine."

"I'll start filling the packs, but what are you going to do?"

"I want to bury your father, Seth, and the gold forever. I'm going to take a big charge of dynamite up above the slide and blow half that canyon wall down on top of them and the gold. I'll save enough to blow up every clue on the way back. After we go through the wall at Pike City, I'll set off a couple sticks and seal up this canyon forever. That ought to please the spirits."

"I sure hope so. I've had more of those spirits than I ever wanted. You go ahead, I'll get started here." Kally found the empty bags in the packs as Chase got a double handful of dynamite sticks and the whole coil of fuse.

He went in a fast walk down off the bench and across the floor of the bowl. He skirted where Seth lay buried under a big rock, and climbed high to the top of the slide. He placed the dynamite under the overhang of the towering cliff and fused it. He unwound the fuse as he worked his way back to the bottom of the pile, and cut it off. He had just enough left for the other places he planned to blow.

When he returned to the bench, it was obvious Kally was in a hurry to leave. The packs were ready and waiting beside the animals. He saddled their horses and tied the light packs onto Maude and the mule. In a short while they were ready to ride. They led all the animals down to the floor of the bowl. Chase lit the fuse and then led the way up the rocky trail over the wall. He rolled the rocks out of the way. When they reached the top, they stopped to look back and waited.

In a few minutes, an ear-shattering explosion echoed from the walls of the bowl, and a great cloud of dust arose. As it lifted, they could see huge sections of the canyon wall crumble and start an avalanche of rock rolling down the slide. Some of the rocks were as big as houses. As the avalanche reached the canyon floor they piled deeper and deeper. The gold, Seth, and Kally's father were soon buried beneath twenty or thirty feet of rock.

"Let's get out of here before that dust catches up with us," Chase said as he turned back toward the trail. "The spirit's gold will be theirs for all eternity now."

Kally managed a smile. "You take the mule and lead the way. Maude and I will be right behind you. I'll be sticking real close to you until we get past those burial grounds."

The animals were well rested, and Chase and Kally no longer had to stop to figure out clues, so they made good time on the return trip. Chase stopped and blew up the clay boulder and the flat rock with the arrow. They stood watches and hobbled the horses each night. Kally didn't like to stand watch alone, but she would have been less comfortable having them both asleep at the same time. She wouldn't be able to really relax until the burial grounds and the strange totems were behind them.

Chase made her take the early watch, and then relieved her early each night. Their meals were light and hastily fixed. At noon they only stopped long enough to rest the horses and chew some jerky.

They rode past the old burial grounds in the early afternoon of the ninth day, and didn't stop riding until dark. They were each able to start relaxing for the first time since they had left the bowl.

"How are you feeling now?" Chase asked as they set up camp and started supper.

"That spooky feeling is finally gone," she confessed. "And just to prove it, I'm going to fix you a good supper tonight." She laughed for the first time in a long while.

Chase hugged her. "I'm feeling a lot better too. I don't think we're going to have to hobble the animals or stand watch anymore. I know we both could use the extra rest."

They enjoyed a relaxed supper and sat around the fire talking and drinking coffee longer than they had for a long while. They talked of their new plans for the ranch.

"With the gold and extra money, we can buy twice as many cattle as I'd planned and be making a good living in a couple of years."

"Don't forget, we have three horses and a mule too," Kally added with a smile.

"We're likely to have more horses than that," Chase reminded her. "Maude's a mare. If we use Ranger or Pacer as a stud, we can start raising our own horses."

"I'd like that." Kally snuggled up closer to Chase as they talked. "I can hardly believe we're so close to having all these dreams come true. We're going to be so happy, Chase. I feel so safe and comfortable with you. I know our life is going to be perfect."

Chase smiled down at her, but something was bothering him again. Old concerns he knew he could bury no longer. "Kally..." he hesitated a moment before going on. "There's something we have to talk about."

Kally sat up straight and looked at him. "What is it, Chase? You sound so serious."

"You know that I love you more than anything or anyone else in the world?"

Kally nodded as a look of concern filled her face. "You're not having second thoughts are you? About us?"

"That's not it, Kally. There's nothing I want more than to fulfill all the plans we've made for our future at the ranch, but I'm afraid."

"There's nothing to be afraid of, Chase," Kally said reassuringly. "We have plenty of money and we already know we have what it takes to work together. We're a good team. And if you're worried about my being a good wife—a complete wife to you—I know now I will be. You've changed my life and my feelings so much, I will never be really happy until I can give myself to you totally. So see, there's nothing to be afraid of." Kally spoke with a sense of urgency in her voice; afraid of losing all she had dreamed of.

"No, Kally, it's not you I'm concerned about, or the ranch. I guess it's me—what I am."

"You're not making sense, Chase," Kally interrupted.

"Let me finish. I need to say this. I'm a gunfighter, Kally, I always have been. Sure I talked of hanging up my gun and starting the ranch even before I met you, but I don't know if I can really do that."

"But I thought you wanted to stop killing." Kally didn't understand.

"I do. I've never wanted anything more, but I don't know if they'll let me—all the young gunfighters out to make a name for themselves. If they could beat Chase Wade to the draw, they could become a legend overnight. They all know that. I'm afraid for you, Kally. There's always the chance you could be killed in the cross fire, or be left a widow. I can't stand the thought of either. It just wouldn't be fair to you."

"Chase Wade, you amaze me," Kally said with a grin on her face. "Just how many men have I seen you fight or kill in the last few months?"

"More than I ever wanted you to."

"And has that made the slightest difference in how I feel about you, or how much I love you?"

"I hope not."

"Of course it hasn't. I knew who and what you were when I fell in love with you. And I've learned enough about what life is really like out here to understand what you're saying is true, but that doesn't make any difference to me. I know we can't erase what you have been and start over fresh, any more than we can erase the things that have happened to me in the past. We can only learn to live with them and be happy in spite of them. I will live the rest of my life with you knowing that each day could be the last that we'll have together, but I'm not going to waste precious time and energy worrying about it. I'll just try to make every day the best and happiest it can be—for both of us. And I can tell you right now, I wouldn't trade a lifetime of safe days in Boston for one day with you surrounded by trigger-happy gunmen." Kally lunged into his arms and kissed him before he could say another word. No more words were necessary.

As the two of them moved to their blankets, the tension of the last few weeks drained from their bodies and they slept longer than they had for days. Neither of them moved until after sunup.

They took their time getting back on the trail, and when they did, they slowed their pace and let the horses travel at a fast walk. As they rode, they talked about heading for the main trail as soon as they left Pike City. They would stop at the first small town or army post to get married.

It was midafternoon by the time they reached the little park where they had left the extra horses and mules. They could have made Pike City before dark if they pushed, but Kally wanted to stay in the park awhile. They would have to wait out the winter in Albuquerque anyway. They were in no hurry.

They unsaddled the animals and turned them loose to graze. Kally suggested they set up camp on the grass next to the pool. She spread out their blankets by the water, while Chase gathered firewood.

Kally fixed a good supper and later they walked hand in hand beside the stream, talking more of the ranch and all their plans for the future. Kally was radiant and full of life again. Chase was happier than he had ever been, and looking forward to the changes this incredible woman would make in his life. Changes he now yearned for.

They turned and walked back toward camp. "I'd like to take a bath before we go to bed," Kally said. "We may not get another chance for a while after we leave Pike City."

"I could use one too," Chase agreed. "Not much privacy here, but we can wait until after dark."

Darkness was already filling the little park, and the moon was starting to come up. They had passed the full moon back in the bowl, but there would soon be enough to light the canyon brightly.

"I trust you'll be a gentleman while I take my bath," she teased. "You'll have to keep your back turned." She walked the few feet to the edge of the pool and undressed. Silently she slipped into the cool water to bathe and wash her hair. By the time she was finished, the moon was shining brightly.

"Throw one of those blankets over here," she said after she had dried off. "I forgot to get clean clothes out of my saddlebag. You can go ahead and get started while I dress. I promise I'll be a lady and not peek either." She laughed as she wrapped in the blanket and Chase traded places with her.

After he had scrubbed good, he stood with his back to Kally as he dried off. He was reaching for his clean pants when Kally called to him.

"Stop right there, mister," she commanded playfully.

Chase stopped and looked in her direction. She was standing on their bedrolls, still wrapped in the blanket, looking straight at him.

"I thought you said you were a lady. I bet you've been watching me all along."

"And if I have?"

"Well, I'm not bashful about you seeing me without my clothes. You're the one who wasn't ready."

"Hush and come to me," Kally demanded in a husky voice.

Chase walked across the grass toward her, and as he did, she let the blanket drop to the ground. He stopped breathing and stood absolutely still. He had dreamed and imagined this moment in his mind for months. Even his dreams couldn't rival the incredible beauty of her naked body in the moonlight. He would no longer have to imagine the exquisite perfection of every curve.

Chase now pulled her into his arms and felt the sensual warmth of her body against his cool skin. "Are you sure?" he whispered.

"I've never been more sure of anything," she answered as they slipped down onto the blankets. She met his opened lips with hers and they exchanged the first of many deep, passionate kisses. Their bodies pulsed and swelled with the passion that engulfed them.

Chase pulled back and looked into Kally's eyes as he spoke. "I want so much to take you, but I have to be sure you're ready."

Kally was already breathing hard as she spoke. "Teach me, Chase. Teach me to be a real woman."

Chase kissed her waiting lips, her face, her eyes, her ears, and moved slowly down her throat as his fingers began to explore the rest of her body. There was no shirt to stop him this time. He caressed Kally's firm, perfect breasts. Gently he drew each nipple into his mouth and it grew firm and erect against his tongue. She rested a hand on the back of his head and her breathing became more labored as he moved his lips down across her flat stomach. Her body was responding fully to every touch of his lips and tongue as he kissed lower and lower.

Kally had both of her hands on the back of Chase's head now as her sudden cry of passion echoed across the silent canyon. Chase had never enjoyed a woman's body as much as Kally's. Slowly he moved back toward her lips. As he kissed her with all the passion he could no longer control, he moved carefully atop her as they became one for the first time. Only ragged breathing could be heard for the next few moments, until Kally's cries again filled the valley. Chase rolled back onto the blankets and held Kally tightly in his arms. It was several moments before she was able to speak.

"Oh, Chase! If I'd known it would be like this I wouldn't have made you wait so long. We wasted so much time you could have spent teaching me. Teach me more, Chase."

"I'll teach you everything you want to know. You've already taught me so much about what real love is. I'll keep on teaching you for the rest of our lives."

There were no clocks or boundaries of time during the next few hours. The only sounds that penetrated the silence of the small park were cries of total fulfillment. Even the night breezes weren't enough to cool two bodies that continued to burn with desire.

Long past midnight, Chase got to his feet and

lifted Kally into his arms. They laughed as he ran toward the pool and plunged into the cool water. Moments later two vibrant bodies, glistening in the moonlight, emerged to love forever.

A long-time resident of the Pacific Northwest, Stuart Dillon is an avid gun enthusiast, and has worked as a cow puncher on the Oregon range.